Dear Reader,

If you are familiar with my work, you probably followed me through the Shadow Falls adventure. You got to know Kylie, Della and Miranda. You watched as these three girls bonded and became amazing friends—the kind of friends who stuck by each other through thick and thin, good times and bad, laughter and tears. Together they tackled parent problems, boy troubles, and, well…the unresolved issues of a few frustrated ghosts. Oh, and let's not forget about the boys they loved. Boys who made our hearts race and long for one more kiss.

I hated to say goodbye to those special friends and their journey, but I'm absolutely thrilled to introduce you to two equally strong teen girls who will have wild adventures of their own.

In this book you'll meet Riley Smith who has her own fair share of tenacious spirits, difficult parents, hot guys, and amazing friendships, just as Kylie did. Riley feels alone, like an outcast, but she's tough and soon finds she has the backbone to face down a murderer, as well as the high school bully.

In the back of this book, you'll find an excerpt from my new contemporary young adult novel featuring Leah McKenzie, a teen who gets a heart transplant and a second chance at life. But what happened to the donor? With the help of his grieving brother, she soon realizes she may hold the clues to how he really died. *This Heart of Mine*, will be released in hardcover and ebook on February 27th from Wednesday Books.

Thank you for continuing to follow me and these inspiring, kickass heroines. Keep reading, laughing, and loving life.

Sincerely,
CC

Other Books by C. C. Hunter

New York Times Bestselling Shadow Falls Series
Born at Midnight
Turned at Dark (free novella)
Awake at Dawn
Taken at Dusk
Whispers at Moonrise
Saved at Sunrise (novella)
Chosen at Nightfall
Spellbinder (novella)
Almost Midnight: Shadow Falls: The Novella Collection
Fighting Back (novella)
Midnight Hour

Shadow Falls: After Dark Series
Reborn
Unbreakable (novella)
Eternal
Unspoken

The Mortician's Daughter
One Foot in the Grave

For more information: www.CCHunterBooks.com
C.C. also writes adult contemporary romance as Christie Craig.
To find out more, visit her at www.christiecraig.com

THE MORTICIAN'S DAUGHTER

ONE FOOT IN THE GRAVE

C.C. HUNTER

everafterROMANCE

EverAfter Romance
A Division of Diversion Publishing Corp.
443 Park Avenue South, Suite 1008
New York, New York 10016
www.EverAfterRomance.com

First EverAfter Romance edition October 2017.
Paperback ISBN: 978-1-63576-417-8

To my niece, Cara Bates, who loves a good ghost story.
This one is for you.

And to my good friend and writing buddy,
Susan Muller, who shares the passion of writing.

CHAPTER ONE

Can I go to jail for this?

The question snakes through my mind as I make my way down Dead Oak Street. The sound of my tennis shoes smacking against the cracked sidewalk fills the cold, almost-dark night. I pull my hoodie closer and hold my purse to my side like a weapon.

A full moon makes its appearance early, hanging in the sky that's still clinging to a spray of gold left over from the sunset. I chose this time purposely, hoping everyone would be in their houses eating dinner, doing homework... not out watching for strangers trying to slip something into their mailbox.

Getting caught isn't an option. Never mind if it's illegal—though it shouldn't be, I'm doing them a favor—it would bring questions down on me that I'm not prepared to answer. That I'll never be prepared to answer.

I spot an address on the street curb. My heart thumps and vibrates against my breastbone.

Three houses to go.

I keep moving and, staring down, remember the old song lyrics, *Step on a crack, break your mother's back.* Since my mom's dead, I don't have to worry. But what was the second chorus? *Step on a line, break your father's spine.*

Maybe I should avoid lines. Dad has enough crap on his plate. Crap I wish I could help him with, but I don't have a clue how to do that.

Taking a deep breath, telling myself this favor is almost done, I keep walking toward house number thirteen. Why did it have to be an unlucky number?

Homes on each side of the street line up like dollhouses and seem to be watching me. Some of them are dark, and have a menacing look. Others have gold light leaking out of their windows like love lives there. Through one, I see a TV airing the evening news. Through another, I spot a family of four having dinner. I wonder what it would be like to have that. To be part of a family. To be more than just "Dad and me." The before-Mom-died memories are so few, and even those are vague. Considering I was four, I guess I'm lucky I have any at all.

Only one house to go.

I see the house. It's dark as if no one's home. The mailbox catches my eye. It's leaning, looking tired and old. The metal door flap is hanging open.

This might be my lucky day.

I reach into my purse and pull out the envelope.

The tightness in my chest releases. I can do this.

I take the last few steps, avoiding cracks and lines. A dog barks from across the street. The barking rings like a warning, announcing a stranger is present. And I'm the stranger.

The yowling grows loud as if the animal is approaching. I accidently let the envelope slip from my fingers. I look over, hoping I'm not about to be mauled. The dog's in the middle of the road, yelping, alerting the neighborhood.

I stomp my foot, and the canine scurries back across the street.

Heart pounding, I kneel down, snatch up the letter, and slip it into the mailbox.

Done. Problem solved. I can go home now.

And so can you, Bessie.

I look up at the bowl of darkening sky. Right then I see a shooting star race across the night, leaving a trail of glitter in its wake. I smile. I know what it means. A rightness enters my chest.

Before I take my first step away from the mailbox, I hear something... someone.

"What are you doing?" The girl's voice rings out.

The rightness is shattered.

I freeze and pray her words are for someone else. Then I see the dark shadow sitting on the edge of the porch, almost hidden behind the hedges. It's from house number thirteen.

The air locks in my throat, a jolt of pin-prickling pain races under my skin.

I am so caught.

The figure pushes off the porch, walking toward me.

I consider running, but my feet feel nailed to the sidewalk. Panic fills my empty stomach.

Even worse is that when she gets closer, I recognize her. Dark hair, light olive skin, dressed in black.

I don't remember her name, but I have two classes with her. English and history. She keeps to herself. Not coming off as shy so much as… a loner. Maybe even someone with a chip on her shoulder.

I saw her roll her eyes at some girls who were being loud and obnoxious in history today. I wanted to roll my eyes too. Their behavior was out of line.

"What are you doing?" she asks again.

Yup. I am so caught. So screwed. My mind races, seeking an answer she'll believe. One that would completely avoid the truth. Not that she would believe the truth. Sometimes I still don't believe it.

I gulp down the knot of panic in my throat. "I, uh… A piece of mail had fallen out of your mailbox."

That sounded convincing, didn't it? I pray she believes me. Pray she hadn't seen the envelope in my hand before I'd dropped it.

Her brow pinches. "Oh." She stares at me, recognition widens her light green eyes. "Aren't you the new girl at school? Riley, right?"

I nod. The fact that she remembers my name when I don't recall hers makes me feel slightly guilty. "Yeah. Sorry I don't remember yours."

"Kelsey," she spouts out matter-of-factly, not in an insulted kind of way, more like in a don't-give-a-damn way. Then she continues to stare at me suspiciously. "You live in the neighborhood?"

"Two blocks over," I say. "I was just… taking a walk." I swallow, again feeling the need to get the hell away from there. Away from her.

"I should… go." I'm ready to step away when I hear a

truck pull into the driveway across the street. Doors open and slam closed, and male voices boom out.

I look over. The streetlight is on, and I recognize one of the two boys. Jacob Adams. Tall, light brown hair, and an oh-so-confident way of carrying himself that most boys his age don't have. He laughs at something the other guy says, and the sound seems swallowed by darkness.

The fact that I know his name says something. It says he's one of the best-looking boys at school. But it's not just that. He's also one of the few kids who's actually spoken to me in my first ten days of school. Not a whole conversation, but just a quick introduction and welcome to Catwalk, Texas. Surprised the hell out of me.

The two boys, almost too loud for the night, go inside the house, and silence falls on the street again. I can hear the streetlights buzzing, spitting out voltage. I feel a similar nervous buzzing inside me.

"So that's why you're here." Kelsey makes a disapproving noise from the back of her throat.

I don't understand what she means at first, and then *bam!* I get it. She thinks I'm stalking Jacob. I start to deny it but then realize I could use this. It's a plausible reason for being there. One that has nothing to do with the real reason. And really, what do I care if she believes I have a thing for Jacob. I kind of do.

"Don't waste your time," Kelsey says. "He's going out with Jami Holmes. Popular, big boobs, and a cheerleader."

Yeah, I kind of knew that too, which is why I wouldn't have bothered stalking Jacob even if I'd known where he lived. I try to think of something to say, but nothing comes out. So I just shrug.

She reaches into her mailbox and pulls out the envelope I just placed there along with two or three other pieces of mail. "But he is nice to look at," she says. "If you like his type."

"Yeah," I say like a confession, and wonder if that's what she was doing, hiding on her front porch. Stalking Jacob.

She holds the mail in one hand and gives me one more look. "See you around."

It feels as if I'm being dismissed. I can take a hint. I walk away. As I hurry back to my house, I wonder if Kelsey is kin to Bessie. Bessie is black and Kelsey's skin is much lighter, though her dark hair and olive complexion could mean she's of mixed race. We're all melting pots. Dad swears he's part Italian.

I'm a block from my house when I feel it. The sensation of being watched. The fine hair on my arms stand up. My skin tightens. My next breath brings in the scent of... I inhale again... of jasmine.

I don't think it's Bessie.

I speed up, hoping whoever it is will take the hint. Right now, all I want is to get home. Not that it feels like a home yet. We've only been in this place two weeks.

The temperature drops. Chills start at the base of my neck and slither down my spine. A new scent—this one spicy, earthy, like aftershave—fills my next breath of air.

I hug myself, watch my feet move, and increase my speed. One foot in front of the other, faster, and faster.

• • •

By the time I cut the corner to my block, the strip of gold

has faded from the sky and the moon hangs bigger and brighter. I look down the street. Dad's car is parked beside my old Mustang in the driveway.

Crap. He's probably worried. I start jogging, my feet slapping against the pavement. The second I reach the driveway, my phone rings.

It's probably Dad. I check. Duh, of course it is. No one else calls me. Well, Shala, my best friend who I left in Dallas a year and two moves ago, occasionally calls. But like Carl, the one-time love of my life, she's moved on. She found a new best friend, leaving me pretty much friendless.

Moving when you're in high school is hard. Everyone already has their confidants and cliques. Add that to what my dad does for a living, and in their eyes, I'm a freak. Or at least a freak's daughter.

Not that I'm pissed at Dad or consider him strange. I'm proud of him. Very few people can do his job. I'm not even really pissed at the kids either. Truth is, I'm not just a freak's daughter, I'm a bigger freak than they could ever guess. Than anyone could guess. But that's my secret.

I bolt inside. "I'm here."

Pumpkin, my red tabby, rushes me, meowing. I pick him up.

Dad walks out of the kitchen, his cell phone in his hand. His dark hair is disheveled as if he ran his fingers through it one too many times. He needs a haircut. Normally, he's as groomed as a guy giving the six o'clock news—camera ready.

Another sign that things are going downhill. Again.

"Where were you?" he asks.

"Walking." It's not an out-and-out lie, but the twinge of guilt tugs on my conscience.

"Alone?" he asks.

"Yeah, just checking out the neighborhood."

"I prefer you do that when it's light," he says. "Or at least leave a note. You scared me."

"It was light when I started out. And you're a little early. But I'm sorry." I put Pumpkin down and go right for a hug. He hesitates, then puts his arms around me.

His smell is so familiar, so comforting. How long has it been since I hugged him?

"Seriously, don't scare me like that."

"I won't." I keep my cheek on his warm chest. Even with his life in chaos, he hasn't stopped parenting. I appreciate that. Not that I'm one of those kids who needs a lot of parenting. Shala used to say I needed to lighten up. That I acted like a nun.

I reminded her that I wasn't the virgin, but she wasn't referring to sex. She meant stuff like drinking, smoking weed, and skipping school. Stuff most kids do. I've never been like most kids.

To make her happy, I finally played hooky a couple of times.

"You okay?" my dad asks when I pull back.

I guess the hug was a little too much. "Yeah. I got dinner ready."

He follows me into the kitchen, but frowns and puts a hand on his stomach. "I ate one of those twelve-inch sub sandwiches, when I should have stopped at six. But I'll sit with you while you eat."

"You should eat a little something," I say. "It's beef stew."

"If I get hungry, I'll fix myself a plate later." He grabs two waters from the fridge and sits at the table. I'm not hungry either. The earlier panic took a bite out of my appetite, but I snag a bowl and dish myself a small helping from the Crock-Pot.

"How's school?" Dad unscrews his water and pushes the other toward me.

"It's okay. The new semester starts next week." I run my spoon around the chunks of beef, carrots, and potatoes before I take a bite. Pumpkin leaps up on the table, landing with feline grace.

"Down," Dad orders.

Of course, Pumpkin doesn't obey. He's a cat. I pick him up and set him down. Then I drop a piece of beef from my bowl onto the floor.

Dad sees me and shakes his head. "You're too soft."

Guilty. I hate disappointing people or even pets.

"You still planning on taking auto tech?" he asks, and almost sounds disapproving.

"Yes. Why?"

"I don't know. I mean, I wonder if there are even any other girls taking it."

"I don't care. I'm not scared of boys."

"You should be. All teenage boys are dogs. I know. I used to be one."

"I'm not afraid of dogs either." As sad as it is, I kind of agree with him. I mean, look how fast Carl moved on.

Dad frowns. "I don't want my little girl to grow up to be a mechanic. You're going to college."

I roll my eyes. "There's nothing wrong with being a mechanic. They make a killing. But for your information

I'm not interested in being a grease monkey. And I am going to college." I say that with confidence, because I've already researched school loans.

The one time I brought up getting a school loan, he said no, that he could afford it. But I know after his time on the unemployment list, money is in short supply.

Which is part of my reason for taking auto tech. I don't want Dad to have to fork out money to fix all the little things that go wrong on an old car. The more I know about the Mustang, the more independent I am. And I kind of like my independence.

But eventually going out on my own means I'll be leaving Dad alone. Who'll watch out for him?

Pumpkin paws at my leg, wanting another taste. I ignore him.

"Besides, you probably already know everything the class covers," Dad says.

"Because I had a good teacher. But I could still learn a few things." I smile. He's right. I spent a lot of time under that car—with Dad. He put himself through college working for a garage. Together we redid the Mustang's engine. It was my fifteenth birthday present. Our neighbor had put a for-sale sign on the car, and the moment I saw it, I wanted it.

Not because I'm a car freak, or a Mustang freak. But I'd seen a picture of one my mom used to own. Honestly, I didn't plan on getting my hands dirty working on that car. At first Dad insisted, and then he didn't have to insist. Not because I enjoyed working on the car, but because of how much I enjoyed spending time with him.

It was our first real bonding experience. Before that,

I'd always gotten a feeling Dad didn't know how
a daughter. My first bra and the whole starting
experience almost killed him. And not once has he said
word "sex."

Working on that Mustang gave us something in
common.

"Speaking of cars," Dad says, smiling, "I'm about to
make your day."

"Really."

"Yup. I got your insurance card in the mail."

"Yes!" I do a little victory dance in my chair. When he
lost his last job, he had to cut the insurance on my car, so I
haven't been able to drive it for almost two months.

"So I can drive it to school tomorrow?" I ask and squeal
a little.

"Yeah." He chuckles. "You and that car."

Thrilled I don't have to walk to school anymore, I dish
a big bite of stew into my mouth and taste it for the first
time. It's good. "You sure you don't want a bowl?"

"No."

He sips his water. I eat. The almost empty echo in the
house reminds me how big it is. All our houses in the past
have been small, older. They seemed to fit us better.

"Have you made any friends at school?" Dad asks.

I almost lie, then decide against it. "Not really."

A sudden puff of steam rises from my bowl. A chill runs
down my spine. I continue to eat and ignore it. Pumpkin
hauls ass out from under the table and darts under the sofa.

Dad frowns. "You should put yourself out there more.
Make some friends."

I point my spoon at him and force my eyes to stay

on him. Just him. "Says the man who never puts himself out there."

"I'm around people all the time."

"Dead people don't count." I lift a brow and take another bite.

"Not just dead people." He turns the water bottle in his hand. "Did you get into the honors classes you wanted for next semester?"

"I think so," I say. Good grades mean a possible scholarship. I'm going to need one.

My next intake of air brings with it a hint of jasmine. I remember smelling it earlier.

Dad leans back in his chair. "There's an antique car show going on downtown this weekend. I thought we'd go. Hang out. Talk cars with people."

"Great idea." I finish my last bite of stew and go rinse out the bowl and put it in the dishwasher. Then I pull out containers to store the leftovers.

I hear his chair scrape across the floor. "I'll put the stew away."

"I can do it." I take a deep breath. The jasmine scent is stronger now.

"Don't you have homework?" he asks.

"Yeah, but it's not—"

"Then go. You do too much around here," he says. "You should be hanging out with girlfriends and not taking care of a household."

"I don't mind."

He steps closer and brushes my hair off my cheek. "I swear you look more and more like your mom every day."

I'm surprised at his words. He hardly ever mentions

her. Right then I see a familiar sadness in his light brown eyes. I go in for another hug. A short one.

When I pull back, I look at him. "You still miss her, don't you?"

"A little." He turns back to the Crock-Pot, away from me. Maybe away from what he's feeling.

I fill Pumpkin's food bowl. The cat comes running. I stare at Dad's back. Even his posture seems extra sad.

"How was work today?" I ask, wondering if that's the problem. Hoping that's the only problem. He swears it doesn't affect him, but I know it does.

"The same." He moves to the counter and lifts the lid off the Crock-Pot. A big puff of steam rises. He looks back. "Go do your homework. I'll close up the downstairs. I think I'm going to retire early with a book."

I stand there and watch him pour the stew into two bowls. "Did you get a new client today?"

He frowns up at me. "I told you, a mortician should never bring his work home with him."

But Dad *does* bring his work home with him. Or maybe his clients just follow him. Like right now.

The young woman stares at Dad, looking as if she's walked out of the yellowed pages of an old photo album. She appears confused and lonely, wearing an orange sundress and jasmine perfume.

Dad can't see her, can't talk to her.

But *I* can.

CHAPTER TWO

Before I go upstairs, I give Dad a shoulder bump, afraid three hugs in a night might be too much. Then I grab a handful of cookies and head upstairs. Once I'm at the landing, I turn and look to see if she's followed me.

She hasn't. But Pumpkin has.

The woman will find me sooner or later. They always do.

It started happening about a year and a half ago, right before we moved from Dallas. At first it freaked me out. Like really freaked me out. But then I realized not one ghost had done anything to hurt me. I'm not sure they could.

Or maybe I just want to believe that.

Most of them just want to talk. Some of them need something. A favor. But that's okay, because I always ask a favor of them too.

So far, none of them have been able to help me. But I still help them. And it's not always easy, either.

Like the favor for Bessie.

She'd bought life insurance six months ago, but neglected to tell her daughter.

I couldn't go up and just tell the family that Bessie had insurance. So I copied and pasted the insurance logo from their website so it'd look legit. I printed a label, addressed the letter to Bessie, put the policy number at the top. I wrote the letter as if it was a reminder to her that they were still waiting for her to pick up a copy of the policy.

I was going to just mail it, but since I'd stolen the logo I feared sending it through the US Postal Service might make it a federal offense. Instead, I spent an hour last night drawing a postmaster seal to make it look like it had been mailed. Then I spent another thirty minutes forging the company president's signature which I'd found on the website.

I thought it looked quite convincing. It's one thing I'm good at: drawing, copying things. Not usually forging signatures. But now I realize that if anyone questions it, Kelsey might be able to point a finger at me, since she'd seen me outside the house.

Great! Something else to worry about.

I get to my bedroom door and leave it open.

Returning to my bed, I sit. Wait.

I'm barely situated when she appears. She looks pretty in the dress. Her hair is blond, hanging in a nice neat wave. Confusion mars her lovely face. I'd had a spirit, an elderly man, last year that hadn't realized he was dead. Giving that bit of news was loads of fun. Not.

I'm hoping this won't be a repeat of that case.

"You can see me, can't you?" she asks.

I nod. When it first started happening, I tried pretending I didn't. But something always gave me away. They'd move. I'd jump. They'd talk. I'd listen.

I discovered it's easier to just deal with them, to get them to pass over. That's the best part. Seeing them go. They are all different. Bessie was that falling star. Some of them become a bolt of color. I can't really explain the feeling, but when I see them cross over, there's this sensation like… I did something really good. Like I've just checked off one item on Destiny's to-do list.

Truthfully, this isn't anything I would have chosen. But that's kind of the point. I didn't choose it. It chose me. And for that reason, it feels like fate. As if turning away from it will screw up some underlying purpose for my life. This doesn't stop me from sometimes resenting it.

The woman gets tears in her eyes. She's young, but older than me. Maybe in her twenties.

"Is he your father?" she asks.

I nod.

"He's a nice man."

They all tell me that. That he respects them when he drains their blood, and when he fills them back up with embalming fluid. They say when he gets them ready for the funeral he takes his time. Looks at photos of them and tries to get it right. They tell me he even talks to them, but he never answers them when they talk back.

I get up to close the door, so Dad won't notice me talking, but then I hear it. The sound. That little noise.

My chest fills with a heaviness. I lean against the doorframe and fight the tears stinging all the way up my sinuses.

Who knew the sound of ice filling a glass could be

so sad? Sad because I know he's pouring himself a drink. Probably the first of many tonight.

This morning I had to wake him up before I went to school. Normally, he beats the sun up. He looked as if the sun had already beaten him up, but at least he went to work. Would he tomorrow? Is he going to mess up and lose this job, too?

He's a good man. He's the only family I have. I love him, but I'm pretty sure he's an alcoholic. And I don't know what to do.

He's so proud that he's hiding it from me. He's so afraid to let me down. And he is. He's letting himself down too.

Anger stirs my gut. I'm tempted to storm downstairs and rip open his secret, try to stop him, but I'm afraid he'll just drink more then. At least if he's hiding it from me, he's not drinking all the time.

I shut the door and turn to face the ghost, but she's gone.

That's fine. I'm not really up to talking right now. I need to figure out how the hell I'm going to help my dad.

• • •

Two hours later, I've finished my cookies, my homework, and my pity party. And I'm no closer to figuring anything out. I go to take a shower. A short one. Wet but clean, I step across the hall with a towel wrapped around me. I can't help stopping to listen for the sound of the fridge spitting out more ice. Thankfully, only silence whispers up the stairway.

I try to tell myself that he's okay. He's not drinking too

much. But from what I've heard about alcoholism, even one drink is too many.

He's never told me he's an alcoholic. I read about it in Mom's diary. I found the small leather journal in a box tucked away in a closet when we moved last year. There were only a few months' worth of entries, but I treasure every word.

The older I get, the more I ache to know everything about her. Did she hate fish like I do? Did she cry at a drop of a hat when she was on her period?

When I told Dad I'd found her diary, he'd seemed upset, but he didn't ask me to return it. And I didn't offer. I kept the photographs, too.

Dad had given me a few photos a couple of years before when I'd asked him about her. I still wonder why he didn't give them all to me then. Does he still miss her that much?

I step back into my room. Pumpkin stands on the edge of my bed, his orange hair puffed up around his neck, his ears tucked back to his head. I know what that means.

"She's back," I say and turn around. Then I see... not her, but him. I almost scream. Air bubbles up in my throat.

I don't even know why I'm so startled, except I was expecting it to be the same woman in orange. It's not.

He's standing there, a good foot taller than me, dark brown hair, blue eyes. Young. My age. Eyes wide. Eyes that are checking me out.

I suddenly feel naked. Oh, hell, I *am* naked, except for a strategically placed towel.

"Get out!" I look down to make sure all of my important parts are covered. Unfortunately, the towel is small, and either my top or my bottom is going to be a little compromised.

His eyes lift up, wide with surprise, and he… smiles.

Smiles.

"Hi," he says.

Hi? You don't say hi when someone yells for you to get out! I scowl at him.

"Sorry," he says, which is better, but he doesn't sound sorry. He doesn't look sorry. He looks happy. Like I'm a present that's already unwrapped.

"I said get out!" I even stomp my foot like an angry two-year-old.

He fades. Only then do I realize another reason I was so startled. He was different. For a fraction of a second I thought he was… real. Alive.

All of the spirits in the past looked like faded photographs, aged and kind of yellowed. He wasn't faded. He was… bright. He was… too young to die.

I hurry to my closet, shut myself in there, take a few deep breaths, then pull on a pair of sweats and a t-shirt.

When I step out, I look around. He's not there. Pumpkin peers at me from under my bed skirt.

"Is he gone?" I ask my cat as if he might answer.

Then I smell it. That same scent I got earlier when walking home. Aftershave. Or deodorant. They all come with their own scent. Each different, like a fingerprint.

But this one is almost familiar. It's a boy smell. A cute-boy smell.

Carl used to smell similar after he showered. I used to really like that scent. When I take another deep breath, I also detect a hint of jasmine.

Oh, crap! Does that mean I have two spirits? I've never had two at a time. I'm not sure I can handle that.

• • •

"Have a good day, Sweetie." Dad squeezes my shoulder and picks up his briefcase and lunch bag. "Be careful driving. I left the insurance card on the coffee table. You have enough lunch money?"

"Yeah. Thanks," I say without enthusiasm and spoon some Lucky Charms into my mouth. I'm still pissed at him.

Although I didn't have to wake him up this morning—he was packing himself some stew for lunch when I came down—he appears to be dragging. I'm not an expert on hangovers, but I saw Carl moving around like a sloth a couple of times after indulging in too many beers.

When Dad walks out, I spoon-chase a pink marshmallow around my bowl, then just drop the utensil with a thump on the table. What am I going to do about him?

I sit there listening to Pumpkin crunch on his kibbles. Then *bam*, I realize I'm not relying on the go-to source that's helped me through most of life's issues—my first period, sex, how to use a condom—hey, I wanted to make sure Carl did it right.

Yup, Google had saved me. I run upstairs, sit at my desk, and type in "alcoholism." Ten minutes later, I'm more confused than when I sat down. It's not that there's not any advice. There's too much.

And reading it makes me aware that I have no proof that Dad's drinking. Or that he's really an alcoholic. I only read it in a diary written before I was born. Yeah, I heard the ice last night, I know he lost his last two jobs after showing signs of irresponsibility—sleeping late, calling in sick—all of which he'd never done before.

But is that enough to draw this conclusion?

Other than the two job losses that he swears were due to other issues, I have no proof. I've never seen him so much as consume a beer. Never seen him stumbling, slurring his words. Never even smelled it on him.

I need proof. But maybe I don't have it because I haven't looked for it.

Snagging my backpack, I run downstairs, drop it on the table, and rummage through the cabinets. Nothing. No liquor. No evidence.

I turn around and stare at Dad's closed bedroom door. I move toward it, reach for the knob. Turning it is so hard. This is Dad's room. He's a private man. Invading his space feels… wrong on every level.

Something else feels wrong, too. Silence. So silent I hear the living room clock counting time. *Tick. Tick. Tick.* It seems to be the only sound in the house.

My heart starts to keep beat with the tiny sound. The slight thump in my chest makes me realize I've stopped breathing. My gaze shifts to the clock on the living room wall.

If I don't leave for school now, I'm going to be late. That's all the motivation I need to let go of the doorknob. Later.

I cut off the kitchen light, throw my insurance card in my backpack, and fly into the entryway.

And come to a rubber-sole-skidding halt.

He's standing in front of the door, blocking it, looking too bright, still smiling. I inhale to confirm his scent. It's there. Still familiar. The aroma takes me back to being close with Carl. Back to being intimate with Carl.

"You going to school?" His voice is deep, almost husky.

"Yeah," I manage, and rub my thumb and index finger on the backpack strap hanging off one shoulder.

He leans against the wall, as if he plans to stay there and visit with me for a long time. "What grade are you in?"

"Twelfth." I realize in my haste to leave, I forgot to brush my teeth. With my luck, I've got a green marshmallow stuck to my pearly whites. I run my tongue over them.

His smile widens. "So am I."

Am, not was. He's speaking in the present tense. Does he not know he's... dead?

The way his blue eyes study me reminds me of how he stared at me almost naked last night. As if he might be envisioning me like that right now.

"We need to... set some rules. You can't just..." I'm tongue-tied, nervous, cute-boy kind of nervous. That's so wrong. Talk about two people being incompatible. "You can't just pop—"

"What's that saying about how rules are meant to be broken?" He grins.

I frown, tighten my eyes, and glare at him.

"Just joking," he says teasingly. "What's your name?"

"Riley." I hitch my backpack up higher on my shoulder. "Yours?"

He pauses one second. "Hayden."

It's different, sort of like him, so I guess it fits him. "I... gotta go."

He tucks his hands deep into his jean pockets. His shoulders round. The muscles in his arms bulge out just a bit. Yup, it's definitely cute-boy kind of nervous that I'm feeling.

"Okay," he says.

Pumpkin hisses behind me.

"Stay away from my cat," I mumble and motion for him to step away from the door.

He inches to the side but not quite enough. Not that it matters—he's not flesh and blood. I switch my backpack onto my other shoulder and head out. I'm one foot out the door when I realize what happened. I felt him. Not like a person, but a light touch as if someone brushed a feather across bare skin. And... he wasn't cold. Why wasn't he... ice cold like the others?

I shut and lock the door. Run my hand over my tingling shoulder. Then, with my heart doing double time, I hurry to my car.

I start the car and drive away. Riding shotgun is the question: What makes this boy so different from all the others?

CHAPTER THREE

I fret about Hayden the whole drive. Now, really close to being late, I take the first school parking spot I can find, unbuckle, grab my backpack and get out. I turn and lock the car. One bad thing about an old car: no automatic locks.

As I'm pulling the key out of the door, I hear steps behind me, and then, "Wow." Followed by, "Is that your car?"

"Yeah," I mutter and swing around, feet ready to run. But the second I see who's standing there, my size sevens aren't so worried about being late.

Jacob and... I think the guy who was with him last night... stand a few feet from me. Jacob is staring at me. His friend is staring at my Mustang.

"Hi," I say and pull out a special smile reserved for good-looking guys. Or I should say, good-looking *living* guys. I didn't smile at Hayden.

"Is it a four-speed?" Jacob's friend asks.

"Yes."

He stares at me as if shocked. "You can drive a manual?"

I nod. It took almost two months and every ounce of patience Dad has for me to master it, but they don't need to know that.

"Does it have a 289 engine?" The friend moves closer to the car.

"No, just a 200, straight six. But I'm not complaining."

He stops staring at my car and now is studying me the way a boy studies a girl. "Tell me you know how to work on it, and I'm going to put a ring on your finger."

A little flattered, but mostly embarrassed, I laugh. Now if it was Jacob saying that...?

The school bell rings.

"Gotta go." I start walking.

Obviously not worried about being late, they both linger to check out my car some more. Before I push through the school doors, I look back... at Jacob, not so much his friend, even though both of them are easy on the eyes.

Not as hot as Hayden.

The instant the thought wiggles through my mind, I reject it and give myself a mental kick in the ass.

I must really be desperate if I'm getting the hots for a dead guy.

• • •

Having flushed most of my Lucky Charms cereal down the garbage disposal this morning, I feel my stomach gnawing on my backbone by lunchtime. I snag a slice of pizza, fries, and a fudge cookie, and try not to count the carbs. Shala, who used to have a bit of a weight problem, was a walking, talking carb meter, and even after all this time, I can still count carbs as fast I can eat them.

It's a good thing I don't gain weight easily because I've never a met a carb I could resist. From the pictures of my mom, she was naturally thin, too.

I hand the cashier my money. She lifts her face. Her blond hair is in a ponytail, and some of it hangs in front of her face, almost as if she's trying to hide. She tucks the loose hair behind her ear, her blue eyes meet mine, and she smiles. I remember her kind of doing that yesterday, too. It's a different kind of smile. As if she recognizes me. Probably has me mixed up with someone else.

"You are extra bright today," she says.

I look down at my navy shirt and jeans. I don't understand what she means, but I smile and take my change. As I walk away, I feel her gaze stuck to my back.

She's an odd duck.

It's only when I look and see my peers, all sitting in groups, laughing and chatting like friends do, that I remember how much I hate lunch period. Why is it that you're never as lonely by yourself as you are in a crowd?

I head to a spot at the end of a table with several empty seats. I'm seated and taking a good long sip of my water when someone drops down next to me.

I almost choke on my H2O when I see it's Kelsey. My first thought is that she's here to confront me about the letter, which causes my appetite to take a dive. I set my water down and wait for her to start accusing me.

But she doesn't even look at me, just starts forking at her salad.

After a few awkward seconds, I throw in the towel and say, "Hi."

"Hi," comes the one-word echo.

She's mentally immersed in her food tray, and not me, so I pick up my pizza and take a bite. It's cardboard with tomato sauce, but the cheese makes it edible.

"Word is you're cool as shit," she says, still studying her salad.

I swallow. "What?"

"Your car. Jacob and Dex were talking about it in math."

Dex must be the other boy.

"I'm not cool as shit," I say. But I remember that almost the same thing happened at the last school. My car makes a big impression on some people. But then they find out my dad is a mortician, and my cool status bites the dust.

Does he have to touch 'em? Does he hug you when he comes home from work? What does he do with the blood he drains from their bodies? Does he smell like dead people?

Verbal jabs have been tossed at me for as long as I can remember. I've basically come to the conclusion that there are some careers that should require sterilization. And mortician is one of them. The only other person who got teased more than me in school about their father's career was Marla Butts.

Her father was a proctologist. The man could have at least changed his name.

"You lived here long?" I ask, a little curious as to why she doesn't seem to have friends.

"A year." She forks a cherry tomato, holds it up and stares at it. "Where did you move from?"

"Dallas." I pop a fry into my mouth. It's cold, but salty and greasy.

"I'm sorry," she says.

Say what? I study her eyeballing her fork. "Sorry for what?" I don't think she's looked at me since she sat down, and it feels weird talking to someone who seems more emotionally invested in a cherry tomato than our conversation.

"Dallas," she says.

"You don't like Dallas?"

She pushes the tomato off her fork and stabs a piece of lettuce. "No, it's great. I lived right outside of Dallas for eight years. I'm sorry for you having to move here. This is a sad, screwed-up, boring town."

I don't know what to say to that, so I just shrug. Not that she sees it. Her attention is now on a cucumber she's chasing around her bowl.

"Why did you move here?" she asks.

I flinch at the question

"My father's job."

Please don't let her ask what he does. I'm not ready for that. And knowing my dad works at the funeral home where Bessie is might connect me to the letter.

"What brought you here?" I toss out, hoping to distract her from the career question.

"My mother got tired of her latest live-in boyfriend beating the shit out of her."

I don't know what to say to that either. But I force out a "Sorry."

"I'm not. Not that she left him. Just sorry that my grandmother lived in this half-ass town."

So, Bessie was her grandmother? I pick up the pizza and as I do I see her bracelet. It reads, *Black Lives Matter.*

"Do your parents like it here?" She's still not looking at me.

"My dad seems to." I hesitate and, sensing she's about to ask, go ahead and say it. "My mom passed away when I was young."

"That sucks." She pauses and then asks, "Does your dad give a shit about you? Word is mine never did."

It's strange to be talking about personal stuff with someone I don't even know. Yet, for a reason I don't understand, I'm compelled to answer.

"Yeah, he does." For all of my problems with my dad, I know he cares about me. And if what I believe is true, it's himself that he doesn't care enough about. For some reason, I feel the need to look up. My gaze goes straight to the cashier, who is staring at me. What's with her?

"My grandmother just died."

Kelsey's confession yanks my attention back to her. Is that sadness I hear in her tone, see in her eyes? Then I realize she's looking at me for the first time.

"Sorry." I mean it. I liked Bessie. And while I don't know what it's like to lose someone—I don't remember losing Mom—I know what it's like to not have someone. To miss them. To feel as if there's an empty spot in your life.

She continues to stare at me. It suddenly feels like too much. I take a bite of my pizza.

"Or did you already know she died?"

I jerk my gaze back to her. *She knows. Damn it! She knows.* I swallow the half-chewed bite of pizza. A big lump rolls down my throat. "Why... why would I know that?"

"Because everyone is talking about it. She died of a heart attack at the grocery store."

"I'm sorry about that. But… I didn't know. I don't talk to anyone." *Except the dead.* I swear I feel the half-chewed glob of pizza hit my mostly-empty stomach.

She continues to look at me, and for some reason I don't believe her. Not about how Bessie died. That makes sense. The first time she came to me, she was holding a can of English peas. What I don't believe is Kelsey's reason she thinks I know about Bessie's death.

Or maybe I'm just being paranoid.

The bell rings. She tosses her napkin onto her lunch tray. I do the same. "I'll see you in history," I say.

"No, you won't," she answers and looks at me again. "I have a funeral to attend." She stands up, her eyes stay on me. "I'll say hi to your dad."

I swallow empty air. "How do you know…?"

She just smiles, then turns and walks away.

• • •

Pumpkin greets me in the entryway when I get home. Which normally means the house is ghost-free. I kind of hope it stays that way. I've got too much rolling around in my mind.

I'm clueless as to how Kelsey knows who my dad is. Well, there's my last name, but face it, Smith is about the most common name there is. I just hope she doesn't suspect my involvement with the letter.

As I move in and toss my backpack on the sofa, my gaze goes to my dad's bedroom door. I recall my earlier determination to figure out if he's drinking. I don't have a clue what I'll do if he is.

Crap. I'm jam-packed with cluelessness.

I stand there staring at the door, again feeling it would be an intrusion into his life. But don't I need to know? I'm about to take a step closer when my phone dings with a text.

I pull it out, thinking it might be Shala. In that second, I consider confiding in her about my dad's problem. We used to talk about everything. Well, not about the ghosts, but everything else.

I kind of need a voice of reason. I need a friend.

Then I look at the phone. It's not Shala. It's Dad.

You home from school safe?

I type *Just got home.*

How did the car drive?

Like a dream.

He texts *Don't cook dinner. We'll order pizza. Stew was good. Thanks.*

He sounds so normal. So okay that I turn away from the door and go give Pumpkin his after-school treat. Then I grab some Rice Krispies Treats for myself. Twenty-five mouth-watering carbs. Yum.

Stomach happy, I grab my backpack and head upstairs. I barely have any homework, but I might as well get it out of the way.

Half an hour later, I'm finished with homework and lying back on my bed watching the ceiling fan spin. I let out a deep breath and think about Kelsey at her grandmother's funeral. I'm sad for her.

I sit up, bend my knees, and wrap my arms around them. "Pumpkin likes you."

He grins. "That's because I'm charming." He continues to stare at me. "Did you know you kinda snore, kinda purr when you're asleep."

I frown.

"It's cute. Not loud or anything." There's a mischievous twinkle in his eyes. "I had to get really close to hear it."

Really close? I sit there imagining him really close to me in bed and I get tingles, and not the kind I normally get from spirits. I open my mouth to say something, but there are no words waiting to come out. I'm never tongue-tied with spirits. It's as if instinctively I know it's my job to help them.

"And I also noticed you only put polka dots on one of your toes. What's with that?"

I hug my knees tighter. I wonder how long he's been here checking me out. "Maybe I just wanted one polka-dotted toe."

His smile deepens. "It's odd, but I'll buy it."

"How nice of you." I sound annoyed and I am, not so much at him, but at my response to him. I glance at the clock. Dad should be home anytime.

"Your dad texted. He's going to be late."

I gasp a little. Can he read my mind? None of the other ghosts could. But I've already concluded that he's different. Oh, please don't let him read my mind.

"How did you know I was thinking about my dad?"

"I didn't. I just… you looked at the time."

"And you read my texts."

"Not intentionally. I was lying in bed beside you, and the phone on the bedside table flashed."

"Remember those rules I mentioned?"

"Yeah," he says.

"Well, add this one. You don't get in bed with me. And don't watch me sleep. It's creepy."

He stands up, but his gaze stays on me. "I didn't touch you." His smile turns mischievous. "It was tempting, but I behaved."

"And you don't pop in unannounced," I spout out.

He rubs his chin. "How do I do that? I can pop and then announce, but I don't think I can announce and then pop."

I'm trying to understand what he means, then I think I get it. It's true, I've never really heard a spirit that I couldn't see.

"How about I pop in with my hands over my eyes." He puts his palms over his eyes, then separates his fingers and peers at me. "Then I'll announce and you can tell me if it's safe to look."

I frown. "And I'm supposed to trust that you won't peek?"

He drops his hands and grins. "Please. Do I look like the guy who would peek?"

"You did more than peek last night." *Crap, did I just say that?* My face grows hot.

"Purely an accident." There's the twinkle in his eyes again and I suddenly feel giddy. I'm flirting. I'm flirting with a dead guy. This is so not good.

"I wasn't aware you were only wearing a towel." He pauses. "Any other rules?"

"No reading my texts," I say.

Right then my phone dings with a new one. I reach for it, but nothing comes through.

I stare at the screen and am about to put it down when it dings again. And again. But there's nothing.

Hayden laughs.

I look up. "Are you... are you doing that?"

"Yeah, cool, huh?"

"How...?"

"Don't really know. Just kind of discovered it one day. Got a lot of time on my hands these days."

I recall watching a ghost investigation—which seemed absurd at the time—that claimed some spirits have energy and are able to interrupt electrical devices. Maybe it wasn't so absurd after all.

"Well, don't be messing with my phone. Or reading my texts. I mean it."

"Got it," he says and for what it's worth, he sounds sincere.

I look at him and remember not finding him on the obituary lists. "What's your full name?"

"Hayden... Parker," he says, and moves in to pet Pumpkin again. "Yours?"

"Riley Smith. But you should know my last name, right?"

He sticks his hands in his pockets and I remember him doing that this morning. "Why would I know your last name?"

"Don't you know my dad?" I ask, hoping to confirm he's from the funeral home.

"No."

"You didn't... uh, follow him here?"

"No."

"Then... how did you find me?"

"A black lady, uh, I think her name was Bessie. I ran across her. She mentioned you."

I nod. "So you know...?"

"Know what?" he asks.

I hesitate. "That... you're not really here."

He blinks and looks away. "Yeah, I know that." There's a somber tone in his answer and it resonates in my chest.

"I'm sorry," I say.

"Me too."

"So what can I do for you?"

He faces me. He's half smiling again, but I see the shadow of unhappiness in his eyes. "What do you mean?"

"Do you just need to talk things through or... do you need something."

"Talking sounds nice."

I nod. "So what's bothering you?"

He looks confused. "Other than being here like this, not much."

My heart hurts for him. He's too young to die. For a girl who got stuck being able to talk to ghosts, I hate death. I inhale and focus on him. "Then let's talk about you being here."

His brows pinch. "I'd rather talk about you."

I've found that rushing them usually doesn't work. "That's a dull subject."

"I doubt that. Any girl who goes around with only one polka-dotted toe isn't dull."

"Okay, I confess, I was going to paint the rest of them, I just... got distracted."

He laughs. It's such a nice sound. I find myself smiling. Yup, I'm flirting alright.

"Fine, but you're still not dull. You're extremely hot. And I know that for certain."

I roll my eyes at him. "We will not talk about—"

"I'm talking about the hot car you drive. The fact that you are taking auto tech? Oh, and you've got a killer smile."

"How did you know that?"

"I'm an expert on killer smiles."

"No, I mean about me taking auto tech."

"You left your list of classes on your desk."

"You know that's snooping," I say and pop up and turn my paperwork over.

"Sorry. I was curious." He pauses. "So, it's true."

"Yeah. And no jokes about how girls can't work on cars."

"I think girls can do anything they want. Before my mom married my stepdad, she and I completely restored our house. If my mom can put in a toilet, I think you can change oil." He moves to the window and looks out. "Do you work on your car?"

"Of course. And I do more than change oil. I helped my dad put the motor in."

"Seriously?"

"Yes."

"So it's like your thing?" He takes a step closer.

Again, I'm amazed I don't feel the cold. "No, spending time with my dad was my thing. But money's tight, so if I can fix my own car, it'll be cheaper to keep it going."

He nods. "Where's your mom?"

"She passed away."

CHAPTER FIVE

"I'd help if I could," he says. "But the only ones I've spoken to are Bessie and you."

Disappointed that his lips are busy talking and not doing other things, I take a step back to gather my wits. But holy smokes, I honestly would have let him kiss me.

What the hell is wrong with me?

"If I see anyone else, I'll ask. I promise," he says.

I look down and force myself to concentrate on the conversation. "Thanks," I tell him. "But don't worry too much. I just thought… I'd ask."

Frankly, I don't know how it all works. The spirits don't really know what to expect either. I mean, I'm told when they see the light it feels like a good place and every time I see one cross over, it's like… like receiving a gift. Truthfully, I don't even know if it's possible for my mom to drop by. But it's the favor I ask every spirit I see.

Pumpkin starts hissing. I look around. Abby is standing there. "Are you going to do it. Are you going to find my ring?"

I rub my hands on the side of my jeans. When I'm nervous my palms itch. And I'm plenty nervous. I hate telling her no. "I… don't know if I can drive that far."

"It's not that far," she pleads and I feel her sorrow again, deep emotional pain that feels too big in my chest. Instantly, I want to cry. I want so badly to help her. But seriously, Dad would kill me if I took off that far.

"What?" Hayden says.

I glance back at him. "I'm talking to Abby."

"Abby?" he says.

I look back at the woman, then back at him. "You can't see or hear her?"

"See or hear who?"

I bite down on my lip. "That's weird."

"What's weird?" He runs a hand up his arm as if he's cold.

Can he feel Abby but not see her? "Wait. You saw Bessie, but you can't see her?"

He takes a step back. "You mean someone's here. Someone that's…"

When he doesn't finish, I look back at Abby. "Can you see Hayden?"

"See who?" she replies. "Please, I'm begging you to help me."

"Riley?" I hear my father call from downstairs. "I brought pizza. Let's eat while it's warm."

I look from the spirit who I almost kissed, to the one who might be the first I let down.

"I should go," I say, happy I don't have to deal with this right now, even if it's just a temporary reprieve.

Abby fades. Hayden, looking nervous, just nods. I leave to go face my dad. My dad, who may or may not be an alcoholic.

Can my life get any more screwed up?

• • •

The pizza was good. Ten times better than the lunchroom's imitation kind. I eat three slices, big ones, before I make myself stop. And it's not because I don't want more. But eating over a hundred carbs in one sitting is too much, even for me.

Dad's chatty and I listen to him talk about the car show this weekend. About Ms. Duarte, his assistant at the funeral home and how she's the best assistant he's ever had.

Dad mentioned when he first got there that she was divorced and about his age. Dare I hope that...

"So how was your day?" he turns the conversation to me.

"Fine," I say.

"You like it here, don't you?"

I pull my bottled water closer. "It's not Dallas." The second I see his expression, I wish I could pull back the words. One time in Banker, Texas, I threw a hissy fit and begged him to move back to Dallas. It hurt him. "But it's not bad. I'm sure I'll get used to it."

He stares at me as if he knows I'm lying. "I'm sorry I uprooted your life, baby."

"You lost your job, Dad. It wasn't your fault." *Well,*

unless you lost it because of the drinking. But right now he seems so normal that I'm inclined to think I've been worrying for nothing.

He goes back to his pizza. I take a bite of my salad. When my fork sinks into the cherry tomato, I recall Kelsey and the bombshell she dropped at lunch.

"You had a funeral today," I say.

"Yeah. How do you know?"

"A girl at school. It's her grandmother."

"Yeah, Bessie Kelly."

I set my fork down. "Did you tell her granddaughter about me?"

"About you? What do you mean?" he asks.

"She knew I was your daughter."

He shakes his head. "I didn't... Wait. I have your picture on my desk. And she came in with her mother several times. She probably saw your picture."

I nod. It makes sense. Complete sense. Maybe my worry about Kelsey figuring things out is another thing I'm blowing out of proportion. I need to learn to chill.

"Is she a possible friend?" Dad asks.

"I don't know," I answer and remember her sitting next to me.

We clean up the kitchen together. I don't want to call it a night. "How about we watch the movie that came in from Netflix?"

"What is it?" he asks.

I make a face, realizing it was a bad idea. "It's a romantic comedy." Considering I almost kissed a dead guy, I probably shouldn't be watching romance. "Or we could see what's on the DVR." I grin. "Something a little violent, with some gore to interest you."

He laughs. "No, let's watch that movie."

"You won't enjoy it." I put the leftover salad in the fridge. I don't know why I don't just toss it. In two days, it'll be wilted mush and I'll feed it to the garbage disposal. But hey, maybe I'll suddenly decide to be heathy, and have it tomorrow as my after-school snack instead of a carb-laden treat. It could happen.

"I'm a romantic." Dad smiles. "I'll enjoy it."

"You're a romantic?" Sarcasm leaks from my voice as I pour food into Pumpkin's bowl. "How long has it been since you've been out on a date? Two years?"

He dated a woman, Tammy, for almost a year in Dallas. I didn't like her, but he seemed to, so I put on a good front. In fact, I kind of blamed Dad's spiral downward on their breakup. It was after that I noticed he started getting up later and started looking disheveled. But maybe it was just mild depression Dad was dealing with and not drinking. That would make sense.

Nevertheless, he lost his job—which he claims was due to personality clashes with the new management. He didn't get another job for almost five months, hence our move to Banker, Texas. At first his attitude and mood were positive in the new town, but after five months of living there, I saw it happening again. This job came only a few months later.

When I realize he hasn't answered, I toss out, "Old people date, too."

"I'm not old. I'm just busy."

"Doing what?"

"Working and being a single parent." He shoots me a frown.

I shoot him one right back. "Oh, great. Blame me."

"I'm not blaming you. Seriously, I just haven't met anyone right for me."

"Maybe you're too picky." I stuff the empty pizza box in the trash. "Tell me you aren't looking for a Victoria's Secret model."

He smiles. "All men are looking for a Victoria's Secret model. Aren't you looking for George Clooney?"

I make a face. "Ugh. He's old."

"Enough with the old shit!" he says.

I laugh, but recall how beautiful Mom was. She could have been a model. I know Dad says I look like her, but I don't see it. The humor lingering in my chest fades when I realize why this conversation is important.

If I get the school loan, I could be packing my shit and leaving soon. Part of me is so ready to claim my independence, another part of me gets sick when I think about it. Thinking about Dad being alone hurts. Thinking about me being without him hurts, too.

I look up. "I'm serious, Dad. You need to meet someone."

"Yeah. Come on, let's watch the movie and see what I'm missing out on."

Dad's asleep less than ten minutes later. I'm glad because there's a sexy scene I'd be uncomfortable watching with him. I'm a little embarrassed just knowing he's in the room. Clothes are coming off. And I get a peek at a man's naked butt.

It is a nice butt, too.

The playful banter and cute ass reminds me of my time with Carl. While I resent that he gave up on us, I understand it was inevitable, and I'm not sorry for what we had. I'm not sorry we had sex. Oh, I was for a while, but recently I've realized that what we had was special, even if it didn't last.

Then I remember Hayden. Our almost kiss. Which is crazy because we can't really kiss. Yeah, I admit I almost feel him, but... My brain takes a U-turn. Can Hayden feel me? I recall how he seemed to feel Abby's presence, but couldn't see or hear her.

The whole ghost spirit thing is a big freaking, fracking mystery. Last year I checked out several books about empaths and dealing with ghosts, but it wasn't anything like what I was experiencing.

Music from the movie catches my attention. Realizing I stopped watching it, I push those thoughts from my mind and crawl back into the story.

An hour and a couple more steamy scenes later, the movie's over. I cried like a baby when the heroine died. I so wouldn't have watched it if I'd known it didn't have a happy ending. I face death way too much in my real life to have to suffer through it in fiction.

I wait to let my eyes unpuff before cutting off the television and waking Dad. It's almost ten. "You really enjoyed it, didn't you?" I tease him.

He makes a funny face and grins. "Sure did. I'd give it five stars." He gets up from his chair, gives my shoulder a squeeze and walks to his bedroom.

I watch him shut the door. "Love you," I say quietly.

He's not drinking, I tell myself, and I almost believe it.

I start to head for the stairs, when I realize I haven't seen Pumpkin. I look around and find him. My heart does a double take.

He's curled up on top of the dining room table. Hayden is sitting there, petting him. Has Hayden been here the whole time? Watching the movie with me? I remember the sex scenes, and blubbering like a baby at the end.

"You didn't announce yourself," I say in a low voice.

"Sorry." He looks up at me and the first thing I notice is he's not smiling. But it's more than that. He appears defeated, lost. I like his cocky look better.

"Is everything okay?" I ask.

"Fine." He's lying. He fades.

I call Pumpkin and head upstairs, stopping right before I walk into my bedroom, listening. No ice clinking into the glass. Only the hum of a sleepy house fills my ears. I latch onto that bit of good news and go to bed.

Too bad I can't sleep. I keep thinking about Hayden and the sadness in his eyes.

• • •

Dad is up and running when I make it downstairs. I'm thrilled to see he's his old perky self this morning. Maybe I can stop worrying about him now.

I down a few more bites of cereal and go rinse out my bowl. This morning I'm the one who's dragging. I stayed up late Googling Hayden Parker, hoping to learn something about him. I found two articles about two different Hayden Parkers. One was a brain surgeon who just won some medical award. I'm pretty sure my Hayden hasn't been cutting open people's brains. The second was an obituary of an eighty-year-old man. So I got nothing.

I get to school without any ghost appearances. Oddly, I'm kind of disappointed. I was hoping Hayden would stop in so I could ask him what was wrong. I realize my concern is a bit over the top. Abby is the one who was really upset. Shouldn't I be worried more about her?

Yeah, I should. But she's not a hot guy.

With my backpack hitched over one shoulder, I make my way through the parking lot to the school entrance when I hear an angry voice.

I look over and see Jami Holmes. She's yelling at whoever's in the truck that she just jumped out of.

Right then I see Jacob behind her. All six feet of him. I think he and Hayden are about the same height.

Jami commences screaming. I hear the f-bomb, "asshole," and "dick" spewed out.

Jacob's eyes meet mine. Realizing it appears as if I'm eavesdropping, I offer an apologetic shrug, and swing around to get the hell out of there, but I drop my purse. It hits the ground and just about everything spills onto the asphalt.

Crap! I kneel down to collect my things, even curl my shoulders, hoping to make myself smaller.

"What are you doing?" Jami screams as I'm scooping my things into my purse as fast as I can.

I'm pretty sure she's talking to me, but I just hurry to collect my things so I can get the heck away.

"She just dropped her purse," Jacob answers.

Yup, she was talking to me.

I glance up and meet his eyes, not hers. "Sorry." I snatch up my purse and hotfoot out of there.

Five minutes later, I'm dumping my books in my locker when I feel someone stop next to me. Thinking it's Kelsey, I glance over.

"Hey," Jacob says.

I open my mouth to say "hey" back but a frog has managed to climb into my throat. I finally croak out something that sounds like "hi." Then I go straight to worrying that he's upset because he thinks I was snooping on him.

"I... I wasn't trying to... butt in. I was just—"

"I know. I'm sorry. Jami gets overheated really easy." He holds out a lipstick.

"Is that mine?" I ask.

His smile crinkles the edges of his eyes. "Well, I don't think it's my color."

That draws a quick smile out of me. "Thanks." I take it. Our fingers meet and I swear I feel a spark. Then I stand there sporting what probably is an all-time goofy grin. I force myself to stop smiling and the silence shifts to awkward, so I turn back to my locker and pretend I'm looking for something.

"Where did you move from?" he asks. His question draws my attention back to him as he leans against the locker next to mine. He's got a real nice lean.

"Originally from Dallas. But I was in Banker, Texas for a while."

"I've been to Dallas quite a few times. It's nice."

"Yeah," I say.

"You like it here?"

"It's okay." I pull out my English book. "Still trying to adjust."

"Yeah, I'll bet that takes a while. I'm sure there was a lot more to do in Dallas."

I nod.

He stares right at me. His brown eyes are nice. *But not as nice as Hayden's blue ones. Shit,* I need to stop thinking about Hayden. Especially when I have a real, live, hot guy standing in front of me.

A real, live hot guy who has a girlfriend, I remind myself.

"Did you know there's a car show here every week? People drive their classic cars in and park at the bank parking lot on Main Street. There's lots of Mustangs. I thought… since you're into cars, well, you might like to go."

My heart stumbles, skips a beat, then starts doing a happy dance. Is he asking me out? But what happened to… *Did he and Jami just break up? Was that why she was yelling?*

While that thought ziplines through my mind, the reality of the situation hits home. *The cutest guy in school is asking me out. But would saying yes, especially this soon after his breakup, put me on the shit list of every popular girl in school?*

This is one of those situations when I know there's a right and wrong thing to do. But isn't being right over-rated? Isn't there something positive about taking a risk?

CHAPTER SIX

Before I can contemplate an answer, he continues, "Jami and I and some other friends are going. If you'd like to tag along."

The reality I believed is yanked out from under me emotionally and I bust my ass. I should've known better. He's so out of my league.

"Oh, uh, well my dad's already planning on taking me."

"Are you going to take your car?"

"I... don't know. Maybe. I mean, we might take... my dad's car." I sound like a fumbling idiot. I feel like an idiot for thinking he was... interested in me. I'm just relieved I didn't say something stupid like, "Wow, I kind of hoped you'd ask me out," or something equally dumb.

"Well, maybe I'll see you there." He smiles. "I'd like to take a look under your hood." He chuckles. "Wow, that didn't sound right."

No it didn't, but I don't have a clue what to say to that so I just nod, then look back to my locker.

"See ya," he says.

"Yeah." I never look at him, but I don't breathe until I hear him walking away. Holy hell, I'm such a dork.

Afraid my dorkiness will explode, I go through the rest of the day without speaking to a soul. Well, other than to say I'm sorry when I bump into someone in the hall. When the get-the-hell-out-of-here bell rings, I shoot to my locker to grab my stuff and practically run to my car.

When I crawl behind the wheel, I sit there, realizing it's Friday and all I have to look forward to is going home to an empty house. And maybe seeing a ghost.

Feeling pathetic, lonely, and a little sorry for myself, I start my car. On the drive home, I decide I'm going to call Shala. We haven't spoken in almost two weeks. A conversation with her always cheers me up, even if it does make me miss my old life.

Pulling into the driveway, I get out my phone and dial her. The phone rings, and rings, then goes to voicemail. "Hey, uh, I haven't heard from you in a while. Just wanted to... chat?"

I hang up and slump back into the seat, feeling the bubble of lonely get heavier in my chest. I know there's a ton of reasons why Shala wouldn't pick up, reasons besides she just didn't want to talk to me anymore. So why do I feel so damn rejected?

• • •

Saturday at 11 am, I pull up at the car show. Dad didn't tell me we'd be part of the show, but that was his plan. He pays the ten bucks for us to park on the lot. I tried to find a reason to bow out, but I couldn't come up with anything. I just really hope I don't see Jacob.

We get out and Dad gets the two lawn chairs out of the trunk. He sets them up beside the front of the car and then opens the hood. Rows upon rows of multi-colored antique and classic cars are parked in the lot. A concession stand in the front is filling the air with the aroma of hotdogs and grilled corn. It's sixty-five degrees and actually a sunny day for January. Big puffy white clouds dance across the blue sky.

I give Dad credit. It *is* kind of nice to be outside. I think the last time I was outside for more than five minutes was when I walked to Bessie's house.

Dad and I are barely settled in when a couple of older guys walk up and start talking to my dad about the Mustang. Dad quickly points out it's my car and I helped him put in the engine, but they aren't interested in talking to me, and vice versa. Dad, however, is more than happy to chat. They move over to make way for people walking by to peek under the hood.

While I know Dad wanted to come here for me, hoping to get me out of the house, he needs it too. Other than work and school, we're a couple of shut-ins.

I really wish Dad would get a life.

I grab a book from my car and start reading. One I almost finished last night. I wasn't even interrupted by a spirit. I'm pretty sure Abby will be back. I don't think she's finished trying to convince me to go find her ring. However, I wonder if Hayden passed over. Normally they say good-bye, and I even get the reward of seeing them cross over, but nothing about Hayden fell into the "normal" category.

"There she is," I hear someone say.

I look up, and Jacob and Dex are moving in. I give the area a quick sweep and I don't see Jami. At least I don't have to face her.

"Hey," Jacob says.

"Hi." Remembering how I thought he'd been asking me out, all kinds of uncomfortable swells in my chest. I stand up and put the book in my chair.

They both walk over to the side of the car to gawk at the engine. We talk a few minutes about transmissions and such. I can tell they are surprised I know my shit. In truth, I'm kind of surprised they know theirs. Not a lot of guys my age really knows about cars.

"Did you buy a new engine or rebuild the one that came in the car?" Jacob asks.

"The car didn't have an engine it. We had to buy one."

"But you guys put it in yourselves?" Dex asks.

"We sure did," my dad says and walks over.

"You must be Mr. Smith," Dex says.

"Yes. So you guys know each other?" He motions between the three of us.

"They go to school with me," I say.

"So tell me the truth," Dex says. "Does Riley really work on the car?"

"Sure does," Dad says with pride, but a little cautiously.

I recognize that tone, too. He used it around Carl. Oh great. Dad thinks Dex is interested in me. They start talking about Dex's old car.

Jacob takes a step closer to me. "It's a nice car," Jacob says. "I'm trying to talk my dad into letting me swap my truck in to get a Mustang. But he's afraid it will take too much upkeep."

"They do require more than... a regular car," I say. "But if you can fix it, it's not too bad."

"How long did it take you to put the thing together?" He eases in a little closer.

"A long time. About nine months. We finished it right before my sixteenth birthday."

The car next to us roars his engine. It's loud. Jacob moves closer. "I'd give anything if my old man had given me a car like this."

"Mr. Smith?" I hear someone call out. "Is that you?" I look up and a man is walking up to my dad. "You're the funeral... I mean the mortician at the funeral home. I'm Daniel Sparks. I was there yesterday with my stepmom."

"Yes," my father says. "And I think you two picked a really nice casket, too." My dad goes into businessman mode. I go into mortification.

Dex and Jacob look at each other. Dex moves in. "Is he really a mortician?"

Oh great. I'm back to being the freak. "Yeah." I look away, not wanting to see their expressions. It's then I feel a chill run down my spine. I glance up and see Abby.

"You have to help me," she says and moves so close, a chill tap dances up my spine and hangs on at the base of my neck. "You have to." She starts crying.

I look at her and shake my head slightly, hoping she gets the message that I can't deal with her now.

"I need you to go there." She steps even closer, as if she thinks I'm ignoring her. And I am, but only because I can't acknowledge her now. "Look at me," she snaps.

"I need... You have to find my ring. You need to... tell them... the truth."

"Is that not a little weird?" Dex asks. "Him dealing with dead people?"

Now I'm ignoring Dex and looking at Abby. *What truth?* I think, but can't say it.

"Where have you been?" I hear someone else say. I think I recognize the voice and hope I'm wrong. I turn my head.

Not wrong. *Crap!*

Jami and another girl from school walk up. Jami's staring at me. I instantly realize how close Jacob is standing next to me and I step back.

"Why aren't you talking to me?" Abby yells.

The car's engine cuts off. The faint smell of exhaust fills the air. Then I catch another scent. Something spicy, earthy.

"You okay?" another voice asks.

I look over and Hayden is standing there. Oh, this is just too much. I put my hand on the car to steady myself.

My head's spinning, and I just want to turn around and run. Run from Abby, run from Hayden, run from Jacob and the accusation I see in his girlfriend's eyes, run from everyone who thinks I'm a freak. Then Abby fades and the icy feeling falls from the air.

"We found Riley," Jacob answers.

I look back at him, then to Jami. "Hi." I force a smile.

"Yeah," Jami says giving me the evil eye. "Can we move on now?" She turns her glare on Jacob.

"Yeah," he says but he looks at me as if to apologize.

I watch them walk off. I hear Dex say the word "mortician" and then laughter. I remain there, my hand on the car holding myself up.

Jacob and Dex stop at the car two spaces down to check out the engine. Jami swings around and hotfoots back to me. She glares at me and says, "He's taken. So back off, bitch."

"I haven't... I don't... I know he's..." But holy hell, what did I do to deserve being called a bitch?

"Good," she says and sashays off.

I gulp down some air. I see Dad, standing alone, staring right at me on the other side of the car.

He comes over. "What's that about?"

"Nothing," I say.

"Really?" From his expression, I can see he's not buying it. He probably heard the "bitch" comment.

"She's screwed up in the head," I seethe out. "She thinks I'm trying to steal her boyfriend."

"The boy in the burgundy jacket?" he asks.

"Yeah." I rub my hands up and down my hips, then sit down. I'm tempted to beg him to leave now, but then he'll know just how upset I am.

"Maybe it's her boyfriend she needs to speak to." Dad drops down in the chair.

I look at him. "What's that mean?"

"He was hitting on you."

"Was not!"

"I'm a guy. Guys know."

"You're an old guy. Young guys do it differently."

He just grins. "Fine, believe what you want."

I suddenly remember Hayden and I look over. He's still there. He still looks upset. He fades.

"I just found out that there's a bigger car show not this Friday but the next in Dayton. I told the guy we might show up."

I nod then grab my book and pretend to read. In reality, I'm too revved up to put words together. I might be sitting in the chair, but my heart's beating to an aerobic tune.

In a few minutes, Dad gets up. "I'm going to get us something to eat. You want a hotdog and fries?"

"Yeah," I say, even though it feels as if my stomach has shut down for business.

Dad walks away. I see people ambling up to my car. I'm so past wanting to talk to anyone that I bury my nose deeper in the book.

The men talk amongst themselves. I squirm and wiggle my butt in the lounge chair and continue to fume about my crazy, insane life. How the frack did I get myself in this mess?

I'm staring at row upon row of words that I'm not reading when I hear someone plop down in Dad's chair. And it doesn't sound like Dad's plop.

Don't let it be Jami. Please don't let it be Jami.

I lower my book just a smidgen and cautiously glance over the novel. My mouth falls open.

It's not Jami. But it might be worse.

"Hi," Kelsey says.

My heart speeds up. "Hi." I drop my book in my lap.

She looks over at the Mustang. "Cool car." She plays with her necklace resting on her shirt. I see what it is: a black fist on Pan-African continent.

"Thanks." I offer the mandatory politeness and then ask, "What are you doing here?"

"I came to see you. You want to hear something weird?"

As if I'm not up to my ass crack in weird. "You mean besides the fact that you knew I was here?"

"Please, that was easy. You drive a cool car and this place is where people with cool cars hang out."

I nod. I guess that makes sense.

"So," she says. "The weird thing is that we got a letter from an insurance company."

She pauses as if for effect. And it works. I'm affected.

I swear she's studying me to see my reaction. I try real hard not to react, yet my heart just stops. I manage to control the outside. I don't even blink. But inside is a different story. My voice of reason is screaming, *You're so screwed. So completely, thoroughly screwed.*

Kelsey continues, "It was addressed to my grandmother and contains information about a life insurance policy." She lifts a brow at me.

I manage to squeeze out a few words. "What's weird about that?"

Was that convincing? I feel as if it was convincing, but I can't be sure. My voice of reason is probably right. I'm so screwed.

"You see," she continues. "We go to the insurance company today because the letter says my grandmother needed to pick up a copy of her life insurance policy." She leans in. Up shoots the brow again.

"I still don't see that as weird," I say.

She leans back in the chair. "Yeah, here's the thing. They look at the letter and say it wasn't from them, someone forged their logo, and it doesn't even look like the letter was really mailed. All I can think about is seeing you that night. You putting an envelope in my mailbox."

My career in forgery is so freaking over.

Panic in my chest starts partying again. "I… I told you it had fallen out of your mailbox."

"Yeah, that's what you say. But this is where it gets weirder. I could swear I saw an envelope in your hand before you knelt down."

"Have… have you had your eyes checked lately?"

She stares at me then laughter spills from her. I'm not sure what kind of laugh it is. I'm not sure if she's being facetious. I'm not sure I can handle facetious. I'm not sure my heart will ever beat again after this crazy fracked up day.

"You know I don't buy that, don't you?" she says.

"Well, what do you buy?"

"Good question, I think I buy—" Footsteps draw near.

Dad walks up. Air catches in my throat. My gaze shoots back to Kelsey. *Please don't say anything. Please.*

CHAPTER SEVEN

I swear Kelsey reads my mind. Then just like that, I'm not
so sure that's a good thing. If she knows I don't want my
dad to hear our conversation, will that lead her to blurt
it out even faster? I've just shown her my kryptonite. I'm
an idiot.

"Hi, it's Kelsey, right?" my dad says.

"Hi Mr. Smith. Yes, it's Kelsey. Thank you for everything you did for my grandmother."

"You're welcome," he says with a touch of pride and
looks at me. "I'm so glad we came here today. I'm meeting
all of your friends."

Friends? I was called a bitch and practically threat-
ened by a girl who thinks I'm after her boyfriend. Now
Kelsey is trying to… To do what? Blackmail me? I don't
even know what she's trying to do, other than make me
admit to something that will make me the laughing stock
of Catwalk, Texas.

"Who else stopped by?" Kelsey asks me.

I mentally plead the fifth and don't answer.

"Jacob?" She looks at me for confirmation that she guessed right. I don't breathe a word—probably because my lungs are on strike again—but she somehow knows. "Really?"

I still don't say a word.

Dad looks down at the hotdog-scented bag he's holding. "Why don't you two eat these and I'll go get me another one."

"Thank you, Sir, but I need to head out. I just stopped by to..." Her gaze lands back on me. She's doing it again, lifting an eyebrow and pausing for effect, and it's still working. "To say hello."

"Well, stop by anytime. You know where we live, don't you?"

"Yes, I do," she says and I almost ask how, then I start praying she's lying. But my gut says she's not. She knows where I live. She knows I'm lying about the letter. Does she know I talk to ghosts?

Staring at me, almost smiling, she says, "We'll talk later." I'm not sure if that's a promise or a threat.

Yup, my voice of reason hit the nail on the head. I'm screwed.

• • •

Sunday morning, I roll over and stare at the swirling ceiling fan. My stomach grumbles, reminding me I barely ate any of my hotdog dinner last night. Dad and I stopped by an ice cream shop on the way home last night, but I guess my belly doesn't consider that double hot fudge sundae, with extra fudge, real food.

Sometimes a girl just has to have chocolate.

Footsteps echo up the hall and a knock sounds on my bedroom door.

"Yeah," I say.

Dad pokes his head in. "I thought I'd go try out the church in the front of the neighborhood. Do you want to join me?"

"Uh, not really. Can I just hang here?"

"Sure," he says, the word ending on a note of disappointment. Dad's not what I would call a religious person, but more Sundays than not, he attends church. He always encourages me to go, too. I do sometimes, but right now I have a bone to pick with the higher power.

Why me? Why am I the lucky one who gets to talk to the dead? Isn't he, or she, the one in charge? Shouldn't that be taken care of by someone who knows what the hell they're doing?

"Maybe next week," Dad says. "I think I'll head on out now and stop for a cup of coffee."

I nod.

"Oh, I'm planning on stopping at the funeral home to make sure Ms. Duarte is on top of the funeral today. I should be back around two. Order something in if you can't find anything to eat. We'll go grocery shopping when I get back."

"Okay," I say and watch him close the door. I stay in bed and listen to him leave. I want to go back to sleep, but I don't think I can. My empty stomach screams *"Feed me!"* I stand up.

The room goes quiet too quickly. I send out my feelers for a drop in the temperature and look around. No cold, just an eerie silence. Neither Hayden or Abby dropped by last night. I'm not complaining. I needed a reprieve, but part of me knows they aren't going anywhere until things are solved. And I'm the one expected to solve shit.

With Hayden, I think it might just be talking the whole dead thing through. With Abby...? I keep remembering what she said about finding the truth. Is there something else she needs besides getting her ring?

I kind of hope so, because me taking off for a two-hour drive across Texas isn't likely.

Still wearing my sleep pants and big t-shirt, I go downstairs. Pumpkin and I share a bowl of cereal. He likes the pink marshmallows. So I set three on the table to keep him from sticking his face in my bowl. I love the cat, but not enough to eat with him. I mean, I've seen him lick his butt. And ever since then I try not to let him kiss me on the lips.

Still hungry, I go to pour myself another bowl, but there's barely any left. Dad's right. We need groceries. I grab a Rice Krispies Treat. Rice is healthy, right? I stop short of counting my carbs.

I hear a weird chiming noise. At first I don't have a freaking clue what it is. Then I realize it's the doorbell. I don't think it's rung since we've lived here. Yeah, that speaks to my popularity.

Who the hell could it...? I remember Kelsey. Remember her saying she knew where I live. Remember her threat that we'd talk later.

Oh shit!

I shoot into the formal dining room, go to the

blind-covered window and very carefully peer out the corner that gives me a clear shot to the front door.

Sure as hell, it's Kelsey.

I let the blinds snap back into place and take off to the kitchen. Once in there, I hide on the other side of the refrigerator.

The doorbell chimes again.

Go away. Go away! I slide down the wall.

My butt hits the cold floor. My bare feet press against the chilled tile. I rest my head on my knees. After last night, I should have been contemplating what to say to her. Should have made a plan, but nope.

All of a sudden I feel something. I pop my eyes open, pretty sure... Yup. Hayden's kneeling down in front of me. For one second I forget about the doorbell. I forget because I can swear I feel his breath. His breath on my lips. As if he's breathing. But that's not possible, is it? Or have they all breathed and I just didn't notice? My mind flips from breathing to... kissing.

His mouth is so close.

"Someone's at your door," he says.

"Duh," I say. "I know."

"Why are you hiding?" he asks.

My frustration shoots up and I'm sure my blood pressure goes with it. "Why do you think I'm hiding?"

"Why don't you want to talk to her?"

The doorbell chimes again, sending my panic up a notch. "Because I think she knows."

"Knows what?"

"That I'm a freak," I snap.

He makes a face. "Why are you a freak?"

"Don't be an idiot! I talk to you, don't I?"

He frowns. "So talking to me makes you a freak?"

"Yes!"

Hurt flashes in his eyes. He's offended.

Of course he's offended. That was mean.

Damn, I just hurt a dead guy who has enough shit on his plate because he's... dead. How rude can I get?

"Sorry," he says.

Before I toss out my own heartfelt apology he's gone. I stare at my toes, my one polka- dotted big toe, and I want to cry.

Fracking hell! I look up to the ceiling. "See," I say speaking to anyone up "there" listening. "I suck at this. Please, just fire my ass and find someone better."

• • •

That night the hot spray of water hits my shoulders and I stand there trying to relax. Today hasn't been a gem of a day. Not that it couldn't have been worse.

Kelsey finally gave up and left. Dad came home and we went out for an early dinner and grocery shopping. We both put away the groceries, then decided to watch the beginning of a new show on Netflix.

When it ended, it was ten. Dad went to his room. I came up to shower and get ready for tomorrow.

Tomorrow when I won't be able to hide and will be forced to see Kelsey. What to say to her has been brewing in the back of my mind all day. But I have nothing. That's when I decided on a plan.

My plan's... nothing.

I'll say nothing. Act as if nothing happened. I'll keep my mouth shut until… What's that saying Dad uses? *Until the cows come home.* Though I don't know when the cows get home. Hopefully, not early.

Only when I feel in jeopardy of turning into a prune do I cut off the water. I start to step out, then stop and peer cautiously out of the shower curtain. Since my near-naked experience with Hayden, I've been extra careful.

The bathroom appears empty, but I still snatch my robe off a hook and wrap it around me before stepping out. I'm almost in my room when I hear it.

Clink. Clink. Clink.

Dad's getting ice again. I close my eyes and lean against the hall wall. It doesn't mean anything, I tell myself. He could be getting juice, water, tea.

I start to walk into my bedroom when suddenly I can't.

Not knowing is killing me. Sticking my head in the sand isn't helping anything.

I turn around and tiptoe down the stairs.

CHAPTER EIGHT

I get to the landing and listen. I hear him. I turn the corner and stop in the archway between the living room and the kitchen.

He's standing at the sink, staring at the drain, as if debating if he should dispose of the glass's contents.

"Hey," I say.

He swings around, several pieces of ice are tossed out of his glass into the sink. "Riley... You scared me. What are you doing?"

"Wondering what you're doing." I rub my palms down my hip.

"Oh, I'm... just getting some water. Is something wrong?"

I stare at his glass. It looks empty save for the ice. "Why don't you get a bottle of water?" Accusation dances on my question, while my heart aches from love, hurt, and concern.

"Because I like ice." He studies me. "You okay?"

I start to say it. To ask if he's drinking, but I suddenly feel like I'm completely overreacting. He's been fine these last few days. I reach up and run my fingers through my wet hair. "Fine. I'm going to bed."

"Me too," he says and sounds relieved.

I take one step then turn back around. He's still standing there, staring at me. "I love you, Daddy." My throat tightens.

"I love you too, baby." Now he looks concerned.

I take off up the stairs before I start crying. When I get to the top I stop and listen. I swear I hear the ice being dumped into the sink.

I stop myself from making conclusions and I go into my room. I get into my bed. My chest is tight. I cut the lamp off and stare into the dark. After rolling over for the tenth time, I give up. I shoot out of bed, turn the overhead light on, and dig the box out of my closet.

I sit on the bed and pull out Mom's photos and her diary.

I go through the pictures one at a time, staring at her face. Missing her so much it hurts. Then I pick up the diary and read. I get to the part where she wrote about confronting my dad about his drinking.

At least he didn't deny it. I hope he meant what he said about getting help. I refuse to live with a drunk. It would be like living with my sorry ass daddy again.

I put the book down. When I was ten and started hearing about my friends going to see their grandmothers, I asked Dad if I had any grandparents. He told that he and my mom had been only children and born late in their parents' lives. So both sets of my grandparents had passed away before I was three.

In other words, death cheated me out of both grandparents and a mom. Now some higher power puts me in charge of helping dead people. How is that fair?

I realize I'm crying. I push the box to the end of the bed, curl up on my side, hug a pillow, and let the tears flow.

Sometimes a girl just needs to cry.

I have a good pathetic sniffle going when I suddenly feel tingly all over.

I glance at my shoulder and see an arm. It's Hayden. He's in bed with me, hugging me. I feel his chest against my back.

My first instinct is to get mad, my next is to just keep crying. His arms aren't flesh and blood, but it feels so damn good to be... touched. I relax back on the pillow, continue crying, and let him hold me.

"I'm sorry," he whispers. "Whatever is hurting you, I'm sorry."

After several minutes, my sniffling slows down, and he says, "What's wrong?"

I roll over and face him. He's on his side facing me. He brushes a finger across my cheek. I feel it. A feathery touch.

"Everything," I say. "On top of the fact that I was mean to you and said you make me a freak. I'm sorry." A big hiccup shakes my breath.

"You weren't rude," he says. "You were just being honest. After I thought about it, I realized how hard this must be on you."

"Not harder than it is on you," I say, meaning that he's dead, but I don't say that. "I'm really sorry."

"Forget that. Why are you crying? Is it me?"

"No, I mean, yeah, I was upset about being rude, but it's not just that. It's everything."

"What's everything?"

"I hate being a new kid, I'm worried about my dad, I miss my mom, and Abby wants something from me that… I can't do. I suck at this."

"Suck at what?"

"Helping you guys." I sit up. "Take right now for example. Here you are trying to help me when I'm the one who's supposed to help you."

He sits up too and leans back on my headboard. It's been a long time since I've been in bed with a guy. Not that we're doing anything wrong, but it still feels… somehow intimate.

"How are you supposed to help me?" he asks.

"I don't know. You're supposed to tell me."

He inhales and runs a hand over his face. "That's what you do, isn't it? Help ghosts."

I nod. "Didn't Bessie tell you that?"

He shakes his head. "No, she just said… said you could talk to me." He hesitates. "So you helped Bessie?"

I nod.

He sits there as if thinking. "You mailed that insurance letter."

I nod. I start to accuse him of eavesdropping on my conversation, but what does it matter? "Bessie hadn't told her daughter about the life insurance and they needed money."

"But that's a good thing," he says. "They should be happy, not upset at you." He pauses. "Wait… I get it. If they find out it was you, they'll want to know how you knew about it."

"Right." I hug one knee closer.

"What other kinds of things have you done for people?"

"Sylvania, an elderly man back in Banker, Texas, needed me to find his cat a new home. Sometimes they just want to talk." And I really think that's what Hayden needs. I think he knows he's dead, but there's a fine line between knowing it and accepting it.

"What does... the woman, Abby, want?"

"She said she wanted me to go find her ring. She lost it in the woods in Lake Canyon State Park."

"Is that where she... died?"

I don't want to tell him, but I realize maybe that will help him open up. "She fell. They said the rain had loosened some of the edge of the overhang." I bite down on my lip. "She was alive when they found her. They said she'd probably been there for over twenty-four hours. But she passed away before they got her to the hospital."

He closes his eyes. "Damn."

"Yeah," I say.

He looks away for a second. "Do you know where the ring would be?"

"She says she knows. But I can't go. Dad would freak if he knew I drove that far. And there's no way I can take him with me and go in search of a ring." I drop back against the head board. "I hate letting her down."

I stare up at the ceiling. "But last night she mentioned something else. Said she wanted everyone to know the truth. I'm hoping that will be easier than driving halfway across Texas. At least I can help her with one thing."

C.C. HUNTER

Pumpkin, with his purr on, jumps up on the bed and curls up beside Hayden. I'm still curious as to why he took to Hayden and none of the others. "It's not that far," Hayden says. "Brian County is less than two hours from here."

"My dad would kill me!"

"Then don't tell him," he says.

I stare at him. "Did you miss the part when I said he would freak?"

"No. Couldn't you just skip school and take a ride there? I'll go with you. We can have a road trip. Spend the day together."

I shake my head. "Just skip school. You sound like Shala. You're a bad influence."

"Who's Shala?"

"My best friend. Or I should say my ex-best friend." I remember I called her and she hasn't yet called back.

But I'm done feeling sorry for myself. I look at Hayden. "Do you know what you need me to help you with?"

He smiles. "Maybe I'm not here for you to help me. Maybe I'm here to help you."

I just look down at Pumpkin purring as Hayden passes his hand over his back. "He's never let any of the others pet him," I say.

He smiles. "I told you, I'm special."

Hayden is special. He's dead and yet he wants to help me. "Why don't you tell me what happened to you?"

"Why don't you tell me a secret about Riley Smith?"

I look at him.

"A secret," he says. "Tell me one. Just one."

"I'm scared my dad is an alcoholic and he's drinking."

86

Don't ask me why I blurted that out, except… he wanted a secret. But no, it wasn't just because of that. I needed to share it. Needed to tell someone.

"Shit," he says. "What are you going to do about it?"

"I don't know. I mean, I can't prove it."

"Prove that he's drinking or that's he an alcoholic?"

"Kind of both." I tell him about Mom's diary and about Dad losing his last two jobs.

He listens and his eyes are so filled with caring that my chest feels achy again. But it also feels lighter. It feels good to have someone to talk to.

"Okay," I finally say. "I told you a secret, now you tell me one."

He thinks a minute. "When I was fourteen, I found a bottle of vodka in my mom's pantry. Me and a friend drank the whole damn thing. My mom came home. She was livid. I got sick, puked all over the house. She didn't clean it up. And the next day she woke my ass up and made me go clean it. It was dry and I had to get a spoon to scrape it up," He makes a funny face. "To this day, I can't stand vodka."

I laugh.

He touches my cheek. "God, you are beautiful. When you laugh, I swear your eyes twinkle."

I swallow.

He smiles. "I think I changed my mind."

"About what?" I ask, feeling a sweet quiver in my stomach.

"About you doing something for me."

I blink and try to regain my wits. "What do you need?"

"This." He leans in and kisses me. I let him. Holy shit, I'm kissing a dead guy.

I start to pull back, but then… I'm pulled in. Into the kiss. Into the fuzzy, fantastic cute-boy sensation fluttering in my chest. I feel his lips, lightly, yet I do feel them. I feel when his tongue slips inside my mouth. I feel myself lean into him. I feel so much. But I want to feel more. I want to touch him.

Before I do, he pulls back.

I look at him, my breathing is raspy and rapid, I push out the words, "We… we shouldn't ever, *ever* do that again."

He laughs and touches my nose. "Because you enjoyed it?"

"Never again," I say.

"Now that sounds like a challenge. And I love a challenge. Actually, I really need one right now." He's smiling. Looking so happy. Looking so… alive. But he's not. "Good night, Riley," he whispers.

"I mean it. We—"

But he's gone. I go straight to missing him, straight to wishing he wasn't dead. And not just for me, but for him. He deserves a life, real challenges. He deserves a real future.

Death. Freaking. Sucks.

I drop back on my bed. A sadness swells inside me. Tears sting my eyes. I touch my lips. I swear I can taste him. A little minty, like he just brushed his teeth. Do spirits brush their teeth?

It hits me again. I just kissed a dead guy. It sounds like a sin, and it felt a little sinful but in a good way. It has to be wrong, doesn't it? I just might go to hell for this.

I scowl up at my ceiling. "Told you, I'm the wrong person for this job!"

• • •

Dad's up and moving when I come down. He's not dragging, his eyes aren't red. He's smiling. See, he's not drinking,
I tell myself. And I believe it a little more than the last
time I told myself that. He's heading out the door when I
remember to stop him.

"Hey, you need to sign my report card."

He walks back into the kitchen. I grab my backpack,
pull it out, and drop back into my chair.

He looks at it. "You got a B on a history test?"

I wrinkle my nose. "I blame the B on the teacher for
being boring. And the fact that I took the test two days
after I got here and didn't even have my book yet."

"Does this mean you aren't going to be in history
honors?"

I frown. I was worried he'd point that out. "But I'm
in honors in math, English, and science. And I really don't
need history because last year instead of taking an elective
I took world history."

He smiles. "I guess I can't complain, then. How did I
get such a smart kid?"

"You just got lucky," I say. In truth, school has never
been hard for me. In fifth grade when the school requested
to test my IQ and Dad said okay, I purposely missed several
because I didn't want to be considered a nerd.

"That I did." He chuckles.

While I pour my cereal, Pumpkin meows at my feet
reminding me to share, and Dad signs the report card. He
gives my shoulder his customary squeeze and then starts
for the door.

"Hey," he says.

With a scoop of cereal in my mouth, I look back at him.

"I'm proud of you." His words are like the hug I needed.

I smile. "Thank you." I speak around the crunch bits and sweet marshmallows.

"Have fun at school." He takes off.

As I sit there, the daddy's-proud vibes fade and I feel Lucky Charms land in the pit of my empty stomach. *Fun?*

Chances of that are slim to none. Considering I'm going to have to face Kelsey, who's out to prove I forged a letter. Then the whole your-daddy-deals-with-dead-people is out of the bag, too. So fun is the last thing I expect today to be.

My goal is to survive.

I keep telling myself that it's just six more months, and I'll never have to darken another high school door in my life.

CHAPTER NINE

First period is auto tech. I'd never been in Building C and it took me a while to find it. I walk in just as the late bell rings. The second I'm in the room, booming with deep male laughter and murmurings about "tits," I start doubting my decision to take the class. It's one big sausage party, and face it, I'm not carrying one in my jeans. And I happen to have two size-C "tits."

All eyes and smiles focus on me. Or at least my tits. I immediately wish I'd worn a looser shirt.

"Damn!" someone says off to the right.

I recognize that voice. My focus shifts that way and yup, I'm right. It's Dex. But my gaze only lingers on him for a second before sliding over to Jacob, sitting next to him. Oddly enough, he doesn't seem nearly as happy to see me as everyone else does in the room.

Dad was obviously wrong about him being interested. That's all good. The last thing I want is to have Jami and her sidekicks against me.

"Can I help you?" a man asks, walking into the room from a back door. I'm assuming he's Mr. Ash, the auto tech teacher.

"I'm here for class," I say.

His brow wrinkles. "Are you Riley Smith?"

"Yes, Sir."

He shakes his head. "I assumed Riley was a boy's name."

"Sorry," I say, then wish I could take it back. Why am I sorry I'm not a boy? I'm fine with who I am.

"I'm not," someone in class snorts out.

The teacher gives the room a scowl. Then, looking concerned, he walks to the desk in the front of the room and nods as if I'm to join him.

He sits down. I stop at the edge of the desk and wait for him to address me.

He straightens his desk as if trying to garner a few seconds to think. He finally looks up. "Uh… Of course you can take this class, but I think it's fair I tell you that you're starting in second semester and we're past doing the easy stuff. Do you think you can keep up?"

I realize this is an opportunity. I can say I'm not sure, and I'll be out. I can take typing or something else equally lame. But then I realize the room's completely silent. Everyone is listening.

If I bail, Dex and Jacob will think I lied about working on the car. The rest of the class will just assume I quit because girls in general can't keep up. Then another realization hits. I honestly don't know what the class has already covered or if I *can* actually keep up. The reason I signed up was to learn, not to show off.

And *bam*, I remember what Hayden said last night

about needing a challenge. It's like a little flame sparks to life in my chest. I feel the need to prove myself. I even feel excited to prove this teacher and the boys in the class wrong.

I tilt my chin up. "I can keep up."

"Okay," he says.

He looks out at the class. "Who is willing to go over where we are and what we're working on now with Riley?"

Everyone's hands go up. Or everyone but one. Jacob sits, still looking unhappy.

Mr. Ash looks out at the class and frowns. "Jacob, can you do that?"

My stomach clinches.

Jacob answers, "Sure," but his frown says something different.

. . .

That afternoon, with dread, I walk into history class. Because I got promoted to honors English, I don't have that class with Kelsey anymore. But chances are, we still have history together.

I peer in and it seems to be all the same students, but Kelsey isn't there. Relief makes my steps lighter. I was so worried about seeing her that I brought a pack of cheese and crackers and a couple of Rice Krispies Treats and hung out in the back of the library while I ate.

But I'm only one step in when I realize that Jami and three of her close friends are there. Jami actually turns in her seat and gives me the wish-you'd-die look.

I wonder if she already knows I'm in Jacob's auto tech class and he was assigned to mentor me. In spite of not appearing happy about being stuck with me, Jacob was nice. A little distant, and less friendly than before, but still nice.

Before I'm in and settled in my regular seat, one of Jami's friends, Candace, pops up from her desk and saunters over to me. She stares down at me the way I look at Pumpkin when he delivers a Texas-sized cockroach the size of a small bird. Then she sets a toy casket on my desk.

I stare at it. Let the freak party begin, I think.

"Saw this and thought of you," she says, smirking.

I'm still debating how to react when I hear footsteps closing in behind me.

"Why do you always have to be like that?" a voice says and before I glance back I know it's Kelsey. Kelsey is staring down Candace.

"Her father is a mortician," Candace says proud and loud. "Ugh." She shudders. "He touches dead people. And she probably touches him."

Obviously, that was what she wanted to accomplish. To let everyone know I'm a freak. And she's done it well, because I hear the murmurs in the class.

I'm still trying to decide on my response to Candace when Kelsey speaks up again.

"You think that's bad?" Kelsey asks.

I'm confused as to why Kelsey's sticking up for me. Is she not trying to blackmail me?

Candace laughs. "Please, it's completely gross."

"Not as gross as what your dad does for a living," Kelsey says. "Oh, did you not know that he came to my house last month and stuck his hand in my toilet? He probably touched some of my shit."

Everyone in the room belts out laughter.

Candace's face turns red and angry. "You bitch."

"Maybe, but at least I'm my own bitch, and not Jami's bitch. We all know she put you up to this."

More murmurs fill the classroom. Candace takes a step toward Kelsey and I'm afraid this is about to get ugly, so I stand up between them. "Why don't we all just sit down."

But Candace isn't done. She leans in, bumping into my shoulder. "At least I know what color I am! You go around pretending you are lily white when we all know you aren't."

The rudeness of that comment has every muscle in my body clenching. "Stop!" I spill out.

"Seriously? Are you blind or are you just an idiot!" Kelsey holds out her necklace that rests on her shirt. It's a black fist on a Pan-African continent. "Or how about my bracelet?" She holds it up and reads it. "Black Lives Matter."

"You haven't told us you're black," Candace announces as if she has an audience. And she does, because everyone is hanging on every word. Then she looks back at Kelsey.

"And you haven't told me you're white. Or that your dad unstops toilets for a living."

Candace takes a side step as if to get to Kelsey. I side step with her—wanting to derail this argument. But anger bubbles inside me at Candace for her rudeness to Kelsey. It's one thing to attack my dad's career, but to attack someone's race? "She's right," I say. "You're a blind bitch."

The next thing I know Kelsey is moving in front of me. I see her eyes, bright with fury.

I try to pull her back, but she doesn't budge.

She appears so mad that she can't speak, but she lifts a finger and puts it in Candace's face.

I see Candace's eyes tighten into angry slits. I shoot between them again, hoping to stop an out-and-out fight.

But I'm too late, because Candace's fist swings and lands right on my face.

Holy shit! Pain explodes in my eye socket, light explodes in my vision.

"What's going on!" I hear someone yell. I'm pretty sure it's the teacher, but I can't respond. I have one hand against my eye and with the other I grab the back of my desk to keep from falling.

"Are you okay?" I hear her say. I think she's talking to me, but I'm not able to answer. If I open my mouth, a whole slew of four letter words are going to spew out.

• • •

Twenty minutes later, the right side of my face is frozen. But at least I don't feel it throbbing anymore. Keeping the ice pack on it, I open one eye and stare at the white ceiling of the school clinic. I'm reclined on the nurse's table trying like hell to figure out what the frack I'm going to tell my dad.

I begged them not to call him, but nothing I said could stop them.

Shit! I can't tell him about the casket. It would only hurt him.

I hear his voice in the front of the office and cringe. My mind races for what to say, but I don't even know what kind of trouble I'm in. I was escorted straight to the nurse's office and stayed here since the fight. I'm pretty sure that Kelsey and Candace were escorted to the principal's office.

I'm not sure who's luckier.

I hear Dad's hurried footstep down the hall. I sit up, but keep the ice pack on my eye.

He storms in. Worry makes his gait stiff. "I don't understand. What happened?"

"I uh... There was a fight and I got hit."

"Who were you fighting?"

"I wasn't fighting. Not really. I just..."

He moves closer. "Let me see your eye."

I lower the ice pack, hoping it's gone down since I took a peek at it in the bathroom mirror. If not, Dad's going to...

"Oh, baby!" Dad says and from his panicked expression I get the idea it hasn't gone down.

He looks back at the nurse who followed him in. "Do I need to take her to the doctor?"

"Honestly, I don't think so. She says she can see just fine. I think it's just a pretty good shiner. But I just got a call from the principal. She wants to see you."

My spine draws tight. My heart shrinks two sizes.

Dad and I head to the office. I swear it's like I'm walking the green mile. Students everywhere are staring at me. Or staring at my black eye.

"Are you in trouble?" Dad asks.

I shrug. "I don't know." My lips tremble. All I want to do is go home, crawl in my bed, and cry with my one good eye.

• • •

We are escorted right into the office. I swear my knees are shaking. I've never in all my life been summoned to the principal's office. And my first time is with my dad. Sporting a shiner. How humiliating is that?

Don't ask me why, but what scares me more is that they are going to tell Dad about the casket. Other than his last two job losses, which may or may not have been his fault, he's always, always done his best by me.

If he thinks I'm getting made fun of because of him…

"Come in. Have a seat. I'm Ms. Hall, principal here," she says. She looks at my eye and flinches.

I've never met Ms. Hall personally, but I've seen her walking the school. It's hard not to notice her. She's at least six feet tall, dark skin, and wears her hair in tightly woven dreads.

Dad and I take the two chairs opposite her desk. My dad starts in. "I really don't know what happened, but I'll say right up front that Riley has never been in trouble like this before. She's a good kid."

The fact that he's defending me pulls at my heartstrings and makes me want to cry.

"Don't worry, Mr. Smith. I already got the scoop and I'm aware that all Riley did was try to prevent a fight. The two other girls have been dealt with."

Then *bam*, I can't sit there and let them blame this on Kelsey. "It wasn't Kelsey's fault," I blurt out. "Candace was… being ugly to me, and Kelsey stood up to her. Then Candace got even uglier to Kelsey. And Candace was the one who hit me."

Ms. Hall nods. "I'm aware of that, too. But it sounds to me as if they both were antagonizing each other. I'm dealing with them. Don't worry."

I shake my head. "I have to worry. Because you

should deal with Candace, not Kelsey. She didn't do anything wrong."

Dad reaches over and squeezes my arm. "Let's let Ms. Hall do her job, baby."

"But she's wrong," I say and my chest gets tighter. My lungs are about the size of golf balls.

I keep my mouth shut for fear I'll start blubbering. Ms. Hall promises to take into account my complaint, but I'm betting she's already dished out punishment.

We leave. Dad says he'll drive me to school to tomorrow, because he's worried about my eye. On the ride home, I hug the door and don't speak. He lets me sulk, or does until we're almost home. "Why was that girl ugly with you?"

I panic for one second and then answer. "Her best friend is the girl who thinks I'm after her boyfriend. They're just a pack of mean bitches."

• • •

"Man, I'd hate to see the other person."

Asleep, I open my one eye—the second is swollen shut—and stare at Hayden who's lying in bed with me again. I'm in such a pissy mood, I almost call him out on not announcing himself again.

I stop short of it and just say, "It's not funny."

He bites back a smile. "Seriously, what happened?"

"What does it look like happened?" I look at the clock. It's almost time for Dad to be home. I probably should go fix some dinner, but then I think getting sucker punched should give me a kitchen pass.

Hayden's eyes widen. "You really got into a fight?

Really? I mean, I was teasing. I thought you... ran into a wall or something."

I almost want to go with that, but I don't have the energy to lie.

"No wall," I say.

"Wow. Riley Smith is a badass. I didn't have you pegged for that."

"I'm not a badass. I just had the misfortune to have to deal with a badass who also happens to be a bitch."

"Damn. What happened?" He lifts up and leans against the headboard.

"What always happens," I say. Then I explain, "Everyone found out what Dad does and started giving me a hard time."

"So you belted someone?"

"No." I shake my head. "Kelsey, Bessie's granddaughter, stood up for me. Then this bitch, Candace, got pissy with her. I got between them, hoping to prevent anyone from getting hurt and I got hit."

"Hmm," he says. "Sorry. She is a bitch."

Something about the way he said that makes me think... "Do you know Candace or Kelsey?" I haven't considered that he could be from here.

He hesitates. "They are the ones who were at the car show, right?"

"No. Well, Kelsey and Jami were there, but not Candace." My eye throbs and I reach up and touch it. "Where are you from?"

"God's country, of course," he answers.

I study him, not sure if he means...?

"From Texas." He reaches up and touches my cheek.

"That's a pretty bad shiner. I know it hurts. Have you iced it?"

"Yes." I look at him. "Have you had one before?"

"I'm a guy. We get them all the time."

"So you're a badass?" I ask. "I hadn't pegged you for one."

He laughs at me for tossing his words back at him.

"Not really a badass. I just have allergies."

"Allergies?"

"I'm allergic to assholes."

I laugh. I can't believe he got one out of me. Especially when it hurts to crinkle my face.

"Actually," he says, "I've only been in three fights. My worst shiner I got from playing basketball. Elbowed right in the eye." He stares at me. "You're kind of cute with it.

"Please," I say.

He laughs. "Really, the bluish-purple bruise brings out the color of your eyes."

I shoot him the bird.

He chuckles. "See, you are a badass." He adjusts the pillow behind him to get more comfortable. I swear he's in my bed as if he has every right to be. Yet I'm not complaining.

"Help me!" The voice draws my attention at the same time the cold lifts goosebumps on my skin.

I look over and Abby is standing there, her back to me. I release a breath and see steam snake up in front of my face. She feels colder this time. It reminds me that Hayden isn't cold.

"I want to help you," I say. "What did you mean by the truth?"

"What?" Hayden asks, then looks around. "Is it Abby?"

I nod.

"Tell her if she can tell you where the ring is, I can go and make sure it's still there. That way when we drive up there to get it, you'll find it faster."

I never told Hayden I'd do it. But right now doesn't seem like the time to say that.

Abby turns around. I gasp and scoot my ass to the other side of the bed. Her face is… It's bad. Bloody. There's a deep gash on her cheek, one on her throat, and blood is pouring down her pale dress. Her arm is dangling downward, a bone is protruding out of her elbow.

I thought my eye was bad, but both of hers are bloody and swollen shut and one side of her head seems caved in, as if her whole cheek bone is crushed.

My heart hurts. My stomach lurches. I look away.

"What is it?" Hayden asks.

"She looks bad," I say. This hasn't ever happened. They always look nice. Nice like my dad leaves them.

Then I know this is what she looked like before Dad fixed her up. Instantly, my heart goes to my dad. How many times has he had to see death this ugly?

"You have to help me. Please," she starts sobbing.

I try to look at her, but I can't. It hurts to see her. I turn away again.

Right then a knock sounds at my door.

I hear it click open. "Riley? You okay?"

I swallow, turn to my dad peering inside my room, and try to hide the horror from my face. "Yeah."

He stares at me and frowns. I hope it's from my eye and not that he sees the sheer horror I'm feeling.

"How about we order Chinese tonight?"

I nod.

"You sure you're okay?"

"Yeah." I stand, refusing to look at Abby.

"You have to help me," she pleads and her words cause a spasm of pain in my chest.

"I'll order for us," Dad says and moves out into the hall.

"Okay," I manage. And I hear Dad's footsteps tapping down the stairs.

I get to the hall. Then I get black spots in my eyes and for one second I'm not in my hall anymore.

I'm running.

I'm in the woods.

I'm on the edge of a high overhang.

I'm terrified.

I'm falling.

Holy shit!

I'm Abby.

Then I'm not.

I put a hand on the hall wall. Force air into my lungs

"What's wrong?" I hear Hayden ask behind me. His arms come around me. I let him hold me. I need someone to hold me. Even if it's a dead guy.

Somewhere in a distant part of my brain I recall he's not cold. I swear he feels real. I need real.

Then Abby appears in front of me. "Please." Blood runs out of her mouth as she speaks. Her cheek is cut so deep I see bone.

I sidestep around Abby and run into the bathroom.

I shut the door, rush to the toilet, and throw up my lunch of Rice Krispies Treats.

There's no way I'm eating Chinese tonight.

CHAPTER TEN

Dad drops me off in front of my school the next morning. He told me I could stay home. But I know the longer I stay away, the harder it will be to go back. And I have to go back. There's even a part of me that doesn't want Candace to think I'm scared of her.

It's true.

I'm not afraid of Candace. Not after what I felt last night. For that flicker of a second, I was Abby, I was falling off that ledge, and I knew I was going to die. The realization that she didn't go quickly makes it worse.

Nope. Not scared of Candace. Now, what Abby went through… *that* scares me.

But holy shit, I don't want that to happen again. Don't want to feel what she felt. But I don't think I can stop it either.

Well, there is one way. I can help her find the ring and whatever truth she needs. And to do that, I'm going to have to go to Lake Canyon State Park. I'm going to take Hayden up on his offer to go with me, too.

Yeah, I know he's dead and he can't really help me. But just his presence makes me feel... not so alone.

I turn around in the parking lot and watch Dad drive away. As I walk inside the school, I remind myself I only have six months left of high school. As the door swishes shut behind me, those six months feel like a prison sentence.

People turn and stare at me. I let them. I just keep walking, remembering that Hayden said I looked like a badass. I wear that shiner like a badge of honor.

I swear if someone says anything to me, I might shoot them the bird.

I put my books in my locker and head to auto tech. I walk in, step into my coveralls to keep the oil off my clothes, and turn around to be seated.

Everyone is staring. Mouths drop open. Haven't they heard what went down? "Stop staring!" I say.

They don't. So I do it. I shoot them the bird.

Laughter explodes. For some reason, so does my tension.

I spot Jacob and the empty seat beside him and go sit down.

When I lower myself in the desk, I see his expression of total discontent. I'm feeling pretty brave, so I just turn to him.

"Look, if you don't want to be the one showing me the ropes, speak up! You afraid of Mr. Ash?" Yeah, I'm playing the badass card really good right now. But you have to go with it while you've got it.

His frown deepens. "I don't mind."

I cut him a cold look. "Then stop scowling at me."

"I'm not..." He exhales. "This isn't my scowling face. It's my I'm sorry face."

"Well, you need to work on your faces!" I say, glance away, and cross my arms.

I hear him chuckle. "I'll try," he says. "Look, I'm sorry about what happened yesterday."

I glance back at him. "Why are you apologizing? You didn't do this."

"No, but I'm pretty sure my girlfriend—or rather, my ex-girlfriend—was behind it. She has this stupid idea that I have something for you."

I didn't miss the "ex" part or the "stupid" part, but I try not to react. I *do* digest what this means. Jami broke up with him. No wonder he's not happy. I just hope he doesn't blame me.

The next few seconds of silence get awkward.

Frankly, I didn't know what to say, so I ask, "Are we doing a brake job today?" I don't even look at him. Instead I inspect my nails. They still have a smidgen of grease on them from taking a starter motor off yesterday. A job I already knew how to do, by the way. But I'm not bragging.

"Yeah. Brake job." He pauses. At least ten conversations are going on around us. Why is it I think we need to be talking?

He speaks up before I do. "I guess I need to say thank you, too."

That draws my gaze back to him. He's just full of surprises. When he doesn't continue, I'm forced to ask, "For what?"

"For making me realize what a bitch Jami is. She had no right to put Candace up to that."

I shrug and look back at my nails. "It's not a big deal."

He leans in and focuses on my eye. "It's a pretty big deal." He grins. "You actually look like a badass, wearing mechanic coveralls and sporting a shiner."

The badass comment takes me right to Hayden. Hayden, who can't attend school, because he doesn't have a life anymore. My thoughts run wild just a second and I wonder if Hayden were alive if he'd be flirting with me.

I realize Jacob is still looking at me. "I'm not a badass," I say. "I'm just a girl who needs to learn to bleed brakes."

• • •

I actually learned something new in auto tech. Now when my car needs new brakes, I've got it covered. But I'm baffled about Jacob. He's being too nice. Even called a guy out when he made some sly remark about me being careful not to break a nail. I recall what Dad said about him liking me. But then why would Jacob say Jami was "stupid" for having the same idea?

I go to lunch hoping to see Kelsey, but she isn't there. The crazy cashier is super friendly again today. I wouldn't have thought much about it if she'd commented about my eye, but nope, her comment is about dealing with difficult situations. What does she know about my situation?

While eating alone, I watch her cash out other people. She never speaks to any of them. What gives?

When I walk into history, Kelsey's not there, but neither is Candace.

I sit down. Jami turns around and frowns at me. Just to confuse her, or maybe to piss her off, I smile and wave. I can't help but wonder if it's the black eye making me so nervy. Heck, if so, I think I finally understand why guys fight so much.

When Kelsey never shows, I start thinking about how unfair it is that she's in trouble because of me. I can't stand by and do nothing.

After school, I hurry to my locker and then head to Principal Hall's office. The front office checks in with her, and she agrees to see me.

I walk into the office. My nerves are strung tight, but I keep thinking about what Candace said to Kelsey. About how unfair it was that she is being punished for something she wasn't responsible for.

Ms. Hall looks at me and frowns. No doubt at my black eye. She waves at the chairs across from her desk. "What can I help you with, Riley?"

I don't sit. I swallow down a nervous breath, even feel it lodge behind my breastbone. "I'm wondering why Kelsey isn't in school today."

"Both she and Candace are suspended for three days."

I frown. "So you didn't consider what I said about Kelsey being blameless? She was standing up for me."

"I considered it, but we have a very strict no-fighting rule. You were only free from punishment because both girls said you were trying to stop the fight."

"But Kelsey didn't fight either," I say.

"She admitted to getting in Candace's face."

I lift my chin. "Okay, she got in her face, but are you aware of what Candace said to Kelsey?"

Ms. Hall looks taken aback. "That didn't come up in the discussion."

"Maybe you should have taken it upon yourself to find out." I lift my chin a notch, feeling a tad more confident. "Candace put Kelsey down for being part black. That's racist. I'm amazed Kelsey didn't go bat shit crazy on the girl."

I bite my lip when I realize I said shit. The black eye really is giving me a case of badass.

Principal Hall tilts her head a little to the left and lifts an eyebrow. I'm not sure if it's because I said shit or because of what Candace said to Kelsey.

• • •

I'm driving home. Ms. Hall asked me if I had anything else to say, preferably without bad language, then dismissed me. I'm almost to my neighborhood when I spot Kelsey's street. I'm tempted to see if she's home, but then I remember her insistence I had something do with the insurance letter.

Is it wise to get any closer to her?

But she's in trouble because she stood up for me. I turn around and head to her house.

After I park in her driveway it takes me a few minutes to get the nerve to go to her door. But I finally do. I knock on her door and mentally scramble on what to say to her.

She doesn't answer. I hear a cat meowing at the door.

I knock again.

Still no answer. But then I think I hear footsteps.

"Kelsey," I say her name. "I just want to talk, please."

I stand there a few more seconds. I'm about to leave

when I hear footsteps behind me, followed by a voice. "Yeah, well that's all I wanted when I knocked on *your* door."

I turn around. She's standing right behind me. Well, damn, she must've known I was home that day. "I'm sorry."

She stares up at me. "Shit. She got you good."

"Yeah," I say and touch my cheek.

She moves up the porch. "It was meant for me. You shouldn't have gotten between us."

"Yeah, and you shouldn't have stood up for me either."

"Okay, so we were both stupid."

"I wouldn't put it that way," I say.

"How would you put it?"

I hesitate. "I don't know. I'm just sorry you got in trouble. I'm sorry about what Candace said, it was uncalled for."

She doesn't say anything, so I continue. "I tried telling Principal Hall yesterday that it wasn't your fault. Then I went back to see her this afternoon."

Her almost-friendly expression disappears. "You told her what Candace said?" Kelsey's accusation seeps out between her clenched teeth. "That's why she just called my mom and said I could come back to school tomorrow."

"Uh, yeah. I was trying to help."

"Then stop trying!" she blurts out and starts toward the door.

"I thought if she knew how rude Candace was then she'd... back off on your punishment," I say to her back as she grips the doorknob.

She swings around. "Why? Because she's black like me?"

The question stuns me. "No. I never thought... I just... It was so rude."

"So was what Candace said to you. Did you tell the

principal that? That she was making fun of what your dad does for a living?"

My mind starts reeling and I'm beginning to see why she's upset. "Uh, no. I just—"

"Well, I didn't tell her what Candace said to you either, because it wasn't any of my damn business! So keep your nose out of mine. I can handle people making comments about my race. I'm proud of what I am, but it shouldn't be used to get me out of trouble."

She storms past me, walks into her house, and slams the door.

I stand there feeling like shit. I had good intentions when I went to Principal Hall, but damn, now I kind of understand why Kelsey's upset.

I start down the steps, then stop. Damn it. I just want to say I'm sorry.

I swing around and knock on the door again.

CHAPTER ELEVEN

For a second, I think Kelsey isn't going to answer the door. But then it swings open.

"What?!" she snaps.

"I'm sorry. You're right, I shouldn't have gone to her, but I didn't do it because she was black and I wasn't using it get you out of trouble. I just thought what Candace said was extremely rude. I thought I was helping."

She stares at me. "Fine. You're forgiven. Now go away."

She starts to shut the door and I don't know what possesses me to say it, but I do. "Can I come in?"

She studies me.

"For what?"

"To talk," I say.

"Like we're friends or something?" she asks and makes a face.

"We could be. Maybe. Let me come in, please."

She rolls her eyes but backs up.

I step inside. The room is small. A comfortable-looking, green, overstuffed sofa and two chairs fill the room. Two cats come running up and circle my ankles. The smell, herby but still a little sweet, like a garden, fills my nose. It reminds me of how Bessie smelled. I wonder if she's still here, or if perhaps the house just still clings to her scent.

"It's not as big or as nice as yours," she says as if thinking I'm judging.

"It's great. Homey."

"You want a Coke, or something to drink?"

"Sure," I say.

I follow her into the kitchen and she opens the fridge. "We've got Coke, Diet Coke, or water."

"Coke," I say.

She pulls out two sodas and hands me one. "You know, friends don't lie to each other."

In a flicker of a second, I know she's talking about the letter. I actually consider telling her the truth, but come to my senses. "When have I lied?"

She studies me. "The letter."

I palm the cold can, then pop the top. I concentrate on the fizzy noise and allow it to fill the silence while I try to come up with something to say. I force out the words, "I told you I saw it on the sidewalk and put it in your mailbox."

She doesn't look convinced.

"I mean, I don't understand why you would even think I'd send that letter. How would I have known your grandmother had life insurance?"

She frowns. "I haven't figured that out yet."

"Well, when you do, explain it to me." I take it upon myself to sit at the kitchen table. Kelsey sits across from me.

Like the living room, the kitchen feels like a home. Not like our house. I don't even think the house we had in Banker ever felt like a home either. The one in Dallas? Yeah, that was home.

That was where Mom lived, too.

It was part of the reason I didn't want to leave it. Because sometimes I could imagine her there. Or maybe I actually remembered her there.

I realize Kelsey and I are just looking at each other and not speaking, so I throw out a question. "Do you have any siblings?"

"No. Only child. You?"

"No," I say. "So it's just you and your mother living here?"

"Yeah." She looks around. "Feels weird without my grandmother." She exhales. "I swear, sometimes in the corner of my eye I think I see her. But that would be crazy. Ghosts don't exist, right?"

I nod and take a long sip of soda. It burns my throat. "You get along with your mom?"

"For the most part," she says. "She can be a pain in the ass sometimes."

"Did she get mad about you getting suspended?"

"Yeah." She frowns. "I had to hear a lecture on how she wasn't letting me go down the same road she did." She exhales. "She thinks because she screwed up, I'm going to, too."

"Sorry," I say.

"Yeah. What's it like with your dad? I mean, he seems okay."

"Yeah, he's... okay. I mean..." I'm not ready to bare

my soul to her about the drinking stuff, even though for some reason I confided in Hayden.

Kelsey is looking at me, waiting for me to finish to offer something personal. So I do. "We butted heads about my boyfriend when I lived in Dallas. He didn't like me dating. But I haven't dated anyone since we moved from there a year and a half ago, so there's really nothing to argue about."

She turns the soda in her hand. "Do you still talk to him, the boyfriend?"

"No. He stopped calling when he started dating someone else less than two months after I left."

"Asshole," she says.

I grin. "You got a boyfriend?"

"Had one before I moved here, but not since. Everyone here seems to have a stick up their ass."

I laugh.

"So what did you do to piss off Jami?" she asks.

"Nothing. Well, Jacob and Dex had stopped off to see my car when I was at the car show. Jami and a friend of hers walked up a few minutes later and Jacob was talking to me. She glared at me as if we were kissing or something. They walked off to look at cars and she ducked back, called me a bitch and told me to stay away from him."

"She's the bitch." Kelsey takes a drink of her soda. "Are you really taking auto tech?"

"Yeah. How did you know?"

"Everyone was talking about it at school yesterday. I'm sure that has Jami all kinds of pissed off."

"She broke up with him," I say.

"Seriously?" Kelsey asks.

"Yeah. Well, I don't who broke up with who, but he told me today that they broke up."

"Shit. Is he hitting on you?"

"No," I say and tell her about his "stupid" comment.

"He could just be playing it cool," she says. "He did stop by to see you at the car show."

"He stopped by to see my car, not me."

"Maybe," she says.

I recall thinking she might have something for Jacob. "Why don't you go for it?"

"Go for what?"

"Jacob."

"Me and Jacob?" She laughs. "That so isn't going to happen. You can have him."

I give her a direct stare. "You said he was nice to look at."

She hesitates as if trying to recall that conversation. "I said if you were into his type. He's not my type."

"Tell me you weren't sitting out there enjoying the view."

She makes a face. "Okay, I was enjoying the view, but it wasn't Jacob I was enjoying."

"Dex?" I ask.

"Yeah. But..." She gives me the evil eye. "If you say anything, I'll blacken your other eye."

Her threat seems harmless. "I wouldn't say anything. But why don't you go for Dex? Or is he going out with someone?"

"No, but... *I'm* not *his* type."

"What's his type?" I ask.

"White." She frowns.

I make a face. "Do you really think that matters?"

"Not to me. I'm proud of it. I wish my skin was darker. But it does matter in this backwoods town."

She changes the subject really fast. We talk about our teachers. About why I like to work on cars—a necessity, not a passion—and we go back to talking about old boyfriends. It's really nice to chat with her. And much to my surprise, I really think we might become friends.

My phone dings and it's from Dad. "Crap," I say. "It's my dad. He's says he on the way home. I told him I was going to fix dinner. I should go."

I stand up and she walks me out to the porch. I'm about to walk down the steps and then I turn around. "Do you want a lift to school tomorrow?"

"If you don't mind, that would be great," she says.

"I'll pick you up around 7:20."

"I'll be ready." She smiles.

Yup, I think we *will* become friends. And that feels nice. Really nice.

When I step off her porch, I see Jacob sitting on the tailgate of his truck. He jumps off and starts walking across the street as if he saw my car and was waiting for me.

I look up and see Kelsey standing at the edge of the porch. "Go get him."

I make a face at her and keep walking toward my car.

"Hey," he says, as he steps onto the driveway.

"Hi."

"You and Kelsey friends?" he asks.

"We're working on it," I say.

"You live around here?" He scrubs his shoe on the concrete.

"Yeah." I pull my keys out of my pocket.

He dips down and looks at my car through the driver's window. "You should take me for a ride."

"Sure," I say. "But later, I need… I gotta go."

"Okay." He backs up. "See you tomorrow."

"Yeah." When I drive away, I look at him in the rear-view mirror. He's standing there watching me. Or watching my car. That has to be it, because it's a *stupid* idea to think he has something for me. But dang, he really is nice to look at.

• • •

I hurry home and heat up two cans of chili and stick some frozen garlic bread in the oven. Thankfully, Dad's not picky.

While we eat, I tell him about learning to change out the brakes. "And Jacob, the guy I'm teamed up with, said the brakes on my car are even easier."

"I could have taught you that," Dad says.

"I know, but now you don't have to." Then I tell him about Kelsey getting suspended and how I went by to see her. "I think we might become friends," I tell him.

He looks up, holding a spoon of chili close to his mouth, and kind of frowns. "Becoming friends with a girl who just got suspended. Uh… I don't know."

I counter his frown with my own. "Dad, I told you the only reason the whole thing happened was because she was standing up for me. I think that makes her good friend material. And I thought you'd be happy. You've been telling me I need to make friends for over a year!"

He sets his spoon back in the bowl. "Okay, I'm sorry. I just don't want you to get mixed up with the wrong crowd."

"She's not the wrong crowd."

"Okay. Time will tell."

I frown at him again. Time will tell about him, too. If he's drinking, sooner or later I'll know.

When I glance up, Dad changes the subject to the upcoming car show.

We're both eating a second helping of chili when I feel the chill surround me. I'm scared to look back, afraid it's Abby.

Dad looks up. "I swear something's up with the heater in this house. It's as cold as my morgue."

Duh, I think, but don't say anything.

I'm just about to scoop up another bite when I notice her. Abby moves around to the other side of the table and stands right behind Dad so I can't help but see her. It's not a pretty sight. She's still bloody and without Dad's makeup job.

Her presence makes it hard to keep up a conversation with Dad. Not that she says anything, but just the sight of all that blood makes me feel queasy and guilty—as if I've let her down.

If she'll just leave and come back later, I'll tell her I'm going to risk really pissing Dad off and taking a road trip to the state park.

She moves closer to the table. I finally drop my spoon and look away.

I'm tempted to run off to my room, but I worry about Dad being alone. Instead, I jump up and start cleaning the kitchen. "You want to watch another episode of the series we started last night?" I ask him, not looking back.

He agrees and we settle down in the living room. Pumpkin, freaking because of Abby, comes and crawls up in my lap.

Abby finally disappears, but when I get up to grab a Rice Krispies Treat, Hayden is sitting at the table again watching the TV with us. A somber feeling tightens my chest. I wonder if he's lonely.

He smiles at me. Damn, he does look lonely.

Before I can stop myself, I smile back. Before I can stop myself, my heart hurts for him. Before I can stop myself, I wish he wasn't dead. I wish I could let myself like him.

CHAPTER TWELVE

When I walk to my room an hour later, Hayden is stretched out on my bed. I should really tell him that it's not acceptable, but I don't have the heart.

"Your eye's even prettier today," he says. Pumpkin, who's following me, jumps up on the bed with him.

I turn and look at myself in my dresser mirror and frown. It looks darker now. "Ugh," I say.

"Any more fist fights?" he asks.

"No. I actually think this makes me look a little scary. People are giving me a wide berth in the hall."

"It's not just the black eye," he says. "It's how you're rocking it. Most girls would have tried to cover it up with makeup or at least wear a pair of sunglasses. But not you. It's like you own it and aren't afraid to get another one, if push comes to shove."

I chuckle. "Actually, I figured trying to hide it would just make it more noticeable." I open my backpack and pull out my English and math books to do my homework.

Because it feels weird crawling into bed with him, I drop my books on my desk and sit down.

"Homework?" he asks.

"Yeah." I start to look back but he's standing beside me. I feel his hand on my shoulder. It instantly brings to mind our kiss.

"Want my help?" he asks.

I look up at him. "I think I can do it."

"Oh, so you're a badass and smart."

I chuckle. "I'm just a temporary badass, but yes, I'm one of the brainy nerd types."

"You in honors classes?"

I nod.

"Me, too," he says. Then his smile wanes. "Or I was."

I set my pencil down. "You want to talk about it?"

"Hell no," he says.

I frown. "You know, I hear it's not bad."

"What's not bad?"

"Heaven, or I guess I should say *the afterlife*. I've been told it looks very peaceful."

"I think I like it better here."

I inhale. "Aren't you lonely?"

"Not anymore. I like the company I've been keeping lately. I like her a lot."

I bite down on my lip. "I don't think that's the way this is supposed to go. I'm supposed to help you move on."

"You don't like my company?"

"No. I do." *Too much.* "But I feel as if I'm not doing my job."

He stands up and sits on the edge of the desk. "Maybe

that's not your job with me." He reaches out and runs a finger over my cheek. "I'm different. You said so."

I nod and push his hand away. "I just wish you'd talk to me."

"I am talking to you."

I frown. "You know what I mean."

"Maybe in time," he says.

I focus back on my paper, unsure how to get him to open up.

"Was Abby here when you were eating dinner?" he asks.

I look up. "Yeah. And so were you, I guess."

"Well, I popped in. It was extra cold. She makes it that way, doesn't she?"

I nod and wonder why he doesn't make it that way, too.

"Is she still asking you to find her ring?"

"Yeah, and I think I'm going to have to do it. Would you really go with me to the state park?"

He smiles. "Are you asking me out on a date?"

"I'm asking you to go with me to find a ring."

"It's a date," he grins.

I turn back and start working. I wonder if he knows how much I wish it *were* a date. How much I wish he were alive.

"When are we going?" he asks.

"I don't know. I have to talk to Abby."

"You're scared of her, aren't you?"

"A little," I say. "But mostly I just feel sorry for her." I remember what I felt last night in the hall. As if I were her. "Maybe I'm scared because she is. Sometimes I feel what a spirit is feeling."

"She's scared?" he asks.

"Yeah. Not that I blame her, because she was lying on the ledge for over twenty-four hours. She had to have been in pain, and alone."

"That would be scary," he says.

I draw in a deep breath. "I have to help her."

"We will help her," Hayden says. "You aren't alone anymore."

"Yeah," I say and look back down to figure out the math problem, knowing sooner or later I'll have to find a way to fix my Hayden problem.

● ● ●

Dad's up and moving when I come downstairs the next morning. I'm starting to seriously think I was wrong about his drinking. He gives my shoulder a squeeze and says goodbye.

I chomp down on cheese toast and give Pumpkin a tiny piece to nibble on.

Abby hadn't returned last night. But I woke up at one point and Hayden was in bed with me. He was sleeping. I didn't know the dead slept.

I started to wake him up to remind him of the rules. But he looked so peaceful. So I just lay there and watched him. I wanted to roll closer so bad. To touch him. To kiss him. But I didn't. Then I remembered what he said: "You aren't alone anymore."

He's right. I haven't felt nearly as lonely. My job is to get him to pass on, but part of me doesn't want him to go. Could that be the reason I haven't been pressing him to talk more about why he might be here? I need to do something about that.

I get my backpack and shut off the lights. While I didn't see Hayden this morning, I have a vague memory of him kissing me early this morning and saying he'd see me later. I reach up and touch my lips.

I leave the house and go pick up Kelsey.

She gets in my car and studies me. Or I should say, she studies my eye. "I swear it's even darker now."

I frown. "I know. They say a black eye can last a week."

"Give me your phone," she says.

"Why?" I ask.

"Because you need a picture of this. Someday, when you're old, you can brag to your grandkids how you were tough as shit and taught a bully a lesson."

I laugh, but hand her my phone. "So I'm going to lie to my grandkids?"

"No. Just embellish it." She snaps a shot, checks it, and laughs. "Yup, tough as shit."

I start the car. I'm not at the end of her street when she says, "So you aren't going to tell me?"

I look at her. "Tell you what?"

"What Jacob said to you yesterday when he walked over to your car."

"Oh." I realize how odd it is that I haven't even thought about that. A week ago, I would have been analyzing the crap out of it, trying to make more out of it than there was.

Deep down I know why I'm not obsessing over Jacob. Hayden.

I tell her what Jacob said about me giving him a ride sometime.

"Damn, he likes you," she says.

"No, he likes my car."

"Are you dense?"

"No."

"Don't you think he's cute?" She looks at me all baffled.

"I did. I mean, I do. It's just…" *I'm hung up on a dead guy.* "He said it was a stupid idea."

"So he lied." She lifts a brow. "People do that sometimes."

I know she's referring to me. I ignore it.

She continues, "I'll bet within two weeks he asks you out on a date."

"I doubt that." We go into school and walk each other to our lockers before splitting up.

It's amazing how much easier school is when you have one person you can look forward to passing in the hall, or lunch. As I walk toward the cafeteria, I look for her. She's waiting just on the other side of the door. We walk in and get in line.

"How was auto tech?" she asks and we move slowly to the front of the line.

I hold up one hand. "I broke a nail."

She laughs. "Seriously, how was Jacob?"

"Friendly," I say, but for some reason I don't mention that he suggested I take him for a ride in my car again, because I think she'll make a big deal out of it. And maybe because I'm wondering if Kelsey and Dad are right. I can't deny there's a part of me that likes the idea. But I don't like it as much as I should.

We get our lunches—Kelsey goes for a salad and water, I go for pizza and chocolate milk—and move in line closer to the cashier. I turn back to Kelsey. "What's up with this cashier?"

"Who?"

"The cashier," I say. "She weirds me out."

Kelsey leans to the left to see the cashier. "Why does she weird you out?"

"She's too friendly."

"Friendly? I don't think she's ever spoken to me."

"Yeah, well she speaks to me."

The line moves up several spaces and we're almost in front of the cash register so we stop talking.

I push my tray and stop in front of her and wait for her to ring it up.

She stops, looks up, then smiles. "It's so good to see you two have made friends." She hits a few keys. "That will be three dollars and fifty cents."

I put four dollars on the counter and cut Kelsey a quick look, who appears all kinds of surprised.

"How do you know we're friends?" Kelsey asks.

She looks up. "Your auras are blending."

"Our auras?" Kelsey asks. The cashier hands me my change and rings up Kelsey without answering.

As we walk away, Kelsey looks at me and chuckles. "Okay, now I'm weirded out."

"Told you." We both laugh and find a spot. "She probably saw us talking," I say and I don't know who I'm trying to convince, Kelsey or myself.

"I know." Kelsey says. "But you're right, she's weird. Who believes in auras?"

"Right?" I say and then I realize something. If I can see spirits, maybe other people can see auras. Then another thought hits. Could the cashier know about me? Know my secret? Does she know I can see dead people?

• • •

I park my car in my driveway. When I dropped off Kelsey, she asked if I wanted to hang out. I told her I had some chores today and suggested we do it tomorrow. It wasn't a lie. I have the chore of being here, hoping Abby comes by. It's much less of a chore if Hayden stops in.

I sit behind the wheel and stare up at the house. I remember Hayden asking if I was scared of Abby. I wish he wasn't so right. Little does he know I'm scared of him, too.

Not the same kind of scared. I'm frightened that I like him too much. Scared the reason I'm not even happy that Jacob might have a thing for me is because of a dead guy who makes me laugh. Makes me feel less lonely. Makes me want to challenge myself. I spent several hours last night staring at him, wishing he was alive.

This sucks.

I get out of my car and go inside. "Hello," I say to the emptiness, thinking, or maybe hoping, Hayden is here.

Silence and bare white walls greet me. I think of Kelsey's house feeling like a home. The walls were covered with artwork or family pictures. The end tables had knickknacks and ceramic cat figurines that gave the place personality. I look around. This house has no personality.

Or maybe it just feels motherless. Mothers are the ones who hang things, who make the nest.

There is no mother here. But I'm here. And I should have worked on our nest.

I remember our old house in Dallas, the one that felt like a home. I suddenly realize that the things in that house could have been put there by my mother. But we still have them, don't we?

Yes, I know we brought them. I know because I recall seeing several boxes of house stuff when we were packing to move here. There was artwork and decorative stuff.

I should find them and make this house feel like a home.

Pumpkin's sweet meow pulls my thoughts away from the bare walls.

I meet him in the kitchen. He's staring at his empty bowl as if hungry. "You're going to get fat," I tell him, but grab the cat food from the cabinet and pour some kibbles out. Then I grab a Rice Krispies Treat. Pumpkin stares at me as if to say, "You're gonna get fat, too."

I put some chicken and potatoes and carrots in the oven for dinner, and still hungry, I grab an apple and sit down at the kitchen table, eating my healthy food for the day. I listen to Pumpkin crunch his kibbles. The house feels too quiet. I remember the crazy vision I had of Abby and I'm suddenly uncomfortable in my own skin. I wish I'd hung out with Kelsey.

I pull my phone over and think about calling her to ask if it's too late. We'd exchanged contact information on the ride home. But I might miss Abby and I need to see this through. I need to get Abby to cross over so I can really concentrate on Hayden.

Exhaling a sad sigh, I toss the half-eaten apple in the garbage and decide to do my homework. I grab my backpack and get busy. I'm almost finished when I turn around and see the light beeping on our home phone. Just another telemarketer, I'm sure. I'm not even sure why Dad feels the need to have a landline, since we both have cell phones.

I hit the message button. "Hi, Bret? This is Nancy Duarte."

Nancy works with dad. Why is she calling him here? Didn't he go to work?

She continues, "I'm just a little worried. It's two and you haven't returned from lunch and I haven't been able to reach you on your cell."

My heart drops. Shit. What happened to my dad?

I grab my phone and dial him. My heart's pounding. I try not to think about him being in an accident. Or in the hospital, hurt. About him…

He's all I've got. My chest feels heavy with all the ugly possibilities.

"Hello?" Dad answers the phone.

The sound of his voice sends a wave of calm over me. "Hey. Are you okay?" I swallow down the raw panic but I'm sure some of it leaked into my voice.

"Yeah, I'm fine. Why?"

"I just found the message that Ms. Duarte left. She was looking for you."

He hesitates one second. And it's that second that makes something feel wrong.

"It was nothing," he says. "I went by to pick up some coffee supplies. I didn't hear her call."

But I do hear something in his voice. A slight aggravation. And something else. It almost feels as if he's… lying. I can't ever remember Dad lying to me.

Did he go to lunch and start drinking?

"Look," he says. "I'm going to stay a little later to catch up on a few things here."

My mind's still racing and I'm trying really hard to convince myself I'm wrong. "I made some baked chicken," I say. "With the red potatoes and carrots that you like."

"Go ahead and eat. It might be eight or nine before I get home."

I stand there in the empty house with bare white walls, without a mother, and I feel as if the foundation beneath me is cracking. "Dad...?"

"Yeah?"

I close my eyes. "Are you really okay?"

"Of course I am. Why would you even ask that?"

"I just worry sometimes."

"Then stop. I'll see you tonight."

He hangs up. It feels abrupt. It feels wrong. My foundation continues to crack.

I put my phone down, stare at the fridge, and remember the sound of ice clinking. Turning around, I stare across the living room. His bedroom door is closed. It's always closed.

I stiffen my spine, square my shoulders, and walk over to that door.

He's my father. I have a right to know.

CHAPTER THIRTEEN

Stepping inside, I find his room is neat and tidy. Dad's always been that way. The bed isn't made but only one side of it looks slept in.

I take a deep breath and my chest hurts. It smells like him. His aftershave. I look around. I've only been in here a couple of times. But the quilt on the bed looks familiar.

There aren't any liquor bottles sitting out. But knowing my dad, he wouldn't leave them out.

I walk over to his bedside table, which has two drawers. My hands are shaking. This feels wrong, but so does not knowing. I open the top drawer.

There's a few books, even a bible, but no bottle.

I open the next one to find magazines. And allergy medicine.

I draw in a deep gulp of air, turn around and go to the other bedside table. I search it. There's some tax forms and a notebook. No alcohol.

I look at the dresser. Then my gaze goes to the door

leading to the master bathroom, a room with cabinets. It makes sense he would keep it there.

I swallow the knot of betrayal down my throat and walk in there. Like the bedroom, it's clean. Only toothpaste and mouthwash litter the counter. I walk up to the cabinet and open it.

It's empty with the exception of some cleaning supplies. I check all of the other cabinets. There's no alcohol.

I'm beginning to feel like a snoop.

I walk back into the bedroom, planning to walk out. But I look at the chest of drawers.

I walk over and open the first drawer. Nothing but underwear. Folded underwear. Dad really is a neatnik. I open the second and find socks. The third drawer has pajama bottoms.

The fourth is empty. The fifth has a few books, the sixth, the last, and bottom drawer, has what looks like two stacks of old jeans.

Nothing.

Does it mean he's not drinking?

I go to close it, but it catches. I push extra hard. When I do, I hear something rattle. Something glass. Something that might just break my heart.

I pull the drawer open and lift the first stack of jeans and find nothing. When I lift the second stack, I feel it. I pick the pile of jeans up and set them on the floor, and my heart drops.

It's not a bottle. It's a framed photograph. My bottom lip trembles. The photograph is of Dad and Mom. Their wedding day, I think, because she's wearing a pretty cream-colored dress and Dad's in dress pants and a button-down shirt with a tie.

Why wouldn't Dad show me this?

I drop back on my butt and pull it out. I stare at Mom's face. For the first time, I see it, the resemblance between Mom and me. And I see my dad's expression. He looks so happy, so much in love. Tears fill my eyes. I think of him pulling out this picture, staring at it, and missing her. I imagine him looking at me and missing her. I imagine how lonely he is.

I wish he could move on. But look at me. I barely remember her and I haven't moved on.

I touch the photograph as if it will somehow be like touching my mom. I continue to stare at it, taking in all of the tiny details. Then I notice something. I blink and look harder. At least now I think I know why I haven't seen the photograph.

Mom's pregnant.

Was that why he'd hidden the picture? I still don't like it. Don't like the secrets.

"You okay?"

I look over and Hayden is sitting on the floor beside me.

"No," I say. I tell him about the phone call and how I ended up finding the photo.

"That's good news, though, right? Maybe he's not drinking."

I nod. I want to believe it. "But he acted so funny on the phone."

He looks at the picture. "Your mom?"

I wipe a few tears from my cheek. "I'm pretty sure it was their wedding day."

He looks up at me. "You look like her."

I start crying again. "I haven't seen the resemblance in any of the other pictures, but I do in this one. Why do people have to die? It friggin' pisses me off!"

He puts his arm around me and holds me.

"I hate death," I say, and I mean both my mom's and his.

Before long we are stretched out on Dad's floor. Spooning. I'm curled up beside him.

"How did she die?" His hand moves over my shoulders. The light fluttering touch feels so good.

"A brain aneurysm."

"Were you there when it happened?"

I shake my head. "I don't think so. I can barely remember when she was alive. But the other day I kind of recalled him telling me she was gone. I didn't even know how she died until I was like twelve and asked him. He didn't want to tell me, but I forced him to."

"At least she didn't linger and suffer."

The way he says that makes me remember my promise to myself that I would try harder to get him to talk.

"Did you? Did you suffer?"

He rolls over and faces me. "You help me forget the bad stuff."

"Maybe you aren't supposed to forget," I say. "Maybe you're supposed to deal with it."

He traces a finger over my lips. "You know, even with a black eye you are so damn beautiful."

His mouth brushes mine and I'm weak enough to let him. The kiss deepens. He's so close that my whole body feels tingly and wonderful. He never touches places he shouldn't, but when his chest comes against my breasts, I wish he would. I ease closer.

Time seems to stop. My pain seems to stop. But we don't.

It's me and Hayden, tempting fate, finding comfort, and forgetting everything bad.

A dinging noise shatters the sweetness and brings me out of that wonderful moment.

I feel as if I've fallen back to earth. It takes several seconds and a few more dings before I recognize the noise. It's the oven, telling me the chicken is done, telling me I'm making a mistake with Hayden.

I sit up, hug my knees and look away from him. "Hayden—"

"Don't say it. Please don't regret it. That's the most I've felt alive in… a long time."

I exhale. "It can't be right."

"But it didn't feel wrong," he says. "You can't say it felt wrong."

I gaze at him. He looks afraid I'm going to reject him. I feel afraid that I have to.

"It didn't feel wrong, but it has to be. You can't stay here."

He looks away for a second, then back. "Not forever, but for a little while. You're good for me, Riley Smith. I think I'm good for you, too. You're smiling more. Sometimes when you see me, you look happy. I make you happy."

But what about when you leave? Loving and losing hurts like a paper cut right across your heart. I loved and lost my mother. I loved and lost all my friends and Carl in Dallas. I'm afraid I might lose my dad. And if I don't put a stop to what's happening between Hayden and me, I'm going to end up loving him. Loving someone who is already lost to me.

With a sore heart and more confused than ever, I get up, and go pull the dinner out of the oven.

The heat of the oven blasts out when I open it. It's only when I see the steam rise around me that I realize I have company. Cold company.

Chills spider up my neck and down my arms and legs.

Sitting the casserole dish on the stove top, I turn around, prepared to see a bloodied Abby.

It's Abby, but she's not bloody. She's just sadder than I've ever seen her. Dark shadows ring her eyes. Her skin's a light grayish blue color. She looks so... dead.

She is dead.

"Hi," I say.

She glances at me. "Please. Please help me. I can't—"

"I'm going to," I say.

Her hollow, lifeless eyes show a touch of hope. "You will?"

"Yes. I'll go to the park tomorrow, but you have to be there. If you aren't, I won't be able to find the ring. You understand?"

She nods. "I'll be there. I'll show you everything." Then she hugs herself as if "everything" is ugly.

"Everything?" I ask. "We're just looking for a ring, right?"

She doesn't answer.

"I can't stay at the park long. So don't be late." I hug myself now too.

She nods.

"Is there something you're not telling me?"

"Tomorrow," she says.

She fades. But now, standing almost where she'd been, is Hayden. He looks unsure of himself. As if he's nervous to face me.

"So we're going to the park tomorrow?" he asks.

I nod.

"What else did she tell you?"

"Nothing. She's being mysterious. She's not telling me everything." I look at him, and I remember us making out on my dad's bedroom floor. "Look, about what happened—"

"Don't be mad," he says.

"I'm not," I say. "It's just… this is hard."

"I'm sorry." He sticks his hands in his pockets. "Please don't ask me to leave."

My tonsils suddenly feel too big for my throat. For the first time, I feel I have some leverage, and I have to use it. I need to do the right thing by him.

"Only if you will tell me what happened to you. I know you don't want to accept it, but the reason you are here is for me to help you." I stop short of saying I'm here to help him "move on," but I think he knows that. "And I can't do that if I don't understand what you are going through."

He swallows. There's a sheen in his eyes. There's tears in mine.

"Talk to me, Hayden. Please."

He shuffles his feet. "It was a car accident. My fault. I wasn't paying attention. I ran a red light. It's killing my mom. We were arguing at home and I jumped into my car and left just to cool off." He swallows. I hear him gulp. "I want to go back to that moment and not screw up. Not even for me, but for her. I know she blames herself and it's not her... It's my fault."

I move so close to him, I feel his energy. I feel his sadness. I feel his pain.

My head leans on his chest. He wraps his arms around me and we stand there in each other's arms.

"I'm sorry," I say.

His face leans down on my head.

"Tell me another secret," he says.

I know he just wants to take the focus off of him, and perhaps I shouldn't let him, but I can't help myself.

"I'm afraid to go away to college. Afraid I'll miss Dad too much. Afraid he'll miss me too much. Afraid of really being completely alone in the world."

His hold tightens. Warm and tender feelings travel through me.

"Tell me one," I say.

"My stepfather is cheating on my mom. I hate him for it. My real dad would never have done that to her."

"I'm sorry," I say.

"Me too."

And I realize in that moment that it might be too late to protect my heart. I'm a whisper away from falling in love with Hayden Parker.

• • •

"Here's another one, *Don't Eat the Yellow Snow*," Hayden says, humor filling his voice. He's riding shotgun and we're on the way to Lake Canyon State Park.

I laugh. "You're making this shit up." The conversation

started with us talking about the different kinds of music we like and then moved to crazy song titles. We'd been laughing about one thing or another since we left.

"I swear it's a real song, by Frank Zappa," he says. "And then there was a group called The Cramps that had one titled, *Don't Eat the Stuff Off the Sidewalk*. Or even better, *Billy Broke My Heart at Walgreens And I Cried All the Way To Sears*."

A laugh pours out of me. "I haven't ever heard of any of those."

"Some of them are from a long time ago."

I look at him and the thought hits. "How do you know about them? You aren't from a long time ago, are you?"

"No," he says. "I wrote an essay on crazy song titles for English last year."

Last year? Does that mean he died last year? I'm still trying to piece together things about his life.

"And," he continues, "There's one, *If My Nose Was Running Money, I'd Blow it All on You*."

I laugh so hard I get tears in my eyes. "Hey, I've got one," I say. "*She Thinks My Tractor Is Sexy*. I forget the artist's name."

"Kenny Chesney. He was on my list, too. In fact, country and western music has some really good ones, like, *You're the Reason Our Kids Are Ugly* or *Did I Shaved My Legs for This?*"

We both laugh and our eyes meet for one second.

I quickly glance back to the road. I think he's going to say something romantic, or sweet, because it just feels right, but nope. "Then there was one, *How Can I Miss You if You Won't Go Away?*"

That one earned a snort from me. But it's short-lived when I realize how much I'm going to miss him. I recall the saying about it being better to have loved and lost than never have loved at all. I think it's the biggest pile of bull-shit I've ever heard.

I'm already grieving his loss.

He continues, "One of my all-time favorites is, *I'm So Miserable Without You It's Almost Like Having You Here.*"

Laughter fills the car. I get tears in my eyes again but this time they're only partly due to my laughter.

We'd started out for Lake Canyon State Park at nine this morning. I'd been a big pile of raw nerves, worrying about lying to Dad, worrying about not finding Abby's ring, but Hayden had made me forget.

Thankfully, convincing Dad I should stay home from school was a cakewalk. All I had to do was say the words "cramps" and "period," and Dad cratered. I hated lying to him, but I didn't see another way to help Abby. If he ever finds out I drove this far, or that I lied to him, my ass will be grass.

That said, I'm pretty sure Dad's lying to me, too.

Last night he hadn't gotten home until almost nine. He hadn't smelled like alcohol. I know. I hugged him twice to find out. But his eyes looked so tired, maybe even a tad bloodshot. He barely ate any dinner. And he went to bed early. I sat halfway down the stairs for an hour waiting to hear ice clinking, swearing if I heard it, I would run down and confront him. That tiny sad noise never happened. I tried to take comfort from it, but it was hard.

Before I went to sleep last night, I texted Kelsey to say I wouldn't be at school, using the same lie I told Dad. I also wrote that if I were feeling better by the afternoon, I'd call her to hang out. I'm just hoping Abby is as good as her word and shows up at the park.

"You're not smiling anymore," Hayden says.

"Sorry. I was just thinking about Abby."

I glance at him. He looks genuinely happy. I wonder if our talk yesterday helped him.

I hope so. Because telling him about my worries for Dad and about leaving for college had taken some of the weight off my shoulders. But there's a chance he's using humor as a ploy to prevent me from asking more questions. If so, it's working. Talking about stupid song titles is much more fun than talking about death.

Or about him crossing over.

"Right up here is where you turn," he says.

I realize what this means. "You said you've been here before, right?"

"Yeah."

I recall he told me he was from Texas. "Did you live close to here?"

"Pretty much," he says. The vagueness in his answer hangs on longer than his words.

I'm about to call him on it, but I see the entrance to the park and I pull in. Discovering Hayden's truth will have to wait until I solve Abby's mystery.

CHAPTER FOURTEEN

I get out of the car. The warm weather trend is over and now the January cold seeps through my hoodie. I pull it closer. The sky is gray and we could use a little sun to lighten up the day.

Hayden appears beside me. "Is she here?"

"I don't see her." I glance around.

"I don't feel the iciness either," he says.

The question tumbles out before I can stop it. "Why aren't you cold like the others?"

"You kidding? Just look at this bod. I'm too hot to be cold." The tease in his tone, in his expression, makes me smile. Then I turn away before I'm tempted to do just as he suggests and look at his body. There's no denying it. He's got the whole muscle thing working for him. I wonder if he worked out, or if he played sports.

I lean against my car. I'm just about to ask him when someone walks up to get in his car. I realize people would think I was talking to myself. It's so easy to forget that he's not really here. That he's not real to anyone but me.

I wait until the man pulls away before speaking up again. "I really hope I haven't come all this way for nothing."

"You're nervous." He inches closer.

I look at him. "If my dad finds out I'm here, I'm up Shit Creek without a paddle."

"Don't worry, I'll throw you a line." He moves even closer and chuckles. "I'll take on a little shit to protect you."

I chuckle. His shoulder comes against mine. I want to lean into him, but I hold myself stiff. At the front of the parking lot, a pregnant woman gets into a car. My thoughts shoot to Mom's baby bump in the photograph I found in Dad's drawer.

"What's on your mind now?" Hayden asks.

I tell him what I noticed in the picture.

"Do you care?" he asks. "It doesn't change anything."

"No, I don't care. It's just… I hate knowing my dad is keeping secrets from me."

"Yeah, but he's a parent. He might think if you knew your mom got pregnant before marriage, it would encourage you to try it."

"That's stupid," I say.

"Yeah, and parents are stupid sometimes."

I can't argue with that. Right then an unnatural cloud of cold falls on me. And it doesn't come from Hayden. I glance around.

"She's here, isn't she?" Hayden asks, and rubs his hands up his arms.

"Yeah." I see her standing a few feet in front of me. She's hugging herself, looking ten times more afraid than

I am. My anxiety builds. I know it's from her, but I feel it like it's my own.

I check to make sure no one is about to walk up, then move forward. "Abby?"

She looks at me. Her eyes are round. She's trembling. Her hands are fisted.

"Are you okay?" I move closer.

"When this is over I will be." Tears fill her eyes and one spills out. As it rolls down her cheek, it takes with it the makeup applied to cover up her deadly pallor. Her blue-tinted skin shines through. She looks toward the paths leading into the park. "Go up Trail A. I'll meet you there."

I reach out and touch her arm.

The burn of cold makes my palm ache. I pull it back. She fades. I rub my hand up and down my hip.

"What's wrong?" Hayden asks.

"She's scared."

"So that's why you're afraid, right?" Hayden asks.

I nod and start walking. "She said to walk up Trail A." With each step, I hear a tiny voice saying "I don't want to do this." I'm obviously still feeling Abby's emotions. Hayden stays close to my side.

"Do they all project emotions?" he asks.

"Yeah, most of them."

"Do I?" The moment the question leaves his lips, he looks as if he was sorry he'd asked.

"A little."

"What kind?"

I debate answering, but then just blurt it out. "Sadness, but only every now and then."

He moves in until his shoulder brushes against mine.

145

I recall the icy cold burn I felt on my palm from touching Abby and again I wonder why he's so different.

"Sorry," he says. "I'll work on that."

I think of our whole song-title conversation, and know he's already been working on that. "You make me laugh more than I feel sadness," I say and it's the truth. He makes me feel a lot of things.

We start up Trail A. Trees hug the path. Their shade makes the day feel damper, darker, denser. The trail leads up. You can tell why they call this the Texas Hill Country.

The vision from the other night, running up and falling off the side of a cliff, starts playing in my head.

Hayden, as if tuned into my fear, slips his hand into mine. It's comforting. The only burn I feel from him is my heart warning me not to let myself care too much.

But I already do.

"Why do you think she's so scared?" he asks.

"She fell and laid there on that path for a long while. I would be scared to come back here, too."

Then I remember something from the vision. "Shit!"

"What?"

"I had a vision or something the other night. She was running when…" My mind continues to collect data and connect dots. "She was already afraid of something when she fell."

"Was she running away from someone?" he asks.

"I don't know." A cold wave of dread circles me, closes in on me.

He exhales. "You don't think that… someone was after her, do you? That someone pushed her off the ledge?"

Cold fear climbs my spine. I stop walking. The ugly

possibilities start crowding my mind, causing a feeling of claustrophobia. Everything feels too close: the trees, the weeds, the truth.

I remember something else. "She said she wanted everyone to know the truth. I hope the truth isn't that... that she was murdered."

He squeezes my hand. "Maybe we shouldn't go there. This might be too dangerous. Let's just turn around," Hayden says.

I consider it, but then I remember Abby and the desperation I saw in her expression. How can I just leave, knowing how frightened she is and that she's up there on that trail now, waiting for me? For help. For peace. And maybe for justice.

"No. I can't let her down."

"What about letting yourself down? You could be hurt."

"That's unlikely. Even if someone did do this to her, a murderer isn't going to hang around a crime scene. Right?"

"I still don't like it, Riley. If something happens, I don't think I can protect you."

• • •

We've walked for about ten minutes. I convinced Hayden it's not that unsafe, but I'm having a harder time convincing myself.

Then it hits me. I'm jumping to conclusions. We don't know that Abby was murdered. Chances are she fell, and that story in the paper got it right.

I attempt to let go of the fear, but most of it follows me up the path. We don't talk. I just listen to the crunch of my feet on the loose rocks and twigs. Occasionally, I think I hear Hayden's steps moving with mine. But that's impossible.

The trail gets steeper. Hayden doesn't let go of my hand.

I remember his words. *If something happens, I don't think I can protect you.* The fact that he wants to protect me pulls at my heartstrings. But knowing why he can't because he's dead gives those strings an even harder yank.

I still feel safer with him here. He's become a touchstone for me this last week.

We reach a fork in the path. Unsure which way to go, I stop.

"Is she here?" Hayden asks.

"I don't see her," I say.

"So, we wait on her?"

"No. We've got a fifty-fifty chance of choosing the right way." I let go of his hand and follow the path to the left.

We walk another five minutes before I catch the strong scent of jasmine. I stop and look around. The cold hits immediately.

"She's here," Hayden says.

"I know." I hug myself and when I glance at him, I notice he seems nervous, almost afraid. Why? Now's not the time to figure it out. It's getting colder.

"Abby?" I do a slow circle, trying to find her. It's only when I'm back facing Hayden that I see her over his shoulder. She's up ahead on the path. "There," I say and hurry toward her.

She's standing right off the trail in thick brush, her gaze directed into the woods.

"Abby?" I say her name again.

She turns. Her face is wet with tears, she's cried her

makeup off. smeared mascara circles her already dark-ringed eyes. I see what looks like clay fall loose from her face. I imagine Dad sculpting it to her face, to hide her crushed cheekbone and make her look like herself, not like a victim.

"Are you okay?" My voice is low, soft, and echoes the empathy I feel for her.

"In there." She points to the woods. "My ring. It's... in there."

I look through the woods and see it. It's a shed, like a tool shed. The outside is painted a greenish tan color, practically camouflaging it in the woodsy surroundings.

I take a step then look back to make sure Hayden's following me. He's already at my side.

"Abby says the ring is in the shed."

We walk through the brush to get a closer look at the outbuilding. Thorns cling to my jeans.

"Shit," Hayden says.

"What?" I ask, my fear multiplying, outgrowing my chest cavity, making it hard to breathe.

"It's locked. The shed's locked."

"How could her ring be..." I gaze at the padlock. My heart skips a beep.

"He locked me in there," I hear Abby say.

My chest grips forcing air out of my lungs. "Someone locked her in there."

Glancing back, I find her still standing by the path.

"Why was she in a locked shed? Ask her," Hayden insists.

I motion for Abby to join us. She shakes her head. Even

from here, I can see her pain. And I can feel it. Terrible things were done to her here.

I move back to the trail and stand close to her. Fingers of cold reach for me. Then her fear soaks through my skin. I can taste it on my tongue. Metallic, bitter. I shiver from the cold, but don't move back. "Abby?"

She doesn't answer, but looks at me. Tears web her lashes.

"Who locked you in there?"

Hayden moves in beside me.

"He… locked me in there." There's a rawness in her voice.

"What did she say?" Hayden asks.

I hold up a hand to silence him for a few minutes and look back at Abby. I imagine what terrible things happened and shiver. "Who did this?"

She blinks, more tears fall to her face. "Just get my ring."

"It's locked. But… I need to know who did this. Tell me."

"No. It's too ugly," she murmurs.

"Please, Abby. I need to make sure he pays for this," I say.

"I can't…" She fades, leaving me soaked in her pain, her desperation.

"Shit!" I bellow out and kick a rock.

"What did she say?" Hayden asks.

"That she couldn't talk about it because it was too ugly." Tears fill my eyes. "I swear to God, I'm going to find out who did this to her."

Hayden's arm comes around me. "And I'll help you. But for now, let's get the hell out of here." He looks around.

"Yeah." We turn to retrace our steps when a blast of cold hits.

Abby appears right in front of me. "Run! Run!"

"Run from what?" Steam billows up from my lips, chills race down my spine.

"Run!" she screams again.

"What's wrong?" Hayden's shoulder comes against mine.

"She said to run." I hug myself against the cold, against the fear growing inside me. Even knowing it's her fear, not mine, I can't control it. I'm scared.

"Then let's do it." He grabs my hand.

I hear footfalls crunching dry leaves and twigs.

Hayden and I both look toward the path and a man emerges. He's a tall, big man, wearing a uniform with the park name spelled out over his front pocket. His nametag reads Bill, Park Custodian. I want to believe that means he's not a threat. I want to believe his job title means he's not the one who locked Abby in the shed. I want to believe the fear turning my skin ice cold is an overreaction.

But my gut says he's the one. I take a step back.

"Run!" Abby screams.

Panic crawls up my spine. Hayden shifts closer.

The man appears shocked to see us. Then I remember, there is no us. He can't see Hayden. He only sees me. Hayden's words play in my head. *If something happens, I don't think I can protect you.*

I'm basically alone with a murderer. My fear quotient shoots up to an astronomical level.

"Hello, young lady," he says. His eyes, a light green—

unnaturally light—move over me, and I feel him assessing me, not in a good way.

"Let's go," Hayden insists.

I want to run, but Evil Bill's blocking my path. I want to scream, but I doubt anyone would hear me. I want to be anywhere but here. I feel dizzy with panic. Then the tiniest bit of logic intervenes. That logic says if I scream or run, he's more likely to come after me.

"Hey," I say, but my voice trembles.

"You okay?" he asks, still staring at me all creepy-like.

"Yeah," I manage. "Just leaving." I start to walk around him.

He shifts to block my path. Abby starts circling him, screaming, "No. No!" I see him run a hand up his arm as if he can feel her coldness.

"Shouldn't you be in school?" he asks. "Are you a bad girl, skipping school?"

The sleaze in his tone has my heart slamming against my chest bone.

Hayden touches my shoulder. "Tell him your dad's here. Tell him he's following you. Do it!"

"No. I'm… my dad's here," I do as Hayden says. "He's right behind me."

The park worker lifts a brow. "I didn't see him on the path."

"He might have stepped off the path." I swallow fear down my throat.

"Really?" Disbelief adds a level of creepiness to his tone. He smiles. "Is that a black eye you've got?" He reaches up as if to touch me and I stumble back.

Right then my phone rings.

"Answer it," Hayden tells me. "Answer it and pretend it's your dad. Tell him you're here with a park attendant. Tell him you are on your way down the trail. Make it sound like your dad is close by."

My mind is rushing and I feel frozen.

"Do it!" Hayden yells.

My phone's still ringing, and I pull it out of my pocket to answer it. The line's silent. I remember Hayden's ability to mess with my phone.

"Hi Dad." I look away as Bill scrutinizes me. "I'm just right up the trail. Yeah, close. I'm with Bill, a park custodian." I take a breath. "Yeah. I'll head that way and we'll meet up in a minute or two." I hang up, certain that the whole thing sounded so fake that he sees right through me.

I lift my eyes to his. "Gotta go." I take another step.

He shifts to block me again. "I'm betting that wasn't your dad."

My chest clutches tighter with panic. Right then his phone rings. Only it's not a normal ring. It's a constant high piercing noise. And it grows louder.

Louder.

Louder.

He pulls his phone out.

"Run! Now!" Hayden screams.

I do it. I dart around Evil Bill and take off in dead run.

Chapter Fifteen

I'm all the way around the curve of the path when I hear a popping sound, like a firecracker. "Fuck!" I hear Bill the custodian yell.

I keep going, running. My feet slap against the ground. The sound echoes in my ears. I don't hear him following, but I can't slow down.

I come to a place where the edge of the path drops off. I remember the vision. I remember Abby running close to the edge. I remember feeling as if I was falling.

That's when I know Abby fell while running from him. My gaze goes to the sharp drop-off. But I still don't stop running. I'm more afraid of Bill than I am of falling. And I know that's exactly how Abby felt.

I turn a corner and almost run smack dab into a couple.

"I'm… sorry," I say, out of breath, with fear still clawing at my insides.

"Is something wrong?" the woman asks.

I'm poised to tell her that a murderer is after me, but

right before the words slip out of my raw throat, I realize how crazy that would sound. I have no proof. Evil Bill never really touched me.

"What happened?" The man asks.

"Nothing. I... I ran into a park custodian and he just... gave me the creeps."

Right then I hear footsteps racing down the path. I move closer to the couple.

Bill comes running around the curve of the trail. He looks angry, mad. He stops when he sees us. His gaze lands on me. I take another step back.

The man standing beside his wife or girlfriend takes a defensive step forward.

Bill lifts his hand. Blood drips from his palm. "My phone exploded while I was holding it." He seethes out. He groans in pain and moves around us to continue down the hill.

I stand there with the couple and watch him leave. As he moves, I see the trail of blood following him. I don't have an ounce of sympathy for him.

"Well, that's probably why he was acting weird," the man says, sounding relieved.

"Yeah," I say, knowing it's not true.

Hayden appears beside me. His posture and his tight expression says he hasn't shaken what's happened either. "Let's go."

I nod. Then I look at the couple. "Thank you."

"Sure," they say as if I didn't owe it. But I know I did. And they aren't the only ones I owe gratitude to.

I start walking with Hayden beside me. I'm holding my side, still winded from the run. I feel like I need to puke.

"Are you okay?" he asks.

I nod, swallow and say, "You were wrong."

"About what?" he asks.

I get tears in my eyes. "You *were* able to protect me. You made his phone explode. Thank you."

His arm comes around me and I feel him pull me closer. It warms my soul. But it's the kind of hug that makes you want to fall against a shoulder and cry.

"Yeah, I did do that," he says. "But let's not try that again. It scared the shit out of me."

• • •

Hayden stayed with me the whole ride home. He talked about funny movies. I know he did it to try to calm me down. And I guess it worked. Because by the time I pull up into my driveway, I no longer need to run to the toilet and throw up. But one question is still heavy on my mind. *Now what?* I can't just let this go. I *won't* let this go.

I recall the skin-crawling look Evil Bill gave me and it gives me the chills all over again. How crazy is it that I deal with death and dead people, and yet none of them have scared me as much as he did?

Hayden fades when I get out of the car, but he's standing in the entryway when I open the door. I start to go up to my room, but the thought of crawling in bed with him, letting him hold me, kiss me, and help me forget everything sounds too tempting. I remember so clearly how it felt to make out with him on Dad's bedroom floor. I can't let that happen again, so I opt for the sofa instead and sink into it. Dropping my head back, I close my eyes.

Hayden drops down beside me. The sofa doesn't sink, but I feel his presence. A tingly sensation. I revel in it. I don't know how I'd have survived this last week if he hadn't been here. My thoughts go back to the bedroom floor and I realize the sofa isn't any safer than the bed.

I recall something he said once: *Maybe I'm not here for you to help me. Maybe I'm here to help you.*

Could that be true? Could Hayden be an angel? That would explain why he's so different. If so, I'm lusting after an angel. I'm for sure going to hell.

I open my eyes and look at him. He looks concerned. He reaches over and brushes a strand of hair off my cheek. His fingertips actually feel warm, comforting. "It's going to be okay," he says. His tone is so tender, I want to cry.

I swallow the weakness down. "How are we going to prove what that man did to Abby? If I thought going to the police and just spilling my guts about seeing ghosts and all this shit would help, I'd do it. I'll let them think I'm battier than bat shit if that would get him arrested and locked away for life. But I don't think it'll help."

"I know," Hayden says.

"I'd consider calling, just making up something to put suspicion on him, but they can trace phones. I see it on all of those cop shows."

"You watch those shows, too?"

"Not by choice. Dad and I take turns picking what to watch." I inhale. "You'd think with what he does for a living, shows about death would be the last thing he'd want to see. But nope."

"It must be a guy thing," he says. "I like them, too."

I nod and think about Dad. I wonder if he took off for

another long lunch today. I swear just the heaviness of that thought has me sinking deeper into the sofa. Deeper into a place where I feel bombarded with problems I can't fix.

I close my eyes again—trying to push everything away. Trying to forget. I'm almost asleep when I feel Hayden's lips on my forehead. It's a feathery touch that says he cares. "Get some rest," he whispers. "We're going to figure this out. I promise."

• • •

I'm jarred awake by a chiming sound. It only takes me a few minutes to realize it's the doorbell. I pop up from the sofa and pull my phone from my pocket to check the time. It's 3:30. I slept for over two hours. I make my way to the door and peer out the peephole.

It's Kelsey. I recall telling her we could hang out. Now I'm not sure I'm in the mood, but I don't feel right turning her down.

I open the door and resign myself to having company. "Hey," I say and step back, letting her know she's invited in.

She walks in and looks around, checking out my house. I almost wait for her to say something about how cold and sterile it looks.

She turns back to me. "Are you feeling better?"

It takes a second to remember I told her Aunt Flow was here. "Yeah, a little."

"Were you sleeping?"

"Yeah, but I needed to wake up." I blow several strands of hair from my face and glance around to make sure we're alone. We are.

"I've got all the medicine you need." She holds up a bag.

"Medicine?" I yawn.

She pulls out a plastic bag that has something brown in it. "Herbal stuff."

My jaw drops open. "What?"

She laughs. "Just wanted to see if you were awake. It's not weed. It's better than weed. We're talking a Chunky Monkey Menstrual Miracle to the rescue."

"Chunky Monkey? Isn't that…?"

"Ice cream. Yeah. Have you ever tried it?"

"No," I say.

"Well, you're about to. Not that this is just ice cream. It's so much more." The smile in her eyes turns sad for a second. "It was my grandmother's cramp remedy." She walks into the kitchen. "Where are your bowls and spoons?"

I move in, point to the drawer, and grab two bowls.

She pulls two spoons out of the drawer, walks to the table and starts emptying the contents of the big bag.

Along with the plastic baggy of unknown contents, there's a quart of Ben & Jerry's ice cream, along with a banana, some cookies, nuts, and a small bag of Reese's Pieces candy.

While I'm not really on my period and I'm unsure of this remedy, most of the ingredients sound yummy and considering I slept through lunch, I'm more than willing to give it a try.

I sit at the breakfast table and watch her prepare two bowls. She cuts up the bananas, adds several spoonfuls of ice cream, nuts, Reese's Pieces, a couple of what looks like ginger cookies, and sprinkles the top with the brown stuff in the baggie.

She pushes one bowl over to me. "Enjoy."

"Dare I ask what's in the powder stuff?"

"Don't worry, it's legal." She grins. "It's mostly cinnamon and ginger with some brown sugar."

"Okay." I dip my spoon in and bring it to my lips. "If I get high or anything, I'll come after your ass."

She laughs.

The second the spoon touches my tongue, I moan. My taste buds fall instantly in love… in lust.

"Holy shit," I say as I savor the different flavors. "This is to die for."

"I know," she says around her own mouthful. "I used to lie and say I was on the rag every time I came to see my grandma. It's like heaven."

"Is it really for cramps?"

"Yup. Look it up. You'll find that bananas, walnuts, peanut butter, cinnamon, and ginger are natural remedies for cramps. My grandmother was into holistic medicines, herbs and such."

"Well, I'd rather eat this than take a Motrin anytime," I say.

She chuckles and looks around the house again. "When you said you lived a couple of blocks away I didn't know you meant you lived in the rich subdivision in front of ours."

"We're not rich," I say. "The house belongs to the owner of the funeral home. Free rent is part of the package." I look around the room and try to see it from her eyes. "Actually, I would prefer your house to this one. This one feels almost like a hospital. White walls, tan furniture, no warmth here." I scoop up another bite and the bareness of the walls taunts me. "I have some artwork to hang. I just haven't done it yet."

We continue to eat when I realize something. "How did you know where I live?"

"ESP," she says.

I point my empty spoon at her. "Try again."

She grins. "I volunteer at the office. I peeked at your file."

"Sneaky," I say.

"Just curious." She licks her spoon. "Guess who else is curious?"

"Huh?"

She gets a big grin on her face.

"What?" I say.

"Jacob pulled me aside in the hall and wanted to know why you weren't in school."

I frown. "You didn't tell him I was on my period, did you?"

She frowns. "I might have. But they know about that stuff. He also asked for your address."

I drop my spoon. "And you gave it to him?"

"Of course I did. But you don't have to thank me."

I roll my eyes. "I'm not sure I'm ready for… that."

She cuts me a sly look. "Are you still hung up on your ex?"

"No, I just…"

"Then who is he? Because no one would push a hot guy away unless there's someone else."

My mind goes to Hayden. "There's no one else," I lie.

"Say that again and make it more believable this time."
I shoot her the bird. She shoots one back.

We spend the next hour laughing about everything from boys to school. The laughing stops when we touch on the subject of parents, and she tells me about her MIA dad. Her mom claims he was a drunk and a womanizer.

"How old were you when he left?" I ask.

"Seven. I remember him. What's crazy is I don't remember him like my mom describes him. I remember him playing with me, watching cartoons with me. I'm not saying my mama is lying, but I need to find out myself."

"How are you going to find out?" I ask.

"Before my grandmother died she gave me an address in Austin where some of his family lives. I mailed a letter two weeks ago."

"And?" I ask, but the flash of sadness in her green eyes tells me the answer before she does.

"I haven't gotten an answer, but when I get a car, I'm going to go there and see if they know where he is."

"Does your mom know you are looking for him?"

"No. She'd freak. And she'd be pissed that Grandmother gave me the address."

She runs her spoon around the melted goo in her bowl. "But I want to meet him. Make my own mind up about him." She looks up. "Is that crazy?"

"No, not at all. I'd give anything if I could learn more about my mom. My dad never talks about her. And when I ask questions I feel... I feel as if it hurts him. I just recently found a picture that looks like a wedding photo." I bite down on my lip. "Mom looked pregnant."

"So?" she asks. "I know my mom was pregnant with me when she married my dad."

"It's not that I care," I tell her. "It just feels like a secret that he's kept from me. And it makes me... makes me wonder what else he isn't telling me."

"I'd confront him. Tell him you saw the photo." She slumps back in her chair. "Well, shit! Listen to me." She sighs. "I tell you to confront him, but I can't confront my own mom. So don't listen to me."

I crater then and tell her about my suspicions that Dad is drinking.

"Oh crap," she says. "What are you going to do?"

"I can't do anything until I prove it. And I'm almost scared to prove it, because if he knows that I know, maybe he won't feel the need to hide it and he'll drink even more."

"I see your point, but you can't help him until the truth is out of the bag. One of my mom's boyfriends was a recovering alcoholic. He went to those meetings three times a week. He was actually a nice guy. I missed him when he moved out."

"That must suck, having people come into your life and then losing them."

"Not anymore. I learned to never care about them."

Which sounds like it sucks even more, I think, but I don't say it.

Our conversation moves everywhere. Back to boys, over to best shopping venues, local hangouts, and then some school gossip. Two girls got pregnant last year by the same guy. Carter, a head basketball player, was brain damaged and hasn't come back to school yet. And the may-

or's son, who was also in twelfth grade, got arrested for drug trafficking.

We move away from the kitchen and I show her my room. We crash on the bed and I show her pictures of Carl and Shala, and my life back in Dallas.

She notices the picture of my mom's and my feet and asks about it. She picks it up and stares at it. "It looks like she loved you. Don't ask me how a picture of two pairs of feet says that, but it does."

Hearing her say that tugs at my heartstrings. "I know. I feel it, too." Right then I'm glad we've become friends. I know school will be out in six months and we might move our separate ways, but for now I have a friend, someone to share with, someone to laugh with, someone to make me feel less like a freak.

I know that sounds dorky, but I don't care. After having been friendless for a year and a half, this feels good. Then I realize I'm discounting how Hayden makes me feel. In some ways, I feel even closer to him.

I push that thought away. Hayden is temporary. That thought is like a paper cut deep into my soul, but it's something I really need to accept.

"Oh," Kelsey says. "Jacob wasn't the only one to ask about you."

Okay, that's a shock. "Who else?"

"Your friendly cashier."

"Seriously?"

"Yup."

"Okay, that's it." I sit up and cross my legs. "She officially freaks me out."

"Maybe you remind her of her daughter or something."

A thought hits and I change the subject. "Have you made a move on Dex?"

"Who?" she says, all innocent-like. I give her the stink eye.

"Fine. He was with Jacob when he stopped me," she confesses. "He said hello and I was friendly."

"How friendly?" I pin her with a look that dares her to lie.

She makes a face. "I didn't frown at him."

I laugh. "That's not a move."

"It's all I got."

I realize how easy it is to talk to Kelsey. Every now and then, Abby and the whole Evil Bill problem bubbles to the surface of my mind. But when it does, I push it down. I know as soon as Kelsey leaves I'll have to deal with it.

With that thought, I feel a chill scurry up my backbone. I sit up and see Abby standing at the foot of my bed. Her shoulders are slumped, and tears are in her eyes. She appears defeated.

"Did it just get extra cold in here?" Kelsey hugs herself, then she leans her head back. "Is that jasmine I smell?"

CHAPTER SIXTEEN

"What are you doing?" Hayden's voice whispers in my ear later that night as I'm sitting on the stairs. Without meaning to, I lean his way, needing his presence, not wanting the loneliness I feel when I think about Dad.

I look at him sitting next to me on the steps. Some of the ache inside me eases. Being with Kelsey was great, but Hayden has become my touchstone.

"You okay?" he asks.

I nod. "Just listening to see if my dad gets a drink."

He slips his arm around my shoulders.

His touch feels so right, but I know it's not. How can I stop this? Then I let myself wonder what would happen if I didn't stop it. Caught between what feels right and what I know is wrong, my chest gets heavy and tight.

I stand up and walk into my bedroom. He follows me. I sit in the desk chair, afraid if I get in the bed he'll join me.

"Was he drunk when he got home this afternoon?"

"No. But he looked tired. He barely ate any dinner. Then he said he had a headache and went to bed early."

I recall too clearly that he'd started doing that right before he lost both jobs. "I don't even know if he went to work today."

"I'm sorry," he says. "Maybe you should talk to him."

"If I had proof, I think I'd have the guts to confront him." I hate sounding so pathetic so I change the subject.

Staring at Hayden, I'm suddenly curious. "Where do you go when you're not here?"

"Just around."

I'm not sure if he's lying, or if that's just what it's like. I swallow. "You know, if you crossed over, you wouldn't be alone."

"I'm not alone. I have you. You need me. I protected you today, remember?"

"I know, but…"

He stares at me, then runs a finger over my lips. "Why do you work so hard to make me leave? Don't you like me?" His smile is crooked, and a bit sad.

Emotion knots in my throat. "Helping you cross over is what I'm supposed to do, Hayden."

"Supposed to do. But you really don't want me to go, do you?"

Hell, no. "I want what's right. For you," I say.

"How do you know what's right for me? I don't know what's right for me." A touch of pain laces his voice. "But when I'm with you, like this, it doesn't feel wrong."

"Crossing over has been right for all the others. You're in this limbo and it's—"

"I'm not like the others."

I don't know what to say. Pumpkin comes slinking into the room, hurries to Hayden, and circles his feet.

"Have you talked to Abby?" Hayden kneels down and pets the persistent feline.

"She dropped in for a few seconds when Kelsey was here. She didn't say anything."

He looks up, almost puzzled, and I go ahead and explain. "Kelsey is Bessie's granddaughter."

"Yeah. I know. So she came over?"

"Yeah, after she got out of school." I exhale again. "Kelsey felt Abby. She asked me why it had turned so cold. She even said it suddenly smelled like jasmine. So she could smell her, too."

Hayden's eyes widen and he stands up. "Does she have the same ability you do?"

"She didn't see her, so I guess not."

He walks to the bed where my photo album is still open.

He's busy studying my album, and then he asks, "Do you think most people can feel spirits, some way or another?"

When I don't answer right away, he asks again, "Do you?"

I consider his question. "In a book I read, it said a lot of people have varying levels of awareness. Maybe Kelsey senses more than some. I've been around other friends who don't seem to feel anything. Then there's people like my dad... he feels the cold, sometimes."

"But I'm not cold, right?"

"Right." And that still bugs me.

The room gets quiet. Too quiet. "Do you think other

people can feel… the emotions? I mean, could I be making others sad?"

I feel it then. His sorrow reaches inside me and I want to cry. But then I realize there's a purpose to his question. "Who are you worried about?"

"It's just a question." His lie is in his voice. In the way, he shrugs. And the way he looks away from me.

"Hayden…?"

He points to the photo album. "This is Piney Woods Camp? Did you go there?"

"Yeah."

"So did I!" He smiles. I sense this is a ploy to change the subject, but I play along. "When did you go?"

"In 2014. I was an assistant counselor to the younger kids."

"Me, too. I was there…" He stops to think, "in 2014 for the month of July."

"I was there in June and half of July that year."

"Did you go to any of the group parties on Friday night? Dances and pizza."

"A couple," I say.

"Do you think we met?" He walks back to me and sits on top of my desk. His knee is brushing up against my arm. I seem to be able to feel him more and more.

I take in his blue eyes, his good looks. "I think I'd remember you."

"I don't know. It took a while for me to get this good looking." His smile is real now. "Wait. I remember I danced with a blonde with light blue eyes. I don't remember her name, but—"

"I don't think it was me."

"You're probably right, because you'd have remembered me. I stepped on the girl's feet and she fell."

I chuckle. "Wasn't me." But I get up to look at my album. I have several group photos from camp. I flip through the pages to find the images. Hayden comes behind me.

"There I am!" he says and points to a picture of everyone waiting to get in canoes.

I look closely and I chuckle. "It *is* you."

"Where are you?" he asks.

"Taking the picture."

He eyes me. "You sure it wasn't you I danced with?"

"I never danced with anyone," I say.

"Why not?" he asked.

I face him. The truth sounds too pathetic, so I lie. "I don't know how to dance."

"Obviously, neither did I, but it didn't stop me. I'll bet you broke my heart when I asked you to dance and said no."

I shake my head.

"How can you be so sure?"

"I wasn't asked to dance."

"Bullshit."

I laugh and just say it. "I was fourteen, gangly, had braces, and…" I glance down at my chest, "the girls hadn't come out to play yet."

He starts laughing and then he moves in. "Dance with me now." His smile is contagious. He puts his hands on my waist.

"I just told you I don't know how."

He holds on. "All you have to do is sway. And get close." He moves in. I feel his breath on cheek.

"By the way," he whispers. "Your girls came out to play real nice."

I slap his chest. He laughs and moves closer. So close the girls are pressed against him.

His feet start shifting. I rest my head on his chest, and inhale his earthy, verdant scent. I feel his hands circling my waist, a tingly light touch. I dance with him, moving slowly around my bedroom. Is it wrong? Probably, but for just a few minutes I allow it.

Or I do until his lips try to find mine. I pull away.

Disappointment brightens his eyes, but I see him push it back. He looks at me. "Your black eye is almost gone."

Lightheaded from being so close to him, I can only offer him a nod.

The silence falls on us like snow. It becomes awkward really fast. "What did you tell Kelsey when she said it was cold?"

"The only thing I could think of. That the heater is on the fritz."

Reaching out, he tucks a strand of hair behind my ear. He smiles and leaves his hand against my cheek. I know it's a test. A test to see if I'll push him away again. I hate tests. And this one, I know I'll fail.

"Did she believe you?"

The temptation to close my eyes and let him keep touching me is so strong. "I don't know. I still don't think she believes me about the letter, so… who knows."

"Is she still asking about that?"

"Not today, but... I could swear she was thinking about it."

I step back and his touch falls away. He tucks both his hands into his pockets. "I've been thinking..."

"About what?"

"About how you could get Abby's ring and get that creep arrested."

And with that, the sexual tension in the room vanishes. "How?" I ask.

• • •

Dad's not in the living room or the kitchen when I go downstairs the next morning. I look at the clock. I'm running late, which means he's *really* running late. Considering he might have already left, I check to see if his car is in the driveway. It's there. Parked. And I get an ugly knot in my stomach.

It's happening again.

I knock on his door. "Dad? You up?"

He says something, words I can't make out, and I try to convince myself this means nothing. Everyone's allowed to sleep late once or twice, right? Moving into the kitchen, I pour some cereal. I sit at the table, pulling pink marshmallows out of my bowl, and dropping them at my feet for Pumpkin. Several times I look at the door, waiting for him to rush out.

I try to figure out what I'm going to say to him. But I can hardly think. That ugly knot gets heavier.

Exhaustion pulls at my mind. Last night I tossed and turned while I considered Hayden's plan of getting Evil Bill arrested and getting Abby's ring back to her family. I don't particularly like the idea, but I don't have a better one, so I'm going for it.

It's going to require writing three more fake letters, and lying three more times. One of those lies will be to the police.

But that's not the hardest part. More difficult than lying is getting the truth. The whole truth. I'm going to have to get Abby to talk to me. Give me the terrible details about what really happened. I'm going to need to include enough of those facts in my letter to make my lie believable.

Sitting there, staring at my bowl with dry cereal, I realize it's been over five minutes and I don't hear Dad showering. I shoot up from my chair.

This time I literally bang my fist on his door.

"Dad, you have to go to work!"

"I'm up," he calls out, and I hear him moving around this time. I don't leave the door until I hear the shower start.

Ten minutes later, when he steps out, his hair isn't combed. His eyes look bloodshot. I feel like my ribs are closing in and strangling my heart.

"Dad? What's going on?" Saying those words scratches my throat.

"Couldn't sleep last night. I gotta run, Hon." He squeezes my shoulder and heads for the door.

What the hell am I going to do?

When I hear the door shut behind him, anger boils inside me. I sling my spoon across the kitchen. It clatters against the cabinet. It clanks against the floor, probably chipping the tile. But I'm more worried about the chip in my heart. Worried what we'll do if he loses this job. Worried about losing my dad.

I jump up and storm into his room. The bed isn't neat like it was before. Blankets are scattered. His suit from yesterday is thrown on the floor. I do another search, and like before, I find nothing.

• • •

"You're quiet today," Jacob says as I watch him take the water hose off of a Chevy Cruze.

Kelsey said the same thing when I picked her up. I almost told her about Dad, but then I suddenly didn't want to talk about it. Or honestly, I was afraid if I talked about it, I'd fall apart. The last thing I wanted to do was show up at school with a red nose to match the fading red ring around my right eye.

"Quiet's good sometimes," I answer.

"Not when you look sad, too." He pulls away from the car.

I force a smile. It feels fake and my cheek muscles protest.

"Good try," he says. "If you want to talk, I'm a good listener. And it's Friday. So I'm open anytime this weekend."

The offer is sweet and it makes my heart do a tiny tumble. "Thank you, but I'm fine."

He rolls the screwdriver in his hands. "I saw Jami talking to you this morning by your locker. What did she say?"

I shrug. "She just wanted to stop by and remind me I was a bitch."

His shoulders drop. "I'm sorry. I'll talk to her."

"Please don't. It'll only make it worse."

"You know it's over between us."

"Yeah. You told me." And there's a part of me that is excited about that. It's not the part that seems to crave being with Hayden.

The bubble of silence around us grows awkward.

After a few seconds, he turns back to the car and starts working. His arms shift as he turns the screwdriver to loosen the hose. Unlike mine, the coveralls he's wearing are short-sleeved and his bicep muscles roll under his skin. While he might not be making my heart sing extra loud, I'm not completely immune to the fact that he's hot. Or that he's being so nice.

"I missed you yesterday," he says. "I had to work with Peter and I swear that guy wouldn't know a sparkplug from a transmission." He shoots me a smile over his shoulder.

I grin. "Sorry." I roll up my coveralls sleeves. The coveralls are about two sizes too big. I move closer to the car. "Do you want me to finish that up?"

"Sure." He lifts up, shifts away from the car, and hands me the screwdriver. His warm brown eyes meet mine for a heartbeat. The soft way he smiles is too much, too intimate, too close to meaning something that I'm drawn to, but somehow don't really want.

I dip under the hood and reach in to finish loosening the hose. "I think you almost got it," I say.

He doesn't answer. With me leaning forward, I feel the loose coveralls pulling tighter over my backside. Then I feel him studying me. Checking me out. I look back and yup, his gaze is on my ass.

He glances up and catches me catching him. Blushing slightly, he turns away.

I put my nose back into the engine, leaning in as far as I can. There's a small part of me that wants to let the cute-guy-likes-me feeling run its course and boost my self-esteem. But there's the other part of me. The part that kind of belongs to a guy I danced with last night. The guy I need to push away.

The hose comes loose and I pull out. "Got it."

He grins and takes two steps closer. "You also got grease, right here."

His finger taps my nose. Our eyes meet and hold again. I'm aware of how close he is. Aware of how everyone else in the shop is on the other side. Aware that my next intake of air is filled with a spicy, earthy boy scent. I think it's his at first, but then it's too familiar. So is the weakness I feel when I smell it. So far, Jacob hasn't made me melt like that. But Hayden...?

I look over his shoulder and see Hayden mid-fade.

The only thing I can see before he completely vanishes is the pain in his expression. "No," I mutter.

"No, what?" Jacob's still smiling, still close, and I'm still so sure I'm making a mess of things.

"Nothing." The next beat my heart takes, I feel a tiny crack, because I know I've hurt Hayden.

CHAPTER SEVENTEEN

After dropping off Kelsey at her house, I head home to filter through my issues. I need to talk to Hayden, tell him I'm sorry. That it's my fault that he's hurt. My fault because I let myself like him. My fault I let myself get too close to him.

Right before I pull into the driveway, my concerns about Dad bubble up to the surface, and I change my mind and drive past our house. I go around the block and head down Locus Street toward Canton's Funeral home. I pull into the parking lot. Dad parks in the gated area around the back, so I can't tell yet if he's even here.

I recall this morning. His bloodshot eyes and the mess in his room. *What the hell am I going to do? Why did I even come here?*

I don't have an answer, but I still pull into a parking spot and cut off my engine. There are several cars parked in front. Not enough to indicate a funeral is in progress, but enough to know that if he's here, he might be with someone.

It doesn't matter.

I get out of the car and head inside. A bell dings, announcing my arrival. My skin immediately feels prickly, too sensitive. The cold air hurts.

The heavy door swishes closed behind me. I inhale and a sharp, almost medicinal, aroma fills my lungs. A character in a book I read once said that funeral homes smell of depression and grief. But for me, it's the smell I've associated with my father all my life. A scent that means Daddy's home.

I stop in the entrance. Murmured voices echo from somewhere in the back.

The walls are painted a pale gray and the floors are white marble. A large glass-top table is pushed against a wall. On it is fresh flowers and some brochures. I've been here a couple of times so I know where my dad's office is. I also know where the dead are kept.

I start in the back as if I have a right to. And I do, don't I? My father works here.

I get to the hall that leads to his office. I hesitate. What am I going to say to him? Is this it? Am I going to confront him about what I read in Mom's diary? Tell him I'm scared he's drinking? Tell him I love him? Beg him to stop before something bad happens?

"He's with someone," a deep, familiar voice says behind me.

Then bam, I feel washed in sadness. Hayden's sadness. I turn around. He's standing there. Guilt swirls around my chest because he saw Jacob flirting with me earlier. Guilt because I let him get too close. I let myself get too close. None of this should have happened.

Then a question comes from the ache in my chest. "What are you doing here?" I whisper.

He doesn't answer. But an ugly answer forms in my mind. He's here. His body is here. He's a new client. He's tucked away inside a casket, in a room that smells of grief, or even worse, in a freezer.

I tell myself this shouldn't hurt so much. I've known he's dead all along. Logically this swell of grief I feel doesn't make sense, but when do matters of the heart make sense?

I hear Dad's voice. I turn toward the office. My dad and a man step out. "Don't worry, Mr. Carter. I'll take care of everything." The two men shake hands.

"Thank you," Mr. Carter says, sounding sincere. "You made this... easier than I ever thought it would be." His voice shakes with pain.

"That's what I'm here for," Dad says in a calm, caring way. It warms me to know he's still taking his job seriously. Mr. Carter starts down the hall, stopping abruptly when he sees me. His eyes are moist, and I sense he's embarrassed.

Dad turns my way, sees me, and concern fills his green eyes.

"This is my daughter," Dad says and moves in. "Riley, this is Mr. Carter."

"Nice to meet you," Mr. Carter says, but the agony in his eyes tells me nothing is really nice for him right now. He's grieving.

I nod. He walks past me. Dad touches my shoulder. "Is everything okay?"

"Yeah." *No. I don't know. Are you drinking, Dad?* I think it, I don't say it—not sure I can even talk. The lump of grief I feel for Hayden makes my chest tight. Another bell rings announcing someone's entrance into the funeral home. Voices from the front carry back into the hall.

"Mr. Smith," I hear someone say behind me. I look back. It's a woman with dark hair and a heart-shaped face. She's familiar. Then it hits me. She looks like Abby.

It's Abby's mother. I just know it. Tears run down the woman's cheeks. I feel the pain in my lungs as I take my next breath. Pain for the woman, and for Abby.

Right then, the scent of jasmine fills my senses. Abby's here.

"Ms. Howard," Dad says, confirming what I already know.

Dad glances at me and gives me the look that asks for another minute.

Ms. Howard seems to take a painful swallow of air. "Something terrible has happened. My father just had a heart attack. Is there any way we can postpone the funeral for a few days?"

"Well, of course. I'm so sorry," he says with empathy.

His concerned gaze moves to me briefly. I nod letting him know it's okay.

"But what about people who show up this afternoon for the funeral?" Ms. Howard asks.

"I'll open the room for a viewing and I'll let everyone know who shows up that the funeral has been postponed. Why don't we go into my office and talk?" he asks Ms. Howard. He glances back at me and mouths the words, *one minute*.

I watch them disappear into Dad's office. My heart's hurting, my head's swimming, and my resolve is weakening. Now that I've seen him working and seeming so on top of things, I think perhaps my worries were unfounded.

"Riley," another voice says behind me.

I look back and the voice belongs to Ms. Duarte, Dad's assistant. Abby is standing beside her.

"Hi. I, uh, wanted to see my dad."

"Why don't you come into my office? I'm sure he'll be done in a few minutes."

I nod. I look at Abby but she's not looking at me. She's looking at the office door. I need to say something to her, but I can't.

I stand there. My next intake of air brings the scent of jasmine, but along with it is Hayden's scent. And Hayden's sadness. Then Abby fades.

Inhaling again, I face Ms. Duarte. "Does Dad have another client?"

"Client?" she asks. Her voice is too mellow, almost like bells, and it seems to float in the funeral-home scented air. "Oh, you mean... Uh, yes, just this morning. Why?"

"A boy? Dark hair, tall?" *A boy who can make you laugh, who can make the loneliness go away?* The back of my eyelids sting.

"No." She appears confused by my question. "It's a man."

I push back the hurt and take in the information. It's not Hayden. Then what was he doing here? Had he followed me? Is he watching out for my dad? Knowing Hayden, he'd do that. He'd do it for me.

"He's at least my age," Ms. Duarte says.

Then, as if that's all it takes, a spirit appears. A man. He's wearing an orange prison uniform. He has red hair, and a tattoo of a spider and a web runs down his neck. His light green eyes are unnaturally bright and angry. He walks toward me, his hands fisted, as if he's walking into a fight. As if he's ready to kill. And I'm his target.

Fear races up my backbone. I take a step back. I've never seen a spirit this mad.

"Can you see me?" he yells. "Someone has to help me. Someone has to help me now!"

I look away from him. Pretend I'm not afraid. Pretend my step back wasn't due to him. Pretend I didn't see him. Please God, I can't handle another one. Especially one that scares me.

"Tell Dad I'll call him?" I run out. Tears fill my eyes as soon as the door swishes closed.

The weight I feel worrying about Hayden and Abby, and my fear of the convict's spirit, have me angry with life. Why couldn't I be a normal teen? One who has a mom at home. One who can worry about simple life issues, like getting pimples, scoring a date for prom, and making it into the right college.

Who the hell thought I could handle this?

• • •

I pull onto my driveway when my phone rings. I know it's Dad.

"Hey," I say.

"Why did you leave? I told you to wait."

"You were busy," I say.

"Hon', I'm never too busy for you. I just needed three minutes to take care of Ms. Howard. What's wrong?"

I swallow the need to cry. "I was worried."

"About?"

"You." My bottom lip trembles.

"What about me?" he asks.

I take a deep breath. "You acted like you didn't feel well this morning."

"Oh, that. No, I'm fine. I just had a restless night."

I think I can hear his chair squeaking.

I think I hear his lie.

I think I hear my heart break.

"It feels like more," I say.

"Don't be silly. Stop worrying. Didn't I seem fine when you were here?"

"Yes."

"See," he says. "Why don't we order in when I get home?"

"Okay." I brush a few tears from my cheeks. But dad-blast it, I'm pathetic.

"You sure you're okay?" he asks.

"Yeah, see you tonight." I hang up.

I walk into the house. It's silent. The bare walls mock me. The soft sound of Pumpkin's purring whispers through the house. I continue down the hall. When I turn the corner, I see Hayden. Pumpkin is stretched out on the table, and Hayden is sitting there, stroking him from head to tail.

"Hey," I say.

He gives me a smile, but it's sad. I drop my backpack on the table and sit across from him. "What were you doing in the funeral home?"

"Hanging," he says, looking at Pumpkin, not at me.

"What you saw today at school—"

"What I saw today doesn't matter. You've been right all along."

"About what?"

"About this…" He waves a hand between me and him. "We're kind of incompatible."

Tears fill my eyes. "And you have no idea how much I wish it wasn't so. I wish we'd danced at the camp. I wish we'd known each other then." *I wish… I wish with all my heart that you were still alive.*

"Me too." He continues to pet Pumpkin. He still hasn't looked at me.

The lump of hurt sits on my chest. But I force myself to say it. "I think you'd be happier if you passed over."

He still doesn't look at me, but he smiles the saddest smile I've ever seen. My breath catches.

"Still trying to get rid of me." His words fill the desolate silence.

"Hayden, I just—"

"I know." He looks up this time. "I think you're right. First, I want to help you get justice for Abby. That guy has to be stopped."

"That's my job."

"I know, but I kinda got pulled into it, too."

My fault again. "I saw Abby at the funeral home, but she didn't say anything. I need to talk to her before I can write the letters."

"Okay, but I thought we could see if we can find out anything about Bill. His last name and stuff. I think there's a park website that might list employees."

I realize I should have already done that. The sooner I take care of Abby, the better I can deal with the other stuff.

I run upstairs and grab my laptop and we settle in at the dining room table. I'm very aware of how he's not touching me. And I suddenly want him to touch me so bad it hurts.

Focusing on what I'm doing and not what I wish I was doing, I Google the park's name. It pulls up a website and even a story about Abby Howard. I click on the website.

"Click on the link, 'Who We Are,'" Hayden says, standing behind me, but not close.

I do and the screen fills with photographs and images. At the bottom is a picture of Evil Bill.

His name is William Griffin. His cold, blank stare in the picture gives me chills. I read his bio, which tells me that he's originally from Tennessee and he worked at several state parks there before he made his way to Texas. I take a deep breath and then go back to Google to search his name.

A lot of links come up. Probably some for another William Griffin. It isn't an uncommon name. Most of the links are over ten years old. I click on a few of the ones that sound like they could be connected to Evil Bill.

I scan one where William Fredrick Griffin caught poachers shooting deer in a state park in Tennessee. One where he worked with a wildlife rescue at the gulf to save animals after the oil spill.

There's nothing here that tells me he's anything but an upstanding guy. But everything inside me tells me he's a murderer.

I glance over at Hayden, who's reading over my shoulder. "I don't buy it. Something's wrong."

Going back to the main list of links, I scan down. One is a wedding notice from California. Another is located in Ohio. Then I see one that...

I almost pass it, but the familiar word I regularly search makes me stop.

Obituary. And it's from Tennessee.

It's from a small-town newspaper outside of Knoxville. It's actually more recent than the other links. I open it. The black and white picture of man staring back at me has dark hair and light eyes. He's Evil Bill. Or I think he is.

I read the obituary for William Griffin. It states he worked as a park ranger and donated time to save wildlife.

It states he died three years ago.

I swallow a gulp of air and look at Hayden again. "How could he be...?"

"This is weirder than shit," Hayden says.

I squint at the picture beside the obituary, thinking I'll see the face and realize it's not him. But I swear it's him. Same eyes. Same jawline.

"Something isn't right."

In spite of the sheer befuddlement ping-ponging inside of me, I look back at Hayden. He gives me a reassuring smile and my heart skips a beat.

My doorbell chimes. I get up, my mind flipping from Dead Evil Bill, to Dead Sweet Hayden. I move into the entryway. There's only one person this could be.

Kelsey.

It rings again. "Coming," I call out.

She didn't tell me she was stopping by, but she's surprised me before.

I open the door. My breath catches.

It's not Kelsey.

Chapter Eighteen

"Hi." Jacob, soft brown eyes, hair a little mussed, wide shoulders, and wearing a warm smile, stands there.

I'm numb. I don't know what to say. My feet feel nailed to the floor. My mind nailed shut.

"Is this a bad time?" he asks.

Yes, but to say it sounds rude and requires my mouth to move. Nothing seems to be working at the second. So I don't say it. I just stand there like a bump on log. *Snap out of it!*

"Hi," I finally manage. The polite thing to do would be to step back and let him come in, but Hayden's here.

Jacob shifts nervously from one foot to the other. I'm making him uncomfortable. *Shit. Shit. Shit.*

He runs a hand over his mouth. "I was... working on my dad's old Falcon and somehow our 7/8 socket must have up and walked out. You mentioned your dad was a mechanic and had a bunch of tools. I was hoping I could borrow one."

He just wants to borrow a socket. It's going to be okay. Hayden can't be upset.

"Sure. Let me see if I can find it. I'll be right—" My plan had been to shut the door, walk through the kitchen and into the garage, then open the garage door to let him in. But he didn't know that.

And when I step back, he steps in.

He's so close, I'm staring at his chest. My hand's still on the door. I ease back and claim a few inches of breathing room. "This way," I say, because shoving people out the door isn't my thing.

When I get past the entryway, my gaze goes to the dining room table. Hayden's gone.

Jacob follows me into the kitchen, looking around at the bare walls and sterile-looking furnishings. I wonder what he's thinking. That I'm motherless, that my life is empty. I open the door that leads to the garage and hit a switch to lift the garage door and shed some light on the darkness.

The door groans loudly as it rises. "What size was it you needed?" I look around. Thankfully, Dad spent some time last weekend getting his tools organized.

"7/8." My heart's thumping. I open up a drawer in one of Dad's toolboxes where he keeps all his sockets. There's *clinking* and *clanking* while I search through the tools for the socket Jacob needs.

"Here," I say.

"Thanks." His hand touches mine when he takes it. It's a casual, accidental touch, but the way his thumb brushes across my wrist doesn't feel casual. Or accidental.

I offer a quick "you're welcome", nod, and rub my wrist over my jeans to stop the tingling.

"You wouldn't want to come over and help me, would you?" Hope plays in his voice.

And there it is. He didn't come here to just borrow a socket. Part of me had that figured out, but the other part just didn't want to face it. Not now. Not when...

"I... can't today."

"Tomorrow?" He smiles and only the slightest bit of insecurity shows.

"Oh, I..."

He scrubs his tennis shoe on the concrete floor. "I'm not going to stop asking. I like you, Riley. A lot."

I cringe. Because deep down, I know I like him, too. But then there's Hayden. Incompatible Hayden. Oh, but there's other reasons. "You just broke up with your girlfriend."

"So I'm free and so are you, right?"

"She thinks I was trying to break you two up."

"But it's not true," he says

"She thinks it is. And if you and I..."

"I personally don't care what she thinks. We didn't do anything wrong. Yeah, I admit I noticed you the first time I saw you. It... would've been hard not to."

Seriously? He's throwing a compliment at me. I hate compliments. Or maybe I just hate the possibility that Hayden might hear them.

"Then I learned you drove a Mustang, and you actually know about cars. Then I was impressed how you owned that black eye and how you walked into a roomful of guys in auto tech and didn't care if they wanted you there or not. You've got guts. I like that."

I shake my head. "No guts."

He grins. "That's another thing I like. You don't... Most pretty girls think they're... all that and a Big Mac. And to us guys, they kind of are, because pretty girls are our kryptonite." He chuckles. "But you don't act like that. You have power but you don't use it. At least not like other girls. I haven't ever seen you judge anyone either. Everyone at school is still talking about how you took up for Kelsey."

"What? No. Kelsey was taking up for me."

"At first, but then you went to bat for her. Took a fist in the eye instead of her. And see," he says. "You don't want credit for it. I like that about you. And I'm hoping in time you'll see I'm not a bad guy either." He holds up the socket. "Thanks. I'll bring it to school tomorrow. Or... I could bring it back tonight and we could hang out."

"I don't..."

"Okay, I'll bring it to school tomorrow." He dips his head, looks up at me through his dark lashes and smiles. "Later." Then he turns and walks out.

I watch him leave. Slowly. My heart's moving faster than he is. Why didn't I tell him it wasn't happening? Not to waste his time? That I'm unattainable?

Because just like Hayden, I need to move on too. I haven't given boys a chance since Carl. Well, except Hayden. And maybe the reason I let him in was because I knew the relationship was doomed from the start.

I fist my hands while uncertainty rushes through my veins. When I turn around Hayden's there, leaning on the doorjamb, looking too good, and offering me a smile that doesn't just tug at my heartstrings, but practically rips them out.

"He's right about you."

I catch my breath. "I'm not—"

"You should be. You deserve someone who appreciates you, Riley. Who can really protect you. Who can be there for you. You shouldn't be lonely."

"And you deserve to cross over and be with your dad," I counter.

He moves in. "Then we'll make a pact. We both have a plan. But first let's help Abby."

I don't say anything. He takes another step and is right in front of me. "Promise me, Riley."

"Promise you what?"

"That the next time Jacob asks you to do something, you'll say yes."

"I don't—"

He places his index finger on my lips. "Promise me."

I get tears in my eyes. "I just wish—"

"He's a good guy," he says.

"How do you know?"

"The way he talks to you. Looks at you."

"I don't—"

"Stop," he says. "You do like him. I see it. And there's nothing wrong with that. I wasn't thinking when I started this. You are… you are in a different place than me. This was… It was fun. But like you say, I have to move on. And so do you."

I nod. There's tears in my eyes. I feel as if I'm losing something special. But he was never mine and I need to remember that.

"Now promise," he says.

"I promise."

• • •

That night, I set the napkins on the table and join Dad there. He came home early with dinner. Hayden and I were still sitting at the kitchen table, trying to find other links on William Griffin. We came up with nothing. We were no closer to finding the truth.

The smell of fried rice and sesame chicken fills the kitchen. All I can think about is the conversation Dad and I need to have. But I hate conflict. The dread curls up in my chest and makes it hard to breathe.

Dad looks at me. "You really worried me when you left without speaking to me today."

I swallow nervously. "You really worried me this morning when you acted... like you didn't feel good." I watch him spoon some fried rice onto his plate. Then he pushes it over to me. The conversation we might be starting makes my hunger vanish, but for show, I spoon a few bites onto my plate.

He helps himself to sesame chicken. "I'm pretty sure I told you I was fine."

I set my fork down. "But you weren't," I say and tell myself it's time. "Your eyes were bloodshot. You looked extra tired. You looked..." *Say it. Just say it,* "hung over." I did it. And I'm proud I did. It had to be said.

Dad looks shocked. "How do you know what a hang-over looks like?"

Since I'm expecting him to be honest, I go for it myself. "Carl sometimes had too many beers."

Dad's eyes round. "I knew I didn't like him." He starts eating as if the conversation is over. It's *not* over.

I chase a pea through my fried rice. "This isn't about him," I say, my heart thumping in my chest.

"You need to stop worrying. I'm the parent." He points his fork at me. There's a touch of anger in his eyes. Anger that I'm afraid means guilt.

"You're my only parent. I have a right to worry."

"I had a sleepless night. With my job, I'm allowed." He says it with a little too much force. He says it without looking at me. "Let's change the subject."

"Dad?"

"I said change the subject."

I pick up my fork and scrape the rice from one side of my plate to the other. I don't even mind the screeching sound the utensil makes on the ceramic plate.

Dad does mind. "Stop that."

After several slow minutes, he speaks up. "I reserved us a spot at the car show in Dayton."

I nod even though the car show isn't what I want to discuss. But when he shuts something down, it's closed. But I'm proud of myself for starting the conversation and if I have to, I'll start it again. Somewhere inside me there's a tiny bit of hope that maybe this is all it takes. That he'll realize his mistake and refuse to let his only daughter down. That he loves me enough to stop. Like he loved Mom enough.

"Why don't you see if Kelsey would like to go with us to the car show?" he says, in an attempt to make peace, but it's a half-ass attempt, because I can still hear the tightness in his voice.

"Sure." I know my answer comes out sounding sullen. I guess I'm not quite ready to make peace either.

"Eat," he says. "Then let's watch something on television."

"I have homework."

"Then stay up late and get it done," he says. "Since you are so concerned about me, maybe a few hours in my company will show you I'm okay."

I force myself to take a few bites and fight back the need to cry. It's going to be a long night.

• • •

It was after ten before Dad allowed me to go to bed. The tension between us lingered and hurt more with every tick of the clock. I felt as if he was punishing me. Punishing me for caring. I was halfway up the stairs when his words, "Love you," caught up with me and hit a sore spot on my heart.

"Love you, too," I reply, and by the time I step into my room, I'm crying.

I crawl into my bed, hug my pillow, and stare at the picture of Mom's and my feet. "Did he do this to you?" I ask. "Make you feel guilty for loving him?"

Rolling over, I run my hand on the spot next to me in the bed. How many times have I woken up to find Hayden there? But damn, I'm gonna miss him. I *already* miss him. And my tears over Dad turn into tears over Hayden.

• • •

Low on sleep, high on emotion, I'm dragging on Saturday morning.

194

Dad's up and running with energy to kill when I mosey downstairs. It's almost as if he's rubbing it in my face a bit. I'll take it if it means he's not drinking. The fact that I'm not one hundred percent sure he ever was drinking isn't important. I'm thankful he's acting normal.

"I have to work today," he says. "You got any plans?"

"I might go see Kelsey," I say.

"Just call me when you leave and get back," he says.

When Dad leaves, I go up to my room and sit on my bed, wishing Hayden would show up. He doesn't.

Bored, I get up and find my sketchpad and charcoal pencils. Drawing calms me.

My hand hangs above the paper. I don't even stop to think about what to draw. I just do it. When the face starts to form, I feel an ache in my chest. I have to redo the eyes several times before I get them just right, but I eventually nail it. Then I get out my chalk pastels and I add color here and there. I finish with the eyes. Blue.

Hayden's blue. But damn, I miss him.

I spend the rest of Saturday afternoon searching for more William Griffin links. I'm still looking for an answer.

I don't go to see Kelsey until Sunday, while Dad's working on the lawn.

I meet her mom. She's pretty and nice. But I sense some unease between her and Kelsey. Part of me wants to shake my friend and insist she appreciate the fact that she has a mom.

Later, reclined on Kelsey's bed, I tell her about confronting Dad. She assures me I did the right thing. I want to tell her about Evil Bill, about the huge freaking mystery of the obituary I found. But that stems from the secret part of my life. I can't share. Not with anyone.

Well, anyone. I shared it with Hayden.

• • •

Monday morning, I get through auto tech with Jacob. I'm nice, but not too nice. Jami and her friends are eyeballing me in the hall after second period. When I walk by them, I smile just to throw them off. I'm not going to let them intimidate me. Or rather, I'm not going to let them know they intimidate me. Truth is, I'm intimidated.

At noon, I'm running low on energy, and I'm late getting to the cafeteria. I'd texted Kelsey and told her go ahead and get her food and I'd be there shortly. Arriving five minutes later, I hurry to the food line. I wave at Kelsey and ignore the almost appetizing smell of spaghetti, because I know it doesn't taste nearly as good as it smells. Instead I go for a turkey sandwich and some chips. A few feet away from the cashier, I feel and then see her smiling at me.

Not again.

She hands change to the person in front of me then quickly turns to me. "You don't give yourself nearly as much credit as you deserve."

"Credit about what?" I ask.

"Everything."

Okay. Her level of weirdness just shot up a notch. I hand her a five for my lunch, wanting to just be done with her. She takes the bill, makes change, then looks up.

"Do you have siblings?" she asks.

"No."

"You know, it's amazing how much siblings can resemble each other. I've met some that you could barely tell apart."

"Yeah," I answer, unsure what to say to that.

"Have faith." She smiles. It's creepy. "It's all going to be okay."

"What's going to be okay?"

"Everything." She turns to the next person in line.

I pick up my tray and hurry away from her to go sit beside Kelsey, who's laughing when I sit down.

"What?" I ask.

"You should've seen the look on your face when you were talking to your weird friend. What did she say?"

"Just more crazy shit." I moan. I make little quotes with my fingers. "'It's all gonna be okay.' Oh, and…" More finger quotes. "She added, 'Did you know siblings can look alike?' I swear she has some screws loose."

"Yeah," Kelsey says, "but for some reason you're the only one who rattles those screws."

She's right, and that's starting to concern me.

• • •

Tuesday, after another day of school, Kelsey asks if I want to come over to her house and do homework. I agree to hang for a short while but suggest we go out to the ice cream shop and do our homework there instead.

When we get to the parlor, we order ice cream and spread our books out on a table. Kelsey starts stabbing her rainbow sherbet and finding the history questions we need to cover. All of a sudden, she looks up. "You were worried

Jacob might come over if we stayed at my house. That's why we came here, isn't it?"

I hate admitting it, but she's got me pegged. "Yeah. It's just... too soon." Deep down I also know the reason I don't want to spend more time with him is because of my promise to Hayden. And if Jacob asks me out or something...

"Please! It's been a year and a half since Carl," Kelsey says.

"But what about Jacob? As it is, Jami hates me. If I start dating her ex right after they've broken up, she might really come after my ass."

"You're scared of her?"

"No... Yes. I just don't want trouble."

"Is that really what's stopping you?"

"Yes... No." I drop my head on the table.

Kelsey chuckles. "Boys rebound fast."

I lift up. "I don't want to be his rebound girl. I'm not sure I want to be his anything." And even as I say it, there's a little part of me that knows I'm kind of lying. But then that little part of me feels guilty because... because I still like Hayden.

She lifts a brow not buying it. "You like him. You said so when we first met."

I scoop up a big spoonful of chocolate turtle ice cream. "Okay, I'm not sure I want to be his anything... right now. I need to focus on me. Make me a better me before I become part of a we."

Kelsey gives me a where-the-shit-did-that-come-from look. "What magazine did you get that crap out of?"

I frown. "Seventeen."

She bursts out laughing, and so do I. It's one of those

friendship moments that soothes life's rough spots. And lord knows, I've got a lot of rough spots right now.

We're barely back to work on homework when the bell over the door dings. I look up and two men walk in wearing coveralls splotched in splatters of color and the smell of fresh paint. They must be working on one of the new constructions nearby. Then suddenly I'm drawn to the fact that they are the same size, have the same... face. They have to be brothers.

And *bam*, I recall the whole weird sibling conversation with my friendly school cashier.

One of the men turns and looks at me. Right at me. Something about him reminds me of Evil Bill. But of course, it's not him. Then another realization dawns, and this one sends chills down my spine.

Evil Bill could have a twin, or at least a brother. I never finished reading the obituary to see if it stated the family that survived him. But that would explain how William "Bill" Griffin could be dead. His brother could've taken his name.

Then an equally puzzling and disturbing question hits. Why did the cashier mention siblings to me? Could she have been trying to give me a clue?

No, right? That couldn't be.

CHAPTER NINETEEN

Hanging on to my one suspicion about Evil Bill, I practically run into my house. Right before I take off upstairs, I look over at the dining room, hoping Hayden is there. He's not.

"You here?" I say and wait, hoping I'll see him. I take a deep breath, searching for his scent.

I see nothing. Smell nothing. The emptiness echoes in my chest. I miss him.

Still on a mission, I take the stairs two at a time, toss my backpack on the bed, and snag my laptop.

In a few keys strokes I'm up and running and typing William Griffin's name into the search engine.

Links come up. I clink on one and the obituary flashes on the screen. I scan it quickly to see if they include the family members of the deceased. And there it is. I read the list of names, including his wife, his kids, and then I find what I suspected: *his brother, Allen Marcus Griffin.*

I jump screens and go back to Google and type in the name.

My heart slams into my chest when the first link I open is an article about Allen Griffin's trial and the seven years he got in prison for rape. Then I see his projected release date: 2017. He's been out of jail almost a year. He's been out and he's using his dead brother's identity.

The fact that I was close enough for him to touch me makes my skin crawl. The fact that we shared the same air makes my lung go on strike. Just thinking about that man makes my blood fizzy. But knowing that he raped Abby just strengthens my resolve to stop him. To make him pay.

I remember Hayden's idea of writing the letter. Of getting Abby to tell me exactly what happened and then writing it in a letter as if Evil Bill had tried the same thing with me, but I escaped. Then I could say that when I saw the news about Abby Howard, I worried that her death wasn't an accident.

Now I can also tell them what I discovered about Bill Griffin. That I believe he's really Allen Griffin. Surely that will be enough evidence for the police to look into him themselves. Hayden also suggested I send a letter to Abby's parents and a reporter. Perhaps the reporter is a good idea, just in case the police don't take my letter seriously, but her parents?

I recall seeing the tears in Ms. Howard's eyes. I think she's been hurt enough. No letter to her mom.

Mind made up, I want to move forward. But there's no moving until... I stand and glance up at the ceiling. "Abby, I need to talk to you. If you're around please come see me."

I don't see her or smell jasmine so I drop back down

on the bed. But then I remember the weird cashier. Chills march like soldiers up my backbone.

What does she know? And how? I exhale the breath I've been holding. There's only one way to find out. I'm going to have to ask.

• • •

The next day before lunch I go hide out in the bathroom and text Kelsey to go ahead and get her food, I'm running late. Truth is, I don't want to explain to her the strange questions I'll be asking the cashier. I tossed and turned last night, coming up with questions. *Why did you bring up siblings? Did you know it was the piece of a puzzle I needed?*

Waiting for a good five minutes, I leave the bathroom. My stomach is in my throat. I'm not so sure why it scares me to even ask the questions, but it does.

When I walk into the lunchroom, I'm assaulted by the smell of fish sticks. Ugh. I spot Kelsey at our regular table and offer her a quick wave, then I get in line. I grab some chicken fingers and fries, and keep moving toward the cashier. I feel my pulse flutter at the base of my neck. I repeat the questions in my head. Once. Twice.

I can do this.

I can.

I avoid looking in the cash register's general direction for fear I'll chicken out. But as I move closer, I realize that before asking the question, I owe her a thank you. It occurs to me that I don't even know her name.

It's only when I'm next in line and I'm reaching for a bottle of water that I allow myself a quick glance at her.

The cold, damp plastic bottle slips through my fingers. I kneel down and pick it up and glance at the cashier again. Sitting in the same seat, taking money is a dark-haired woman. She isn't the blonde, blue-eyed, forty-something-year-old woman who's usually there. I stand up, relieved she's not here, but somehow disturbed as well. I want answers.

I need answers.

The student in front of me pockets her change and walks off. When I step in front of the new cashier, I force myself to ask, "Uh, where's the woman who usually works here?"

The new cashier looks up. "She had a family emergency and has taken a leave of absence. That'll be four dollars and fifty-two cents."

I hand her my five-dollar bill and fight the crazy feeling that the weird cashier's absence is a strange coincidence. Is she avoiding me? But how could she know I'd get up the nerve to ask questions?

The answer tiptoes over my mind. Perhaps the same way she had clues for me.

I take my change and turn away, trying to tell myself I'm making more of this than I should.

"Wait," she says.

I turn around.

"You aren't Riley Smith, are you?" the new cashier asks.

I hold my breath. "Yes. Why?"

"This was left in the register with your name on it." She pulls out a small envelope and holds it out to me.

I grip my tray tight with one hand and take the small invitation-sized envelope and stick it in my pocket.

"Thank you," I say and turn away, hoping I don't appear as shocked as I feel.

I take two steps away from the register and glance at the cafeteria doors. I want to take off out of the lunchroom and go read it, now. Right now. Then I see Kelsey looking up as if she's waiting on me. My gut says it wouldn't be wise to read it in front of Kelsey. My gut also says that someway, somehow, the old cashier knows my secrets.

"I wonder what happened to your friendly cashier," Kelsey says when I join her.

"She took a family leave," I say.

"You asked?" She sounds surprised.

"Yeah." I look away, hoping to derail the conversation.

Time passes with the speed of a turtle on muscle relaxers. My mind is on what's in the envelope in my pocket and not on my barely-touched now-cold fries and chicken fingers still on my tray. The clink and clatter of lunchroom noises accompanied by a crescendo of teen voices echoes around us.

I'm literally counting the seconds to the bell when I realize that Kelsey isn't her chatty self.

"You're quiet," I say.

"So," she snaps.

"What's with you?" I ask. When she doesn't answer, I look away.

After a few seconds, she blurts out, "Today's my grandmother's birthday."

I look back at her. "I'm sorry."

"Not as much as me." She glances around as if checking to make sure no one is eavesdropping, then she leans in. "It feels like a part of me is missing. I've always felt like that because of my dad. Now my grandmother's gone too. And she was like this link to the African American part of me. Now that link's gone and I'm not sure I'll ever figure myself out."

Her words echo inside me. "I kind of feel that way too. About my mom. I don't know exactly who I am because I don't know who she was."

"So we're both messed up," Kelsey says. "That's why we're friends."

She's trying to make light of it, but I know it's heavy. "Yeah. I guess. Or maybe it just takes time. When we get older we'll figure it out."

Kelsey makes a face. "You say that as if adults have all the answers. I personally think they are screwed up worse than us. Look where my mom's choices landed her and me. She has shoes that have lasted longer than most of her relationships. She's been beaten. I don't have a father and I've cohabitated with four of her live-in boyfriends, who've walked in and then out of my life."

I think about my dad and realize I can't disagree with Kelsey's assessment. Parents are just as screwed up as us. "Then maybe our only choice is to learn from their mistakes, and our own."

My first mistake to come to mind is letting things go as far as they did with Hayden. At least I'm trying to fix that one. I just wish it didn't hurt so much.

The bell rings and I'm ready to run to see what's in that envelope, but looking up, I see hurt and grief in Kelsey's eyes. Wanting to end on a good note, I recall Dad's invitation for Kelsey to come with us to the car show on Friday.

I throw it out there and she accepts immediately, even sounds a little excited about it. Then we go our separate ways.

I head straight to the bathroom, lock myself in a stall and pull the note out.

Standing there, my almost-empty stomach fluttering with nerves, I finally open it. I rip the seal and get a damn paper cut. I pull air in through my teeth, making a hissing sound.

I stare at the line of blood appearing on the pad of my index finger. It stings badly, but that's not going to stop me for one more second. I pull the card out and open it up, eager to see what the weird cashier wrote to me.

I stare at the neat handwriting and read the two words, *only two words*, written on the card.

You're welcome.

I don't know whether to be pissed, amused, or disturbed.

I'm going with disturbed.

• • •

That afternoon, I find my house empty again, except for Pumpkin. No Hayden. No Abby. "Abby, I need to see you," I say aloud. My voice seems to echo on the empty white walls.

I feed my cat and finish my homework. It only takes fifteen minutes. Then I'm bored. I recall Kelsey being so quiet on the ride home from school. No doubt thinking about Bessie's birthday.

I suddenly feel like a terrible friend for not suggesting we hang out. Mind made up, I grab my purse and keys and take off. When I pass the grocery store, I get an idea and pull in. I buy a marble cake and some birthday candles.

I drive to Kelsey's house, and before getting out I check

to see if Jacob's truck is parked next door. It isn't. I can only hope he doesn't come home and decide to pay me a visit over here.

Supplies in hand, I knock on the door. Kelsey answers, her eyes a bit puffy. She's been crying. I suddenly wonder if the cake and candles are a bad idea. But it's too late to change my mind.

"Hey," I say.

"Hi." She glances down at the cake. "What's this?"

"I thought we should celebrate your grandmother's birthday."

Tears instantly well up in her eyes.

"I'm sorry," I blurt out. "I thought it'd help. I guess it's a stupid idea."

She sighs. "Not stupid," she says. "Come in."

I follow her into the kitchen and set the cake on the table. Then I pull out the pack of candles. She looks at me. "Thanks."

"It's nothing," I say.

"No, it's *something*. It's you being a friend. I forgot how nice that can be."

• • •

Thursday, after the last school bell rings, I head to my locker, feeling generally pissed. I haven't seen Hayden or Abby, but last night the ghost of that angry convict followed Dad home. I managed to pretend I didn't see or hear him, but his rage rubbed off on me. I feel it buzzing in my blood. Part of it may be from what I'm going through with Dad. Oh, he's waking up on his own now, but he walks around with this look of guilt on his face and he's being extra nice. I know something is up, I just don't how to approach it, to make him face it, to fix it.

The school's-out hall noises echo around me. Everyone just wants to go home. Me included. I grab my books from my locker and slam my door a little hard.

"Hmm, what did that door do to you?" Jacob asks, appearing at my side.

"Nothing," I say, trying to blow off steam, and meet his eyes.

He smiles. "I'm a good listener."

"I'll remember that," I say.

"Want to hang out after school?" His shoulder comes against mine. The touch is warm, but not completely welcome. His scent reaches my nose. It's a boy smell, but not the one I'm missing so much.

I immediately recall my promise to Hayden, but... "Can't today," I say. And it's true. I need to stay home and wait for Abby and Hayden.

He leans closer. "Still not giving up." His breath whispers across my cheek.

His next move leaves me stunned. He presses his lips to my cheek. It's quick, so fast that to complain about it sounds silly, and then he's gone. I stand there for several seconds, then brush my hand over my cheek, wishing he hadn't done that. Wishing my heart hadn't responded so much when he did it. I'm so damn confused!

I walk to the parking lot, and there's a cold breeze that my light hoodie isn't holding up against. I crawl into my car, grip the steering wheel, and just sit there. Kelsey had a dentist appointment and left early. I'm alone. I'm lonely.

I miss Hayden. I lean my forehead against my steering wheel and fight back the tears.

. . .

At five o'clock that afternoon, the stark silence in the house finally breaks me. My patience snaps with it. I have to write that letter to stop Evil Allen. I grab my keys and head out. I'm done waiting for Abby. Since she isn't coming to me, I'm going to her.

As I drive, I try to come up with a reason to just show up at Dad's work. The only one I can come up with is wanting to go out to dinner and thinking meeting him would be a better option. It's not as if we haven't done that before. The fact that I didn't call or ask first is another matter.

I'm hoping in his guilt-ridden eager-to-please mood, he won't think anything of it.

I walk into the funeral home. It feels like a tomb. The cold attacks me. Chills race down my back. I'm hoping Dad is with someone, so I can search for Abby.

Standing in the entryway, no one comes to greet me, which is a good thing. Maybe Ms. Duarte is out. I walk toward the back and hear Dad talking. I almost turn around so that I can find Abby before he sees me, but then his words stop me.

"Everyone makes mistakes. God knows I've made my share." His voice is quiet, soft, even comforting. I move closer, curious to see who he's speaking with. The door, left ajar, has a sign posted on it: *Personnel Only*.

I know this is where Dad works on the bodies.

Dad's voice reaches my ears again. "I like to think we are judged by the good we do as well as our mistakes."

I inch closer and peer through the small opening. Dad's working on the convict. Applying makeup to his face.

The spirit is standing on the other side of his body, listening to every word my dad says. Both are so intent on the conversation that they don't know I'm there.

"One day at a time," Dads says. "That's how I try to take it. There's a lot of days I'm not successful. And part of me hates myself because of it." He exhales. "But this isn't about me, is it? It's about you. And I'm betting if you took a closer look at your life you'd see the good things you did too. I helped write the obituary, and it says you have a daughter. I have one, too. They're precious."

Dad's words tug at my heartstrings.

"I know," the convict's voice answers.

"There's this movie," Dad continues, not hearing his client. "I'll bet you saw it. I can't remember what it was called, I think it's more of comedy, but it has heart, too. It's the one where a man looked back at his life and saw the good he'd done."

"I don't want to talk about damn movies!" the spirit says, his tone half-pleading, half-angry. "You have to hear me. It's life or death. I need you to hear me!"

I step back before I'm noticed. When I look back down the hallway, I see Abby standing there. She turns and walks into another room.

I go after her. The door's closed. Quietly, I turn the knob, hoping it's not locked. It slips open. Nothing but darkness greets me. I blink and my eyes adjust enough to see two rows of pews. I ease in and carefully close the door behind me. It still clicks when it shuts. That clunk-clack resonates in the darkness. It's a dead sound. And it sends chills spidering up my back. Or is Abby's cold presence doing that?

Where is she?

I stand there frozen for several seconds, then I move in.

"Abby?" I say her name then sit down in a pew.

"I'm sorry." The words seem to float from the looming shadows. I hear her pain in those two words. Then I see her standing a few feet from me.

"We need to talk." My words slip out in a whisper.

She drops down beside me. She's back in her nice dress and makeup. But she sits so close, her coldness causes my skin to burn. If I move, though, I'm afraid she'll leave. So I push the icy sting from my mind.

"I need for you to tell—"

"No," she says. "I shouldn't have told you. I put you in danger. He could have... He could've hurt you like he hurt me."

"But he didn't. I'm fine. And I found something out. He's not who he says he is. He's already been arrested for... bad things. With this information, I think I can stop him. Get him in jail so he can't hurt anyone else. But I need you to tell me exactly what happened."

"No. It's too ugly." She stands up.

Right before my eyes her face changes and becomes a swollen mess. Blood stains her dress.

I try not to react. "Abby, I don't mean the details about what he did to you. I need to know how he got you into the shed. How you got away. I'm going to write an anonymous letter as if it happened to me, but I got away, and I'm going to send it to a reporter and to the police. Help me stop him," I say, my voice a mere whisper.

The sound of the door opening shatters the room's solemnity.

"Riley?" My father's voice rings out in panic.

"I'm here." I look at Abby. "Come by the house tonight," I whisper to her.

Light explodes in the room. "What were you thinking. You scared me to death. Ms. Duarte arrived and said your car was here, but we couldn't find you."

I stand up and face him. "Sorry. I got here and you were busy with a client, so I came in here to wait."

"You should have told me."

"Sorry," I say again. "I was hoping we could do dinner out. That's why I stopped by." I hate lying to him.

"Why didn't you turn the lights on?" he asks, walking up beside me.

"It was kind of peaceful," I say.

He rakes a hand through his hair and I see the worry wrinkling his forehead. "I didn't mean to scare you."

I stand up, remembering how kind he was with the convict. And I can't help but wonder if he can sense that they hear him. Why else would he talk to them?

CHAPTER TWENTY

Abby doesn't show until almost eleven. She's right. What she has to tell me is ugly, but I sit there trying not to cry for fear she'll stop. Even still, I know she's leaving out some parts. I know she's trying to protect me. I'm going to stop this guy if it's the last thing I do.

"Please do not put yourself in any more danger," she says.

"I won't." When she starts to fade I ask, "By any chance, have you seen Hayden? The boy, the other spirit, I told you about?"

"No. I'm sorry. I've never been able to see him. But I remember what you asked me to do. To see if I could find your mother. When I cross over, I promise you I'll do it."

"Thank you." They all try, and they all seem to fail.

When Abby leaves, my eyes well up with tears. Tears for her. Tears for me. Tears for my mom and for Hayden.

I want to roll over and forget. To wipe the ugly smear of Abby's story from my mind. My soul.

I can't. It's like gum on the bottom of my shoe. No matter how hard I try to scrape it off, it's still there. Sticky, ugly goo.

I fall back on the bed, feel my pulse race and tell myself to sleep. I can write the letter tomorrow. But each time I close my eyes, I see Evil Allen. My skin crawls and I keep envisioning what Abby endured. What I might have endured, if Hayden hadn't saved me.

Hayden who's done so much to help me, but I haven't even managed to help him pass over. There's a part of me that wonders if the reason I haven't been successful is because I don't want him to leave.

God, that's so wrong.

Then it hits me. Maybe he did cross over, and I just don't know it.

After five more minutes staring at the ceiling, I get up, walk to my desk, and turn on my laptop. If I'm not going to sleep, I might as well write the letter. I think I recall the name of the reporter Hayden said I should send it to. To be sure, I search the newspaper's website. Then I go to the local police website and find the name of a homicide detective.

Heart hurting, hands on the keyboard, I start writing.

I write for two hours straight, trying to get it perfect. The letter's a lie, a huge one, but I pray the police and the reporter will find the truth behind my words. The ugly truth of what really happened to Abby. The truth that a monster is on the loose.

When I finish, I print it out and read through it again.

Dear Detective Holloway,

It happened over a month ago. At first, I vowed to never tell anyone. Then I saw the news a couple of weeks ago about

Abby Howard. I wasn't sure if telling my story would make a difference, but in the end, I knew I had to try.

You see, something very bad happened to me at Lake Canyon State Park. A man, a custodian, wearing a nametag that read Bill, happened upon me while I was hiking. He was very friendly. Even flirted a little. After my recent argument with my boyfriend, I sort of found it nice. I told him I was looking for arrowheads. He said he wanted to show me his collection.

I followed him up Trail A. Almost all the way to the top. He opened a shed and waved me in. I don't know why, maybe it was the way he looked at me, but suddenly I realized I shouldn't trust him.

I made up an excuse about realizing the time and having to go. He didn't look happy. As a matter of fact, he looked very angry. I turned to leave, but he caught me by my arm. I struggled and screamed but it was right at the park's closing time and no one heard me. Then he hit me. Hard on the jaw. With his fist.

I almost passed out. The next thing I knew he was pulling me into the shed. I found a rock on the ground and hit him with it. He fell back long enough for me to scramble up and run. At first, he chased me. But some voices rang out from somewhere and he stopped.

I was going to report him, but I was so scared, I just wanted to go home. I blamed myself for flirting back with him. I blamed myself for trusting him.

I had almost put it out of my mind until I saw the news story about Abby Howard. I couldn't help but wonder if perhaps he was involved with her death. So I got on the park's website and did a little investigation. I found his name. But when I

Googled him, I found an obituary of a man with his face and the same name. William Fredrick Griffin died six years ago. I was confused, but then I read it carefully and discovered William had a brother. A man named Allen Marcus Griffin.

When I did a search on him, I discovered he had recently gotten out of jail for rape. I think it's likely that Allen took over his brother's identity. I'm really hoping you will look into this and stop this man, this monster, from hurting anyone else.

I signed it, *Sincerely, a concerned citizen.*

Then I printed one out for the reporter.

I read it again. So much of the story includes things Abby shared with me, like the rock she used to hit him. Her own story. Her own nightmare. Unfortunately, though, Abby didn't get away. He caught her and pulled her back into that shed. He raped her. It was only when he reached for the same rock to hit her that she managed to get away. But she'd been so shaken and badly beaten by him that she slipped off the edge of the trail, just like I imagined her doing when I was running from the same man.

It doesn't matter that he hadn't pushed her off that ledge. He'd planned to kill her in that shed. She knew that. I can still hear and feel the pain in her words. Feel the fear that she felt while that man hurt her.

After I read the letter, I rip it up into tiny little pieces. Holding my hand over the trashcan, I watch as the shreds of paper cascade downward. After closing my eyes a minute, I print two more. Then I print labels for the letters. Finding gloves in my desk drawer, I stick the labels to the two envelopes, then fold the letters and stuff them inside. Remembering one of Dad's shows about how DNA can be found in licked envelopes, I find a washcloth, dampen it, and seal them shut.

A feeling of accomplishment fills my chest, but the ugliness of it all hangs like a piece of rotten meat on a mental hook. It isn't until I have them sealed that I realize a problem. I can't just stick them into my mailbox. The police could probably follow them right back to me. I need to find a place across town to mail them. No, I need to find a place *out* of town to mail them.

All of a sudden, I'm exhausted. My eyes are heavy. My heart's heavier. A quick glance at the clock tells me it's three a.m. Still wearing gloves, I hide the letters in a drawer. Tomorrow I'll figure this out.

But as soon as my head hits the pillow, my mind starts spinning again. I try counting sheep, but that doesn't work. I open my eyes and stare at the side of the bed that I so often caught Hayden sleeping on. Reaching for the pillow, I pull it to my chest and bury my nose in the soft cotton. The slightest scent of Hayden lingers there. I haven't a clue how that's possible, but I hug the pillow and swallow a lump of loneliness down my throat.

• • •

The next day, with less than one hour of sleep, I drag myself to auto tech and put on a coveralls. It's a big day. We're taking out a transmission. It's something I've really wanted to learn, considering I had to have my transmission over-hauled six months after we got the car running, and it cost an arm and a leg. Six months of my babysitting money, to be exact.

After a good five-minute cautionary tutorial on how people have died working on cars, Mr. Ash finally allows us to get to work. Jacob and I grab a creeper, a rolling board to lie on while working under a car, and position ourselves under the jacked-up 1964 Falcon. The only old car in the shop.

I can't be sure how we were lucky enough to get it, but I'm guessing luck had nothing to do with it. I'm sure Jacob pleaded with Mr. Ash to let us have the older car. We are practically shoulder to shoulder. The smell of the engine and old oil fills the little breathing room we have. If I were claustrophobic, I'd be freaking right now.

Jacob glances over at me. "You look tired."

"You're never supposed to tell a girl that," I spit out.

He chuckles. "Something tells me you're the kind of girl who doesn't appreciate lies."

If only he knew how often I'm forced to lie. My mind quickly goes to the lies I've told and written lately. Of course, all of them were to protect my secret or to help the spirits. But somehow, I think lying, even for a good cause, stains a person's soul. I worry that one day mine will turn jet black.

Jacob offers to do the first part of the job. Since lack of sleep is making my arms feel like they're made of lead, I agree, but I'm intent on watching and learning.

The next thing I know, I hear Jacob whispering in my ear. "Wake up, sleepyhead."

I open my eyes. "Oh, sorry." I blink a couple of times, and then glance at him. "How long have I…"

"Been asleep?" He finishes for me, smiling. "About forty minutes. Mr. Ash just gave us the five-minute warning."

"Sorry," I say.

"You should be," he says, teasingly. "I've been so busy watching you sleep that I barely got anything done."

"You should have woken me."

"I don't know. As pretty as you are, I figure you need your beauty sleep. Bad night?"

"Something like that." I start to roll out but he catches me.

"There's this dinner of sorts tonight. A fundraiser. To raise money to pay for Carter's hospital bill. He was... is a friend of mine."

I start to speak up and he presses a gentle finger over my lips.

"It's not a date. There's several of us going. I thought maybe you and Kelsey would like to join us."

I remember the promise.

"Come on, it's Friday. Live a little," he says.

It's Friday. The thought scurries around my head and herds two thoughts from the corners of my mind. First, I don't have to conjure up a lie. I can't go. Even if I wanted to. I have a completely honest excuse. Second, tonight would be the perfect time to mail the letter.

"I can't. I'm... Dad and Kelsey and I are going to the car show in Dayton. Sorry," I say.

"Damn." Disappointment echoes in his voice. "Then the least you can do is agree to come up here tomorrow and help me work on this transmission."

"Tomorrow's Saturday."

"I guess you were asleep when Mr. Ash said he was going to be here tomorrow working on his car and if any of us want to come up and get a head start, we could."

"Yup, I was asleep," I say.

"So you'll come tomorrow?" He sounds hopeful. I feel hopeless.

Again I recall my promise. "Okay."

"Okay," he says and his brown eyes light up. "Great. Yeah. I think Ash said he'd be here around eleven. Is that good for you?"

I so want to back out. I so don't know if I'm ready for this. I so wish Jacob was Hayden. "Yeah," I force myself to say. "Eleven's good."

• • •

I finish my classwork early in English and ask to use the restroom. I've got to make a plan. Hiding out in a stall, I do a search for public mailboxes in Dayton, Texas. It gives me two addresses. A post office and a blue box outside of a UPS store.

Multitasking, I pee and do a quick search for the car show location at the same time. Luckily, the UPS office is just down the street from car show. I still don't know how I'm going to get the letters mailed while I have Kelsey with me, but I'm determined to try. Determined to get justice for Abby. And equally determined to get Evil Allen behind bars. I get a chill just thinking about him.

I flush, zip, and am almost ready to walk out of the stall, when I hear someone coming in. Correction. More than one. They're talking. I stick my phone in my back pocket, ready to leave when I hear, "Are you going to the fundraiser tonight?"

I know the voice. And in an oh-shit-I-know-that-voice way. It's Candace. The girl who gave me the black eye.

"I'm thinking about it," the second person answers and I know that voice too. It's Jami, Jacob's ex.

I debate walking out now. But my gut says it would end badly. Am I being a coward by hiding out, or am I being smart to avoid trouble? Decision made, I quietly sit down on the toilet. It feels so odd, sitting on the throne with my pants up.

"Do you know if Jacob is going?" Candace asks.

"I do now," Jami says. "I asked Dex to go with me."

"Seriously?" Candace asks. "Are you just trying to make Jacob jealous?"

"Like I could actually be interested in that dork Dex," Jami answers, sounding like a bitch on wheels. "I just wanted to piss off Jacob, but it didn't work. Dex said he was already going with Jacob and a group of people."

"Who's he going with?" Candace's voice is too shrill, almost excited.

"I don't know, but if that little mortician's twit is with him, I'm gonna flip."

I'm little? I'm a twit? I curl my hands into fists.

"I bet if you'd undone your second shirt button Dex would've said yes. You've got great boobs."

I roll my eyes. I just can't see Kelsey and me complimenting each other's boobs.

"I don't know." Jami's voice echoes around the bathroom. "I think he's too loyal to Jacob."

"Do you really want Jacob back?" Candace asks.

"No, but I want to hurt him. Bad."

"Well, I know a way we can do that," Candace says.

CHAPTER TWENTY-ONE

"How?" Jami's voice sounds a few octaves higher, as if the thought of hurting Jacob makes her excited and happy.

"Remember the weed we didn't smoke last weekend?"

"Yeah," Jami says.

"Let's plant it in his locker. Then send an anonymous tip that he has drugs. They always bring in the drug sniffing dogs every two weeks. We can even make sure to plant it when we know they are going to show up."

Jami giggles and I swear it sounds like a witch. "You might be on to something."

My mouth drops open. I can't freaking believe they'd do that.

I hear them walk into the stalls. I wait just a second and then quietly hurry out, praying they didn't hear me – or worse yet, see me – through the stall cracks.

• • •

"What are you going to do?" Kelsey asks me when I tell her before history gets started. The teacher's not here yet, so there's still a lot of noise in the classroom.

"I'm going to tell him. I have to."

"Not because you like him or anything?" Kelsey says with a look that says "duh."

"I like him enough to not let him get suspended for drugs." I don't mention I'm meeting him tomorrow. She'll have a cow when she hears that. And she'll read more into it than there is. Or maybe there is more to it, and I'm lying to myself. Whatever it is, I'll deal with it later.

A piece of wadded paper flies by my face. Two guys in the front of the class are dancing. I swear, sometimes I feel so much older than my peers.

"Okay. Why don't we meet him and Dex by his truck after school?" Kelsey says.

I nod, unable to look away from the two guys dirty dancing. Then I look at Kelsey. "What if he doesn't believe me?"

"Why wouldn't he believe you?"

"I don't know," I say and I know I'll worry about this until it's said and done. "Are we still on for tonight?" I ask.

"Yeah." She frowns. "Mom's going out with Charles. Third date. So she probably won't be home. She goes by the three-date rule before she gives it up."

I hear the discontent in her tone. I kind of remember feeling that way when Dad started dating. "You don't like him?"

"I don't feel anything. It's her business who she wants to screw. I just hate it because I know he'll probably be moving in with us in two months."

I hurt for her. At least Dad never had anyone live with us. "Do you want to stay the night with me?" I ask, because I sense she wants me to ask.

"Do you mind?"

"No," I say. And I don't, but if Hayden shows up, I might regret it.

• • •

"Speak of the devil," Dex says when he looks up from talking to Jacob and sees Kelsey and me walking toward them. The parking lot is alive with a Friday's-here buzz. I remember feeling that when I was dating Carl—the excitement of being free from school and exploring what it meant to be young and alive. Not that I explored all that much. No weed, like Jami and Candace. But Carl and I would almost always go have sex on the weekends. And I can't even say I regret it.

Jacob gives Dex an elbow while smiling right at me and I blush, because I'm thinking of sex. Jeepers, I'm really exhausted.

Dex flinches. "Uh, Jacob was just telling me you are meeting him tomorrow to work on the transmission."

"Yeah," I say and hope Kelsey missed that.

She doesn't miss shit. She gives me a you-didn't-tell-me look. Great. Now I'm going to be in trouble.

It gets quiet and I realize I need to start talking. "Uh," I look at Jacob. "I... kinda overheard something and I thought you should know."

"What?" Jacob asks, smiling at me as if pleased I walked up.

I skip the part about Jami coming on to Dex and go straight to the whole weed plan.

Jacob's smile slips off his lips and a look of shock replaces it. "She... she wouldn't do that."

Dex exhales. "Yes, she would. She was coming on to me today. She's out to hurt you, man."

"What the hell did I do to her?" Jacob spits out.

"You broke up with her," Kelsey says the obvious.

"It's not like she likes me," Dex continues, as if worried he'd overspoken. "She's just out to make you jealous. I walked away, man."

Jacob's jaw tightens. "Flirting is one thing, but setting me up to get caught with weed... That could... That bitch," he fumes. He looks at me. "Sorry. It's just..."

"I know," I say.

He kicks at some gravel at his feet. His frustration tightens his stance. "Thanks for telling me." He starts walking away.

"Where are you going?" Kelsey blurts out. Jacob turns around. "Don't tell anyone Riley told you. She's already taken a punch for me and I'd have to defend her this time."

Jacob's soft brown eyes meet mine. "I'm not. I wouldn't. I'm going to talk to the counselor. If Jami does this shit, I want her to pay." He hesitates. "Thanks again. And I won't get you involved in this. I promise."

I nod and watch him leave. I'm glad I told him. He really is a nice guy.

"So you two are going to the car show tonight?" Dex asks, his gaze on Kelsey.

"Yeah," she says, glancing at me a little surprised that Dex knows.

"You into cars too?" he asks her, and he sticks one hand in his pocket and shrugs his shoulders as if uncomfortable.

"I know a cool one when I see one," she says.

"So no," he says and grins, still looking right at her. "So what are you into?"

"Nothing." She actually takes a step back as if she realizes she's actually speaking to Dex and he seems interested. Her brows tighten and her mouth thins. I swear I see fear. She's afraid to care about him. I can't help but wonder if that's what she sees on my face when I think about Jacob. I'm afraid to care about him, too.

"She reads the same kinds of books you do. You know, fantasy stuff." I know because I saw Dex's books in auto tech and recognized some of the same titles from Kelsey's room.

"Really?" he asks.

"Yeah." She cuts me a tight-lipped frown. "We should go."

We're not halfway to the car, when Kelsey starts in, "Why did you tell him that?"

"Why wouldn't I tell him?" I ask, playing innocent.

"Don't," she says.

"Don't what?"

"You know." She shoots me another pissy glare and then says, "So you and Jacob, huh?"

"Don't," I toss back at her using her same tone.

"It's not the same with Dex and me," she says.

"Yes, it is," I say.

"Pretend like it's not," she mutters.

I give up, or partly do. "I only agreed to come work on the car tomorrow. It's school. It's not like a date or anything."

She studies me. "You know your voice gets all floaty and soft-like when you lie, don't you?"

"Does not," I say, and damn if I don't hear the softness whisper across my words.

She cuts me her signature "duh" look. "I can't believe my best friend is a liar." She smiles a little. I smile back.

When I get in the car, I start it, but then glance at her. "You're afraid."

"Of what?"

"Of caring for someone."

"Bullshit," she snaps.

"Not bullshit. I know because I'm the same way. But we need to get past that."

She exhales and looks down at her lap. "Maybe I just don't want to be like my mom. She cares so easily, they use her, and then they leave her in pieces. And I have to help her pick up those pieces. I hate that."

I hear her pain. I feel her pain. "Maybe I'm just too much like my dad, who refuses to care about anyone because... because he lost someone he loves. But either way, we're wrong."

She leans back in the seat and moans. "It's Friday. Didn't you get the memo? Psychoanalyzing crap is not permitted on Fridays."

• • •

We stop by Kelsey's house to grab her stuff and then she comes straight home with me. Dad never really said when we'd leave. But he's home when we get there. He's in a chipper mood, which seems as real as tattooed eyebrows.

It's a little chilly, so I grab an extra hoodie and we make a thermos of hot chocolate to take with us. Something about the smell of it reminds me of my mom. I take in a deep breath of it. The scent curls up inside me and somehow feels like love. Did my mother used to fix it for me?

A few minutes later, we're about to leave when I realize I've forgotten to bring the letters. That's how exhausted I am.

While Dad and Kelsey are putting chairs in the trunk of my car, I say, "Gonna go to the bathroom before we hit the road."

Taking the steps two at a time up to my bedroom, I shoot over to my desk. Remembering I can't touch them, I grab one of the plastic gloves from my drawer, and drop them, and the glove, into my purse before heading back downstairs.

Right before I close the front door of the house to leave, I smell the spicy boy scent. My breath catches. I look over and see Kelsey and Dad now waiting for me, standing by my car.

"One minute," I yell and scurry back inside. The sound of the door clicking shut sounds like an omen. The omen of an end. The end of what?

"Hayden?" I say his name, and the sound seems to echo in the empty house. Then it crawls back into my empty heart. A heart I've vowed is going to give Jacob a chance. A heart that's not sure that's the right thing.

I draw in another deep gulp of oxygen. Blended with the lingering scent of hot chocolate is Hayden's scent. His aroma is there, but he isn't. Dad's calling my name and I reach for the doorknob.

"Please come see me later," I say and rush out.

• • •

We've been at the show for a good twenty minutes. The temperature is dropping. I zip up my gray hoodie, glad I changed into a sweater for tonight. Darkness is crawling up on us, creeping into the sky and turning it shades of orange and pink. As night falls, the lights overhead are hissing as the voltage increases.

The silky-smooth taste of hot chocolate rests on my tongue. I two-hand the warm cup and pull it to my lips, inhaling the cocoa scent and trying to recall any memory of Mom.

People amble around, stopping and admiring the cars. In the distance, I hear conversations on transmissions, water hoses, and horsepower. Dad and Kelsey are talking about Dallas. My mind shifts from one thing to the next and inevitably gets stuck on something darker, deeper. On murder. Abby's murder.

This might be my chance. I set my cup down, and pop up. "Bathroom break."

I don't wait to give Kelsey a chance to say she'll join me. Purse over my shoulder, letters and glove tucked inside, I hotfoot it away.

I walk toward the bathrooms, stop, and look around to get my bearings. I see where we pulled in and know the name of the street. Pulling out my phone, I confirm the directions to the UPS store, then set out.

Realizing Kelsey might come looking for me, I pause

and text her. *Need ice cream to go with hot chocolate. Gonna grab us some. Be back soon.*

I almost hit send when I hear my name. *Crap!* Turning around, I spot Kelsey hurrying over.

"Where are you going?" she asks. "Bathrooms are over there."

"Yeah, I… I was texting you." I hold up my phone. "I wanted some ice cream and someone said there was a great parlor right up the road." I worry she can hear in my voice that I'm lying again.

For some much-needed evidence, I hit send on my phone. "See," I say when her text dings.

She pulls out her phone and reads it.

"If you'll let my dad know, I'll be—"

"Just text him," she says. "I'll go with you."

Friggin' great! I have no choice but to start walking.

She falls in step beside me. I feel her studying me. She knows. She knows I'm lying.

"How far is it?" Her words hang in the cold air, sounding like an accusation.

Guilty, I pull myself deeper into my hoodie. "The lady I asked didn't say." I work at sounding normal. "Said it was up the road on the right."

We walk the half block. Even with the sun almost set, I see the UPS store and the blue mailbox out front. I keep walking, moving closer to the edge of the sidewalk. I need to do this. I don't know when I'll get another chance to drive out of town. Even if Kelsey's here, I've gotta do it. Even if she starts asking questions.

My insides shake. How the hell am I going to accomplish this?

Suddenly I don't care how. It's going to get done.

"Look, a mailbox," I say. Rushing to take the last steps to the blue structure, I twist so my purse is hidden out of sight from Kelsey. I reach into my purse, feel for the glove, and use it to pull out the two letters. Quickly, I push the envelopes through the slot and shove the glove back into my purse. I take a deep breath.

"What are you...?" She moves in and stares at me.

"Mailing a letter," I say through the frog-sized lump in my throat and do one quick glance down to make sure the glove is all the way in my purse.

It's not. It's lying at my feet. *Shit!*

I glance up quickly, hoping she didn't see. Her gaze is on my face, not the glove at my feet. My hands are shaking and in spite of the cold, my palms are sweating.

What if Kelsey starts connecting the dots? Connects the letter I put in her mailbox to the letters I just mailed? Fear that she will flutters inside me. Mostly though, I'm just relieved I did it. I finally did something to help Abby.

Now I just have to pray the letters are taken seriously. And pray that Kelsey isn't on to me.

She continues watching me with suspicion in her eyes.

I look away from her and glance up and down the street, finding something that gives me a huge-ass sigh of relief. "There's a yogurt shop. I'll bet that's the place the lady told me about. Is yogurt okay?" I meet her eyes, begging her to take the bait, begging her not to ask questions.

"Yeah." Her voice is noncommittal, as if she's placating me. But that's okay. Placate the hell out of me. I don't care. I had to help Abby. Just like I helped Bessie. But I don't want to lose the only friend I have right now.

We walk into the shop. It smells sweet and pink, like cotton candy. I'm staring at the list of flavors, but my mind wanders to the letters. When will they be delivered? Did I word it right? Should I have written more? Not as much?

"You're quiet," Kelsey says.

"What do you want?" I ask as if nothing strange has happened.

"Isn't it too cold for ice cream?" she asks as if the idea of ice cream is bothering her. Is that the only thing she's questioning?

"It's never too cold for ice cream," I say.

We both order and I get one for Dad, too.

As we head out, Kelsey's quiet as if still thinking. We walk, occasionally dipping spoons of cold frozen yogurt into our mouths. She finally speaks up. "You are beginning to freak me out."

"Why?" I ask, because I can't come up with anything else.

"Because you, Riley Smith, are one odd duck."

"Says one odd duck to the other." I lick my spoon and try not to shiver.

She's right. It's too cold for ice cream.

She's right. I'm an odd duck.

She's right to be freaked because I am a freak.

I see, talk to, and help dead people.

I'm the mortician's daughter.

CHAPTER TWENTY-TWO

The next day around eleven a.m., I slip on my auto tech coveralls over my jeans and top, trying to come up with an excuse for leaving early. I could go with the truth. I'm tired. Kelsey and I stayed up until one in the morning talking and laughing.

We'd discussed old crushes, first periods, and college dreams. We're both considering a business major. But I confessed to her, if I thought my dad wouldn't shit a brick, I'd do an art degree. I mentioned it once in tenth grade, and he almost got angry, telling me he wouldn't pay for a degree where I'd end up asking people if they wanted fries with their burger for the rest of my life.

Neither of us have made a decision on where we'll go. She's still not sure how she's going to pay for it. I'd encouraged her to look into school loans. It's what I plan to do.

Even after Kelsey went to sleep, I'd stayed awake hoping Hayden would show up. He didn't. It hurt.

Then, staring at the ceiling last night, I remember

thinking that Hayden could be gone. That he crossed over. He told me he'd try to say goodbye, but maybe he wasn't able to.

Damn that hurt. I spent the rest of the night hugging my pillow and telling myself I needed to be happy for him. I need to find a way to be happy for me, too.

I zip up my coveralls.

"Good morning!"

I jump out of my skin when Jacob's words brush against the back of my neck. Swinging around, I face him.

He's smiling. His eyes are so warm and welcome. He's standing close. So close I can smell his toothpaste. I notice the soft curve of his bottom lip. I recall the quick kiss he gave me in the hall that I haven't called him on.

I take an automatic step back, but then regret it. "Morning." The cute-boy flutters stir in my stomach.

"Where's Mr. Ash?" he asks.

"He's pulling his car around."

"Oh." He reaches for a coverall, then he pulls his jacket off. I stand there watching. The muscles in his chest bunch up as he pulls his arms out. Suddenly it feels too intimate. I don't know what's so intimate about watching someone pull his coat off, but I feel it and react to it.

My face heats up.

I look away, then remember overhearing Candace and Jami yesterday. I turn around.

"What happened? Did you tell the counselor about … what Jami and Candace said?"

"Yeah." His smile weakens. "She said she doesn't think they would carry through with it, but if they do, she'll react accordingly." He hangs his coat on a hook beside mine. "I didn't mention your name, by the way."

I smile. "Thanks."

"No. Thank you. You could have kept it to yourself." He exhales. "I can't believe I fell for Jami. I mean, what the hell was I thinking?"

"She's pretty. She's a cheerleader." *She probably unbuttoned the second button on her top. Because, you know, she has amazing boobs. Just ask Candace.* "That's what you were thinking." I bite into my lip, wishing I hadn't said that.

He sighs. "Yeah, I won't make that mistake again. I'm learning that not all pretty girls are bitches." He motions to me as if I'm being held up as an example.

When I don't say anything, he asks, "How was the car show?" He steps into the coveralls and zips them up.

"Good"

"Were there lots of other Mustangs there?"

"Some," I say.

He tilts his head and studies me. "Nice ones?"

"I think so."

He chuckles. "I swear, sometimes you don't seem like you're into cars."

"I hate to disappoint you, but I'm really not. I mean, I love my car and I want to know how to work on it. But I'm not a car fanatic."

"So what are you a fanatic about?"

I start to just shrug. "I like to read… and draw."

"Do you take art?" he asks.

"I did at the other schools. Here it was auto tech or art. But I'm thinking of taking some classes in college."

"What kind of art?"

"I don't know yet. Maybe painting or drawing."

"Where are you going to school?"

"I don't really know yet. I have to get some school loans first."

He studies me and smiles softly. "You are an enigma. Sooner or later I'm going to figure you out. Uncover all your secrets."

I hope not. The garage door opens and Mr. Ash is standing there. He gets back in his car to drive it inside.

Jacob is still staring at me. "So why did you get a Mustang? Why that car?"

Hesitating, I watch Mr. Ash pulling in, and then tell the truth. "Because my mom had one when she was young."

"Does she still have it?"

"She died when I was four."

Empathy fills his expression. "Damn. Sorry."

I nod.

"So it's just you and your dad?"

"Yeah."

"At least you don't have siblings. I have a younger brother and sister. They are a pain in my ass."

I grin. But I don't agree. I spent many years wishing I had a sibling. Someone besides just me and Dad. Because when you just have one family member, you are more panicked about losing them.

"Not that I wouldn't kick anyone's ass if they hurt them," Jacob says.

Again, I think about him being a good guy. My heart feels a slight thrill at being here with him.

Mr. Ash gets out of his car. "You two can get started. Just be careful, remember the safety rules."

We both nod.

In a few minutes, we're under the car on our creepers. The space is so small it feels intimate. It's quieter than on regular school days. I start working first and I feel his gaze on me. I keep trying to loosen a bolt that doesn't want to be loosened.

"What was his name?" he asks.

I glance at him. "Whose name?"

"The guy who broke your heart. The guy who's stopping you from giving me a chance."

My mind goes to Carl, but is it Hayden standing in my way? I don't even know. Shit. I am an enigma even to myself.

"It's not like that," I say.

"Yes it is. And whoever it is, he's an idiot. I wouldn't do you wrong."

• • •

"This is nice," I say, and look around at the pond. The sun is out and it's almost warm. I think of last night and the cold. Crazy Texas weather. I watch some geese float past. Their squawking follows them down a slow ride on the water. Occasionally, I hear a splash. It's peaceful.

Don't ask me why I agreed to come here, but I did. Jacob pleaded for me to go grab lunch with him and all I could think about was that damn promise to Hayden. Then I thought about going home to an empty house. To being alone and worrying about the letter I wrote, worrying about Dad. Missing Mom. Alone to accept that Hayden is never coming back.

So here I am. With Jacob. Because Kelsey and her mom are going to see a cousin and won't be back until tomorrow and Dad told me this morning that he had to work.

Jacob, holding a fast food bag, tosses me the blanket he pulled out of his trunk.

I shake it out and sit down on it. "I didn't even know this park was here."

He drops down beside me and hands me my hamburger and drink.

The burger's still warm in my hand. I find a place my drink won't fall over and unwrap the sandwich to take a bite.

He does the same. We eat in silence. After a few minutes, he crumples up his sandwich paper and looks around. "I can't come here without thinking of Carter."

I remember this is the guy with brain damage. "You two were friends?"

"Yeah." A sad smile widens his lips. "Last summer I had this grand idea to come fish the pond. Carter had just put a worm on his hook and was grabbing the rod to cast it in when a goose came up and snatched up the worm and hook. The thing started squawking. I screamed for him to cut the line and he did. But then he said the goose would die with a hook in his mouth."

Jacob takes a deep breath as if breathing in the memory. "So Carter jumps up and goes after the goose. The thing is fighting like crazy but he holds this huge bird up and brings him back here. The goose is squawking like mad, I'm laughing my ass off and Carter's yelling at me to get the pliers out of the tackle box. I hand them to him and he puts the bird between his knees and uses the pliers to attempt to pull the hook out."

Jacob laughs again, but there's a whisper of loneliness in it. I wonder if that's part of the reason I like him. I sense that like me, he's dealt with loss.

He looks down a second. "The goose never shuts up and it's as if he's calling for help. Because all of a sudden we are surrounded by geese. I mean a huge flock of them. Like they are out to save their friend. Carter doesn't care. He just keeps working. I have to stand up to wave them away. I swear, right before we get flogged by a hundred geese, he gets the hook out and lets the damn bird go. It goes squawking off, but not before it stands there and gives Carter a piece of his mind. I swear that bird called Carter every name in the book."

I laugh, getting the image of him and his friend being surrounded by geese.

He lets go of a deep sigh. "That's Carter for you. He loved animals. He'd have been flogged by a shit load of geese before he'd let that bird die."

"Loved?" I ask. "Has he passed away?"

"Not yet, but I saw his stepdad and he told me he's not doing well." He swallows hard. I can see he hurts for his friend. I think of how I hurt for Hayden and I can relate to how he feels.

"What happened to him?" I ask, remembering the man at Dad's work, a Mr. Carter. I wonder if that's a coincidence? Was Carter the boy's last name, not his first? If so, should I worry I might have Jacob's friend stopping in to see me next.

I start to ask about the name thing, when my phone

rings. I check the number. "It's my dad. Excuse me a second."

I take the call. "Hey Dad."

"Where are you?"

"I called and left a message. I went to lunch with Jacob, my auto tech partner."

"I know. I got that message. So you're on a date?"

"No." I pull the phone tighter to my ear just in case Jacob can hear him. "Just lunch."

"Is it just you and him?"

"Yes."

"Then it's a date. And you know the rules, before you date anyone I need to meet them."

I almost tell him he has met Jacob at the car show, but then Jacob will know this is about him. I frown, remembering all the issues I had with Dad when I dated Carl. "I'll be home soon," I say in an unhappy voice.

"You'd better. I'm at work. Call me when you get there. And this won't happen again, young lady. Understand?"

I hang up. I'm fuming. Now that I know Mom got pregnant when she was young, I wonder if that's why he's so hard on me. He thinks I'm going to get pregnant?

I suddenly realize Jacob is staring. "Sorry," I say.

"Your dad?" he asks.

"Yeah."

He looks at me and grins while a little guilt plays in his eyes. "So he's a little overprotective?"

He must've heard what Dad said. I frown. "That's an understatement."

He shrugs. "Then let me come over and talk to him.

I actually do pretty well with dads. I can talk cars, sports. Dads trust me. I've got one of those faces."

I sweep a strand of blond hair behind my ear. "I don't think—"

He presses a finger to my lips. "I know you're fighting this. But give me a chance, Riley. We can take it slow. Just hang out some. I won't push you. I just... You are unlike any girl I've ever known. I want to get to know you. I want to know what makes you tick. What makes you laugh. And it's not just... because you're beautiful. It's... everything about you appeals to me. The way you think, the way you treat people. Give me a chance, please? Next Saturday my parents are throwing a party down by our lake house. It's not a grand place, but the lake is scenic and we cook out and it's a lot of fun. Come with me."

I'm speechless. Or I think I am, but then I hear the two syllables slip from my lips. "Okay." *Shit!* Did I actually agree to this? What the hell am I doing?

Oh, yeah. I'm moving on. I'm keeping my promise to Hayden.

Jacob grins. "Yes!"

Then he kisses me. His mouth is soft. His lips are moist and they ease across mine. His tongue slips across my bottom lip.

I'm pulled in at the same time I force myself to pull back. I feel the flutters in my stomach, good flutters, but nothing like I felt with Hayden. I push that thought away. I have to let go of Hayden. Hayden's dead. I'm alive and I need to start living like I am.

I meet Jacob's eyes. "What happened to slow?"

He shrugs, guilt flashes in his eyes, but he still smiles. "I don't think I can kiss slower than that."

I give him the evil eye.

"Okay. Sorry. Sorry. I promise to behave. How about this?"

Before I know what he's intending, he leans in and kisses my cheek, then whispers that kiss over the corner of my lips. I feel frozen again. But the temptation is there to let go and let it happen.

"Is that slow enough?" he asks pulling back, studying me as if he knows I'm mesmerized. And I am mesmerized. I sit up straight.

"How about no kissing for a while." I lift a brow.

"Wow. That is slow." He reaches out and brushes another strand of hair off my cheek.

I swat at his hand. "And no touching."

"Fine." He's still smiling and I want so bad to let his smile become important to me. To let it take me to a happy place. To follow this thing, this temptation, to a place where I feel normal again. I remember it being hard to juggle ghosts and a social life. But now I miss juggling. I miss being more than the mortician's daughter.

"I'm good with it." He holds up his palm. "Really good with it. Promise."

• • •

"Wake up! Get up."

That night I feel the cold pain in my forearms at the same time I hear Abby's screams. I bolt up to escape her hands and her panic that are gripping me. Hurting me.

"What is it?" I ask, running my hands over the ache in my arms. Then I gasp when I see her. She's back to being bloody and beaten.

I feel bad that I'd kind of yelled at her. "What is it?" I repeat in a calmer voice.

"You're in trouble. I'm so sorry I did this to you."

"How am I in trouble?"

"He's trying to find you."

"Who?" I ask, but deep down I'm afraid I know. I just don't see why or how.

Abby lifts her chin and I see the gleam of tears in her eyes. "The man who raped me. He's trying to find you."

CHAPTER TWENTY-THREE

"Wait. Calm down." I get out of bed. "How do you know that he's trying to find me?"

"I went back there. He was in the park office. They have a security camera in the front of the building and he was scanning the footage of you getting out of your car. He wrote down your license plate number and muttered, 'I got you now, bitch.' He must know that you were there looking for my ring."

"He couldn't know that," I say.

"Then he must blame you for his phone blowing up. His hand is all bandaged."

"He couldn't know that either!"

"Then he's just upset because you got away. I don't know why he's out to get you, but he is. You have to believe me."

"I do," I say and the coldness is back, sinking bone-deep and traveling up and down my arms. Up and down my spine. It reaches my heart and it skips a few beats, then starts racing.

Hard.

Fast.

Pounding.

I feel my chest bone vibrating.

Shit. Crap. Damn.

What can I do? I can't tell Dad. I can't go to the police. What the hell am I going to do?

"I sent the letters," I tell her, trying to calm her, trying to pretend it calms me. But is that going to be enough?

• • •

"Something interesting?"

I look up from my phone to Jacob leaning on the locker next to mine.

"Not really," I say and close the link before it opens. For the last three days I've been a nervous wreck, obsessively checking the news for any information on Abby's case, desperate for my letter to reach the right hands. On top of that, I've just been flat-out scared that Allen Griffin really is looking for me.

"We're still on for next Saturday, right?" Today Mr. Ash had us watching videos so we hadn't had an opportunity to talk in class.

"Yeah," I say, and realize I haven't mentioned the date to Dad. That will be fun. Not.

Jacob has kept his going-slow promise. We see each other at auto tech every morning and off-and-on during school. Jami sees us, too. I've caught her glaring at me several times, as if with a warning. But let's be honest. I have bigger fish to be afraid of—Allen Griffin.

Jacob and Dex have also been meeting up with Kelsey and me at my car after school. We've hung out and chat for about fifteen minutes the last couple of days. Kelsey isn't happy about it. Or she says she's not. But I see the way she looks at Dex, when he's not looking at her.

It's probably the same way I look at Jacob. Interested, but uneasy. I'm not sure if my world is about to get rocked or if it's about to fall off its axis.

"I should go," I say, feeling like an idiot, unable to find anything else to say to the guy I have a date with next Saturday.

I run to the bathroom, hide in a stall and open the website for the local newspaper. Surely they've received my letter by now.

Will they open it right away? Will the letters go into a pile of mail to be opened God only knows when? Will they even take my accusations seriously?

Will Evil Allen find me before the truth is out?

As I wait for website to come up, I'm hoping the reporter has looked into the story quickly and written his article. But nope.

There are no articles or news about Abby's death. I hate this feeling brewing inside me. It's fear.

It hasn't helped that Abby has shown up every night trying to get me to leave town. Like I could just pick up and leave. Her other suggestion to go to the police is just as crazy. What the hell could I say that wouldn't have them blasting me with questions I can't answer? And if I told them the truth, I'd end up in the crazy house.

My best bet is to be on guard. Pray the letters work.

Pray really hard.

• • •

After school, Jacob and Dex are at my car again. Jacob asks me if I want to hang out. I tell them that Kelsey and I have to study for a history test and have tons of homework to do. We do have a test, but I'm exaggerating on the homework.

He accepts with a sigh of disappointment.

Kelsey crawls into my car. "So where are we going to go again today so that you don't have to go home? And why are you so scared to be at your house these days?"

I look at her and frown. Have I been that obvious? Shit, I'm clueless how to explain anything. So I just don't.

"I thought we'd go to Running Water Park. I tossed a blanket and some marshmallow treats and waters in my car to snack on while we study."

When we get there, it's so pleasant that Kelsey forgets to call me out on being so weird lately. We munch on the snacks, finish studying, and are about to start on our homework when a couple of geese swim past.

I'd told Kelsey about Jacob bringing me here. Even told her about the kiss. But I remember the crazy story Jacob told me about the geese. I recount it to Kelsey and we lie there looking up at the sky and laughing.

"You really like Jacob, don't you?"

"Yeah. Sort of, kind of, a little."

She laughs again. "You know, he cornered me at my locker today, wanting to know what happened between you and your old boyfriend."

I frown. "What did you tell him?"

"The truth as I know it. That you had to move away. And that he moved on before you thought he should."

I cringe thinking about her passing on this information. "You could have told him it was none of his business."

"I'll try to remember that next time," she says, not sounding guilty at all.

I don't know if she's getting even with me for telling Dex she reads the same books as him, or if she's trying to help me just like I was trying to help her that time.

She looks back up at the sky. "Is Carl really the reason you're holding back on Jacob?"

"Yeah." *Along with a few other reasons.*

"He seems to really like you."

"I know, and I'm going out with him on Saturday. But don't start on me when you're giving Dex the cold shoulder. You didn't say two words to him today."

"That's different."

"How?"

She sits up. "I don't expect you to understand."

"Understand what?" When she doesn't answer, I sit up. "This isn't just about your mom's failed relationships, is it? Is this a race thing?"

I see her shoulders draw back, but she doesn't answer.

"What makes you think he cares about that?" I ask.

"Everyone cares," she snaps.

"Really? So you think I care?"

She looks at me. "You're different."

"Maybe you only feel that way about me because you gave me a chance. If you give Dex a chance, you might learn—"

"Not everyone's like you."

"And not everyone is like Candace and Jami."

She moans. "I don't give a shit how Candace or Jami

feel about me. Part of me doesn't give a shit how anyone feels. I'm so damn proud of both of my heritages and when someone rejects me because of one of them, I get so freaking pissed."

I look at her and think I know what happened. "What boy rejected you?"

She exhales. For a minute, I don't think she's going to answer and then she does. "Brad. We dated for like six months. We even had sex. His parents invited me over for a barbeque. He asked me to remove my necklace and bracelet, told me I couldn't tell them that I was part black. It hurt so bad!"

"And that's why you push people away," I say.

"I don't push, I just don't invite anyone to get close."

"But you shouldn't judge everyone just because of him."

"And you should get over Carl."

"I'm working on it," I say and I really am. I'm ready, I think. Ready to hit the restart button.

We get quiet for a few minutes, listening to the sound of the park. A few kids are playing on the swings, and ducks and geese are splashing in the water.

"Did I tell you I think I have a job?" Kelsey says.

I know it's an effort to defuse the tension, but I let it pass. "No. I didn't know you were looking for a job."

"I wasn't. But Mom's work needs someone to help them with their social media. She suggested me. I'm supposed to go Thursday morning for an interview."

"So does that mean you'd have to work after school every day?" I try not to feel sorry for myself for losing my after-school buddy.

"No. I'll work from home. Make my own hours, sort of."

I pull my knees closer. "I wanted to get a job before we moved here, but Dad said it was only okay if I could find something that was just on the weekends."

My phone rings. I glance at it. "Speak of the devil," I say and take the call.

"Where are you?" Dad's voice, sounding stern, flows through the line.

"At the park with Kelsey."

"Just Kelsey?" he asks.

"Yes." I frown and worry about getting his permission for Saturday. I'd better mention it tonight and get it over with.

"So you didn't fix dinner?"

I cringe a little. "Uh, no."

I think he's about to chastise me, but instead he says, "Well, why don't you pick up a pizza on your way home. I should be home soon."

"What time?" I ask, not wanting to go home and be alone.

"Soon." He hangs up and his tone takes me back to worrying about him. I'd pushed my Dad concerns to the back burner with everything else going on. But they are back.

Just what I need. Something else to eat at my sanity.

• • •

When I pull up to the house, Dad's car isn't parked in the driveway. Thinking that Evil Allen might have gotten my address, I'm nervous to be home alone. What are the chances Dad pulled into the garage? Not great, since he's never done that.

I actually consider just driving around the block until I see his car, but then I feel like a coward. Plus, I want to watch the news, in case there's something about Abby and a new investigation.

Before I pull into the driveway, I check up and down the street for any strange cars. Nothing. I pull into the drive, grab the pizza, and hurry inside.

I don't breathe until I hear the click of the lock. Even then I stand in the hallway listening for any noise telling me to run like hell.

I don't hear anything, until Pumpkin turns the corner purring and demanding love.

If someone were in the house, well, anyone but Hayden, Pumpkin would be hiding. I hold the pizza in one hand and pick up Pumpkin with the other, snuggling him with my cheek. He purrs louder.

I make my way into the kitchen, checking for Hayden just in case he's still here, and drop off the pizza. I'm so busy loving on Pumpkin that I almost don't notice the light beeping on the phone. My first thought is that Dad went MIA at work again and Ms. Duarte was hunting him down.

I rush over and hit rewind on the antique answering machine. "Four new messages," the machine says in an automated voice.

Four?

The first three are hang-ups. I feel the unease start at the base of my neck.

The fourth message is Dad. "Where are you? I'll call your cell."

I think about the hang-ups. Could Evil Allen have tracked down my phone number? How hard would it be, since Dad still lists us in the phone book?

I breathe in. Breathe out. Tell myself not to panic. But I grab my cell and call Dad. He answers on the second ring.

"Hey, I'm here with the pizza."

"Sorry, I got hung up on something. I should be there in about an hour."

An hour. Shit.

"Okay. See you then." What else can I say? *Can you hurry up because I think a serial rapist is after me?* Not good.

I hang up and go check all the locks. Then I snatch up Pumpkin as if he will keep me safe. I walk to the living room, find the remote and drop on the couch.

I find my soft spot between the sofa's cushions, but I'm so tense it doesn't feel comfortable. Still snuggling Pumpkin, I turn the television on.

The news is already on. When I see the reporter standing in front of Lake Canyon State Park, my attention is revved up, I catch my breath and drop Pumpkin in my lap. This has to be about Abby, doesn't it?

"Brian County Police Department has refused to comment thus far, but they aren't denying that they are relooking into the cause of death in the Abby Howard case and that William Griffin, a park employee, is now considered a person of interest."

"Yes!" I pump a fist in the air. Pumpkin, taken by surprise, bolts off my lap.

I'm literally doing a happy dance on the sofa... until

the reporter continues. "When a detective spoke with the park attendant briefly this morning over the phone, he agreed to come down to the station for an interview. We're told that Griffin never showed. And according to his boss at the park, Griffin disappeared from work shortly after that conversation and has not been seen since."

"Freaking hell!" I yell. "Why the heck did you call him and give him a chance to run? Are you idiots?"

I'm furious. Livid.

And then I hear banging on my front door.

CHAPTER TWENTY-FOUR

I bolt to the kitchen and grab a butcher knife. The doorbell rings again.

Knife in hand, I move to the dining room to peer through the blinds. I feel like an idiot when I see a kid standing there.

I forget I'm holding the knife and rush to open the door. The kid looks scared. "Uh, sorry, I was cutting vegetables," I say.

I feel so bad that I order candy from the boy for his school fundraiser.

By the time Dad gets home, my heart is almost back to beating normally.

"You didn't have to wait for me," Dad says as he puts paper plates on the table.

"I wasn't that hungry." I pull the pizza from the oven and place it on the table. Then I snag a couple of water bottles from the fridge.

"How was your day?" I ask.

"Busy," Dad says.

"Bad busy?" I ask.

"I work at a funeral home."

I'm a little shocked by his answer. This is only the second time I've ever heard him complain about the job. That tells me Dad's mood hasn't improved since I spoke to him on the phone. I need to change that, because I need to bring up Saturday.

We eat. I talk about how the video we saw today in auto tech. Dad feigns interest in what I'm saying, but I can tell he isn't really into it.

Finally, I pick up my third slice of pizza and right before I take a big bite I drop the bomb. "I've been invited to a party Saturday night."

"Whose party? Kelsey's?"

"No. Jacob Adams."

Dad sets his half-eaten slice down and the scowl that's been waiting to come out makes an appearance. "The same guy you went out with already without introducing him to me?"

"It wasn't…" I bite my lip. "Yes, he's my auto tech partner. And you met him at the car show."

"I thought he had a girlfriend."

"They broke up. Look, Dad, he's a nice guy and the party is at his parents' lake house and they will be there. So it's completely safe."

"I think you should have him over for dinner sometime before you go out with him."

I so don't like his tone. "He's planning on coming over early so you can officially meet him."

"Did you hear what I just said?" His frown is firm,

but damn it, he doesn't have a right to be like this. I'm a good kid. I help out around the house and, until I had a serial rapist after me, I'd cooked dinner most nights. I never break curfew. Heck, for the last year, I haven't even gone out. I finally get asked to do something and he's saying no.

"Dad, you aren't being fair."

"I don't have to be fair."

I'm stunned by that answer. "I'll be eighteen in two months. And like I said, his parents will be at the party."

"I already said what I have to say!" he spouts out.

His bad attitude spills all over me and I soak it up. "Why are you doing this?" Now my tone is sharp.

"Because I'm your father."

"No, that's not why. It's because you got Mom pregnant before you got married."

Dad's eyes round and his mouth hangs open. He's not used to me talking back. Normally I don't. Because I *am* a good kid.

"How... do you know that?" he asks.

How do I know that? Because I was snooping in your room looking for alcohol and found the wedding picture you never showed me! I literally bite into my lip to keep from spilling my guts. I need to think fast because he's waiting for an answer.

"When we were unpacking I saw the picture of you and Mom when you got married. She had a baby bump. Is that why you've never let me see the picture? What else are you hiding from me, Dad?"

He doesn't deny my accusation, but instead says, "We made a mistake."

"So you're afraid I'll make the same mistake."

"The answer is still no." His firm tone escalates to anger.

Now it's my mouth that falls open. "This is so unfair. I'm not going to have sex with Jacob when his parents are around."

His eyes widen. His cheeks redden.

"Yeah, it's a word, Dad. It's spelled S-E-X. And if you ever allowed yourself to talk to me about it, you'd know I'm the kind of kid you can trust. You'd learn that I know all about condoms and protection. About safe sex. But no. You sit here on your high horse judging me and telling me I can't do something just because you and Mom made a mistake. That's all kinds of wrong. I shouldn't have to pay for your mistakes."

"Don't talk to me like that, young lady!"

"Again, I'm not that young!" I jump up. I fist my hands. Unfortunately, I'm still holding a slice of pepperoni pizza, so my fingers dig into the crust. "I'm going to that party, Dad. And unless you can get a lock on my door between now and then, you can't stop me."

I swing around and storm off, carrying my anger, my attitude, and a slice of mangled pizza.

"Riley," he calls after me.

I ignore him and march myself up the stairs. My chest is hurting. I've never talked to my dad like that before. But he's never been so unreasonable before.

When I get to my room, the pizza lands with a *thud* in my garage can, and I land face down on my bed. I moan, kick my feet like a two-year-old for one second, then roll over and stare at the ceiling. I feel my phone in my back pocket. I almost pull it out to call Kelsey and tell her what a dick my dad's being.

But I don't want to talk to Kelsey. I want to talk to... Hayden. I want him to show up and lay on the bed to have one of our long talks with me. I want him to make me laugh. To make me forget how shitty my life is.

But that's not happening.

Pumpkin jumps up in my bed and starts licking the pizza sauce and cheese goo from my fingers. I should go wash my hands. Brush my teeth. But I don't move. I don't care.

My life really is shitty.

. . .

I wake up and roll over when my phone's alarm dings to tell me it's time to get up. I snuggle back under my blanket, hoping to wait until I hear Dad leave. Facing him this morning is not on my desired to-do list.

I stay there for ten minutes listening. Did he get up early and leave? Maybe seeing me wasn't on his desired to-do list either.

Then I recall the mornings he overslept. *Crap.*

I pop up, throw on my clothes and head downstairs. I run to the dining room window to see if his car's gone. It's not.

I walk to his door and knock. "Dad, do you know what time it is?"

He doesn't answer. "Dad?" I knock harder. "It's after seven."

I hear him mutter something and then he yelps, "Fuck."

I cringe. I've never heard him drop the f-bomb. *Really*

good, Dad, a great example for me to live by. I guess I'm still pissed at him.

I listen, to make sure he's up. He is. I hear him scrambling.

I walk back to the breakfast table.

In only a few minutes, he storms out. He's shirtless, but has on his suit pants and is holding a jacket and shirt in his arm.

"I'm supposed to be there early." He hauls ass to the door.

"Dad?" I say.

He swings around. "We'll talk tonight. I may... I may have been wrong about the party." He starts back toward the door.

I breathe a sigh of relief. At least the man can see reason when it's thrown at him, but...

"Dad," I say.

"Gotta go!"

I pop up and chase him into the entry room. "Dad."

"What?" He turns around.

That's when I notice his bloodshot eyes.

"Your shoes," I say.

He looks down at his bare feet, then up. "Thanks."

He runs back to his room and comes out holding his shoes. I watch him leave.

Who forgets his shoes? Someone with a hangover.

The worry I feel over what he's doing to himself takes up too much space in my chest. Damn it. What's going to happen to him? What's going to happen to him when I leave for college? Will he just drink himself to death?

Damn! Damn! Damn!

Tears fill my eyes.

All of a sudden, Pumpkin comes hauling butt through the kitchen as if something scared him. And bam. I'm suddenly scared.

Shit! I didn't lock the door. I take off, tears in my eyes, and throw the deadbolt.

Leaning against the door, I let go and the tears flow. I'm scared. I'm worried. I'm confused.

"Are you okay?"

The voice... the oh-so-welcome voice reaching my ears goes right to my heart. I swing around. Hayden is standing there.

"Where... have you... been?" My voice shakes.

His blue eyes meet mine. "Trying to stay away."

"Why? I needed you." I put my hand over my trembling lips.

"We talked about that. You need to move on. You promised me."

"I am, but..." I walk right into his arms and let my head rest on his chest. It feels so right, so safe. *Please don't leave me again*, I want to beg. Instead I just let myself cry.

"What's wrong?" I can feel his hands moving across my back. The touch is comforting, caring, cautious. I can tell he's not sure he should be here. His hold is hesitant, as if he doesn't know if he should push me away or pull me closer.

I vote for closer, but then logic intervenes and I step back. I tell him about the letters I wrote, about Abby telling me the guy's looking for me.

"Damn," he says. He takes both of my hands and holds them. "You're going to have to go to the police."

"And say what? There's not any part of the truth that they will believe." My voice shakes and my heart trembles.

"Riley, you're not safe."

"I've tried to figure it out. I have nothing. I'm just praying they catch him." Then all of my other issues spill out of me and I tell Hayden about Dad this morning, looking like he has a hangover again. "I don't know what to do. I'd confront him again if I had any proof. But I don't."

"Do you really want that proof?" he asks and stares at me as if he knows something, but isn't sharing it.

"What?" I ask.

When he remains silent, I say, "What do you know, Hayden?"

He glances back at my dad's bedroom door. "He keeps the liquor in his dirty clothes hamper."

"Are you kidding me?"

"No."

"How long have you known?"

"Just since last night."

Emotions are storming inside me. I'm furious that Dad's drinking, and I'm angry that Hayden wasn't going to tell me. I'm also hurt he was here last night and didn't come see me.

I rush past Hayden and swing open Dad's bedroom door, bolting into the bathroom. I yank the top off his hamper and toss his dirty clothes out. Sure as hell, there are two bottles buried under some clothes and a blanket.

Without thinking, I pull the tops off of both bottles and pour the contents down the sink. "You can't drink it if it's not here!" I seethe out the words, feeling justified, feeling righteous.

No sooner do I watch the last swirl of alcohol circle the drain, than my sense of justice gets sucked down with it.

Now the truth's out. The genie's out of the bottle. The devil's loose. How is Dad going to deal with that? How will I deal with Dad dealing with that? What if now he just starts drinking in front of me?

I look up at the ceiling feeling overwhelmed. "Mom, please help me. Tell me what to do."

But like every damn time I ask for her help, I get nothing. Nothing. Why the hell did she have to die?

My home phone starts to ring. I think of Dad. Did he have an accident on the way to work? Was he still drunk? Should I have stopped him from driving? I can't lose Dad. He's all I've got.

I bolt into the kitchen to answer it. "Hello?" My heart's rocking against my chest bone. *Be okay, Dad. Please be okay.*

I hear nothing but breathing. Then a click. The line is dead.

Shit. Was that…?

I glance at Hayden. "I've been getting hang-ups. I don't know if it's him or if I'm jumping to conclusions. Probably just jumping to conclusions, right?"

He doesn't answer. The color of his clothing starts fading. Everything about him is muted, like an… old photograph. Like all the other ghosts.

"What is it?" I ask, sensing something is happening. Something… not good.

"I have to go," he says. "I can't…"

"Will you come back? Are you crossing over? Talk to me, Hayden."

"Call the police to protect you."

Emotion swells in my chest. "You... *you* protect me."

"At least tell Jacob."

"Jacob? Are you crazy? I can't tell Jacob about any of this. He wouldn't believe me. The only reason you believe me is because..."

"And that's the same reason I can't protect you. Please..." He fades even more. "I have to..." He never finishes the words.

"Hayden?" I say his name, but he's gone.

I'm alone.

CHAPTER TWENTY-FIVE

Fear curls up in my empty stomach. Fear for Hayden. Fear for myself.

I dash upstairs and grab my backpack, storm downstairs, grab my keys, turn the lock on the door and fly outside.

Jumping in my car, I start the engine and drive off. I start driving to Kelsey's, only to remember today is Thursday and she went for that interview and won't get to school until after second period.

I force myself to take deep breaths and tell myself I'm simply overreacting. It wasn't a serial rapist on the phone. But I can't deny that it was liquor in Dad's clothes hamper. What the hell am I going to do about that?

I look in the rearview mirror, something I've been doing a lot since Abby told me Evil Allen was looking for me. A dark blue older Honda is about four car spaces behind me.

I squint into the mirror. It has tinted windows and I can't see who's driving. It's not him. It can't be him. But just to make sure, I turn off the main drag to confirm he won't follow. My eyes are skipping from the windshield to the rearview mirror.

Then I see it. The blue car. It's behind me.

"Fuck!" I say, borrowing Dad's word from this morning. I turn down another street, and hold my breath. I feel the *thump thumping* of my heart as I watch to see if the blue car follows.

It does!

I hit the gas and turn down another street that I know will lead me back to the main road. I don't have a freaking clue where I'm going. I just want to be with more cars, more people.

I get back to the main road, driving with one eye on the road and one on the rearview mirror. He's still there, but lagging behind as if he knows I'm on to him. I look back up just in time to see the red light in front of me. I slam on my brakes. The tires squeal.

My eyes are glued to the rearview mirror. The blue car moves closer, closer.

I start remembering everything Abby told me he did to her. Fear turns my skin cold. I look back at the car again. I still can't see the driver through the tinted windows, but I can see his license plate number. I glance down. There's a pen in the console.

I pick it up and start writing his license plate number on the back of my hand. The light changes, and I take off. The next thing I know I'm hit from behind. The idiot just hits my Mustang and knocks me into the oncoming traffic. Tires squeal, a car swerves to avoid hitting me—then a horn blasts out. I slam my car into reverse. I push on the gas. I get a few feet back, then my car seems to stall. It sputters as the engine dies. And that's when I see him. He's getting out of his car and walking toward my Mustang.

I try to start my car and it won't start. "Shit!" I go to lock my doors, but I don't know if the back ones are locked.

I try to start the car again and it still won't start.

He appears at my window and looks down at me. My blood runs cold. I blow my horn, hoping someone will hear and come to my rescue.

And that's when see the truck pull over. Not just any truck. But Jacob's truck.

Evil Allen turns around and bolts back to his car. Jacob is walking toward me. Allen drives around me, even runs over the curb to get away. His tires burn rubber in his escape.

I'm gripping the steering wheel and have tears in eyes.

Jacob knocks on my window. I'm so shaken, I don't want to remove my hands from the steering wheel.

"Are you okay? Did you he just hit your car?" He knocks on the window. "Riley, open the door."

Now hearing more car horns, I pull myself together. I roll down the window. I realize if that man was brave enough to hit me in broad daylight, he might also try to hurt Jacob. "Let's go to school and I'll tell you about it there."

"You're crying. Are you sure you're okay?"

I nod and I start my car. Jacob runs back to his car. He follows me.

I'm pulling into the school parking lot. There are kids mulling around. Surely he wouldn't try to follow me here.

I park, spill out of my car, and go hauling ass across the

parking lot, wanting to be inside. Jacob steps out between two cars and catches me.

"What happened back there?" he asks. "Your car looks hit in the back. Did he hit you?"

I catch my breath and nod. "He was following me. Then he hit me when I stopped at a red light."

"Who was he?"

I'm back to lying. "I don't know. It was a blue Honda."

"Shit, I should have gotten his license plate," he says.

"I have it," I say and hold up my hand.

"Come on," he says and with his arm around me, he leads me into the school.

"Where are we going?" I ask.

"To report it."

I stop. Jacob stops beside me.

"What?" he asks.

My mind races. Will this lead the police to find out I wrote the letters?

"Come on. Before he gets too far away."

I suddenly know I don't have a choice. He needs to be caught. He has to be stopped.

I jog the rest of the way into the building with Jacob.

When we get to the office Jacob rushes the desk, breaking in front of other students. I stand back, still a little unsure if this is the right thing.

"Someone was following Riley to school and even rear ended her," he tells the desk clerk.

She looks up, and finds me in the crowd. I move in.

"Who was following you?"

"I don't know."

"Did he pull over and talk to you? Did you get his insurance card?"

"He walked to my car, but he looked angry. I was scared because he'd been following me."

She frowns. "Are you okay? You aren't hurt, are you?"

"No," I answer.

"When I pulled over, the man saw me and ran," Jacob said. "He drove over the curb to get away. Riley got his license plate." He grabs my hand and holds it up.

The clerk looks from Jacob to me. She pulls a pen and a notepad out. "Show me your hand, and I'll report it to the school police."

• • •

"You going to be okay?" Jacob asks five minutes into auto tech as we find our coveralls and slip them on.

"Yeah," I say. I still feel the rush of my pulse fluttering at my neck.

"Do you have any idea who it could have been?"

"No," I lie. "But thanks for being there."

"Any time." He squeezes my hand. I remember what Hayden said about Jacob protecting me.

In five minutes, Jacob and I crawl under the car. We spend the next fifteen minutes loosening the last bolts of the transmission. Jacob manages to get the transmission loose. "Transmission out!" he calls out and smiles at me, proud of our accomplishment.

"Be careful. It's heavy," Mr. Ash says.

Jacob is beaming. I should be excited, but I'm still

trying to breathe normally. We manage to pull it out and put it down between us.

"We make a good team," Jacob says.

I nod.

"Is it down?" Mr. Ash asks and I see his feet at the edge of the left tire.

"Yeah," Jacob says.

"In that case, Riley, can you come out here? Someone needs to speak to you."

"Okay." I start rolling out from under the car.

When my head finally clears, I see a school policeman standing by Mr. Ash's desk and any chance of getting my pulse back to normal is lost. I stand up on weak knees.

"What is it?" I ask and feel everyone's eyes on me.

"Let's step out in the hall," the officer says.

I follow him, and feel as if my stomach shrinks to the size of a peanut.

"The car that followed you this morning... Did you ever see the driver's face?"

"Yes."

He nods. "Can you describe him?"

I give the man his description.

He jots down notes as I tell him. He pulls out his phone. "Give me a few minutes." He dials and says, "She can describe him. It's him."

I swallow. Relief starts to flutter in my stomach. "Did you catch him?"

"The local police did. Thanks to you. And he was wanted in a case the Brian County Police are investigating."

I feel the weight on my shoulders lift. A knot forms in my throat. He's caught. I did it. I stopped him. The police have him. Abby might get her justice. Emotion floods my chest. Good emotion, but tears still try to climb up my sinuses.

"The police will want to talk to you. We're trying to reach your dad, but he's not available right now."

"He's at work," I say. "But you don't need to call him."

"Yes, we do. And we already tried to reach him. We called his work phone and someone there gave us his cell. But he's not picking up now. We left a message for him to call us. When something like this happens, we're required to call the parents. And he'll have to be there when the police speak to you."

I nod and go straight to worrying. Not worrying about the police finding out. It's all about Dad. *Where the hell is he? Did he go somewhere to drink?*

"You okay?" the officer asks.

"Yeah. Fine. It just freaked me out... a little." *I shouldn't have let Dad go to work. What if he got in an accident?*

"Well, you don't have to worry now. The police have this guy. We're hoping your dad will get our message and we'll get the police here to speak with you. If you need to you can go and just rest at the nurse's office."

"No, I'm fine now. Thanks," I say.

"Okay." He walks away. I'm standing there, part of me wanting to jump in the air and click my heels. Another part is fixated on Dad.

I force myself to remain calm and watch the officer turn down the hall. As soon as he cuts the corner, I grab my phone and dial Dad's number.

It rings then goes to voicemail. I bite down on my lip

so hard I taste blood and I don't even leave a message. I find the number of the funeral home and call.

"Canton's Funeral Home," Ms. Duarte answers.

"This is Riley. Where's my dad?"

"Hi Riley. Is everything okay? The school called and—"

"Everything's fine. Where's my dad?" I know I sound rude, but right now I don't care. He's my dad. He's all I have.

"He was meeting Mr. Canton this morning."

"Bad news?" I ask, now worried Dad's getting fired.

"No, Mr. Canton is thinking about buying another business in Berry Town and wanted your dad's opinion of the place. I called his cell after the school called, but he must have it turned off."

"Oh," I say. It makes sense Dad might not answer while he's with his boss.

I hang up, stick my phone in my back pocket, and feel better. He's alive. Surely he won't blame me for the accident, right? Then again, he'll probably be furious that I poured out his liquor. I turn back to the door, but before I grab the knob the cold hits me. I swing around.

Abby's there. She looks good. Her makeup is perfect, and her hair looks as if she just walked out of a salon. She's smiling. There's a glow around her, an aura.

"You did it," she says. "You caught him. He's not going to hurt anyone else ever again. Some officers went to the park this morning. They found my ring."

"That's good." I feel this heaviness that I've been carrying around with me lift.

"I can go now," she says. "It's because of you that I can let go. You did that for me. Saying thank you doesn't seem like enough. All I can say is that I won't stop looking for your mom. If she's there, I'll find her."

I smile. Abby disappears, but where she stood I see a rainbow. Beautiful colors dance in the air.

I breathe in and feel the rush of peace, the rush of rightness. I cross my arms and give myself a hug. I realize I'm smiling.

Right then, all of my other woes feel manageable. The sensation grounds me. I feel stronger. Strong enough to face Dad and his demons. Strong enough to lie to the police about how I already knew Allen Griffin. Strong enough to help another ghost. And probably another after that.

Strong enough to accept that in some crazy way this is my destiny.

I don't know what it really means, but I need to own it.

Then I think of Hayden and I hope he's passed over, too. Hope that he's there with the colors. Where only peace lives.

"You okay?" a voice asks. I swing around and see Jacob.

"I'm working on it," I answer.

"Working on what?"

I offer a smile. "On being okay."

"Good." He looks at me, a little uncertain.

"Yeah. It's good. I'm going to be okay." And for the first time in a long time I actually feel it. It may not be easy, but if I can manage to get a serial rapist and murderer caught, I'm sure I'll be able to tackle whatever comes next. Whatever happens between Jacob and me.

"Thank you." I lean in and kiss him. On the side of his lips. It's short but sweet.

"Wow!" he says when the kiss ends. "That's promising." He pulls me closer and kisses me again. It's longer than mine. It's right on my lips, his tongue even slips softly between mine. I realize this is the "real" first in-school kiss I've gotten. Carl kissed me plenty, but never at school. He was a private kisser.

Jacob passes a finger over my wet, swollen lips. I can still taste him on my tongue. I still feel the just-been-kissed flutters in my stomach. The kiss, the public kiss, felt secret and little sinful, but all in a good way.

Pulling back, he asks, "What did the officer say?"

"They caught the guy. He's wanted for questioning in another case."

"Good. Are you going to have to testify or anything?"

"I don't know about that, but the police want to talk to me. But they are waiting for my dad to show up."

He moves in and slips his hand in mine. His palm is warm, comforting.

Right then my phone rings. I pull it out and see Dad's number.

"Excuse me," I say to Jacob, and then, "Hey," I say to Dad.

"Are you okay? The school just called me and told me what happened."

"Yeah, I'm fine. But they want to talk to me and you have to be present."

"I'm already on my way. But should you be at the hospital?"

"Dad, I'm fine. Really."

"Oh, Riley. You're my baby girl. Nothing can happen to you."

I hope you feel that way when you find out I've been in your dirty clothes hamper. "I love you, too."

CHAPTER TWENTY-SIX

Dad walks into my English class. He goes straight to the teacher's desk, but his worried gaze finds me. I see it in his eyes. His love for me. Then I hear murmurs in the class and the word mortician floats from those whispers. I pop up, hoping to get the hell out of there. Fast. The last thing I want is for Dad to know they make fun of me because of him.

The second we walk out into the hall, he turns and grabs me. His hug lasts longer than any I've gotten in a long time. Tears sting my eyes.

They are waiting for us in the counselor's office.

The closer we get to that office, the faster my heart beats. Have they somehow figured out that I was the one to send the letter? Will I get caught in a lie?

I breathe in. Trying to recall the feeling of seeing Abby pass over, I keep putting one foot in front of the other.

We walk into the school office and are led to the

counselor's office. The officer shakes my dad's hand and introduces himself.

I nod, my mind already going over what I can tell the truth about, and what I have to lie about.

We sit down and the officer asks me to start at the beginning. Of course, I don't. Not the real beginning. I start when I saw the blue Honda following me, leaving out that I was afraid I knew who it was. In a tight voice, I tell them about the car hitting me, about him coming to my window and looking angry and evil.

My voice starts to shake, tears fill my eyes, roll down my cheeks. I'm not sure if it's because I'm lying or if... if I'm just realizing how close I was to the person who raped and caused Abby's death.

"You were so smart not to get out of that car," the officer says and he tells us that the man was a known rapist and that I fit the profile of his victims. Blondes with light eyes.

I start shaking, praying he doesn't say Abby's name so Dad won't learn the connection.

The officer doesn't say her name but mentions a girl's death at the park.

"Wait," Dad says. "Is that Abby Howard?"

The officer nods. Dad explains how he knows her. I panic.

Dad puts his arm around me and hugs me tight. Air is knotted in my lungs.

The officer looks at me. "Have you been to the funeral home lately?"

I nod.

"I'll bet he saw you there."

"Why would he go to the funeral home?" my dad asks.

"Murderers do that sometimes."

I don't think I've breathed since Abby's name was mentioned, but I try to pull in air.

"Will she need to testify?" my dad asks.

"We don't know right now. There's a better chance you might not because we have other evidence. But we are going to take your car to the police station to confirm a match with the paint. We should have that done in a couple of days. Oh, and he does have insurance." He glances at my dad. "I'll make sure you get that information."

Dad insists I come home with him. I tell him I think I can make the day, but he's insistent. And probably right. I think it's just hitting me what happened. So I don't argue.

As we drive away from the school, Dad says, "You did good today, Riley. Oh, God, I can't imagine what I would do if something terrible happened to you."

I'm still upset, but I realize what an opportunity this is. I swallow the knot of dread down my throat.

"I know how you feel, Dad. I worry everyday about you. About your drinking."

He glances at me with a bit of shock. "We already discussed that, Riley."

"I know. And I also know you lied. I found the bottles in your dirty clothes hamper."

His mouth drops open. "What were you doing…"

"In your room?" I ask. Then I answer it. "I was looking for your liquor. I'm sorry that I invaded your space, but in a way, I'm not sorry. You need help."

He turns back to the road and I can see his frown in his profile. His hands tighten on the wheel. My heart tightens with it.

We drive the rest of the way in silence. When he pulls into the drive, he just sits there and so do I. I know this conversation isn't over.

Silence thickens the air in the car. He finally clears his throat and speaks. "You are right. I've been drinking too much. I'll cut back."

"Cut back? No, Dad. You can't drink. You're an alcoholic."

He makes this sound that comes from the back of his throat. "Why would you think that?"

"You've lost two jobs in the last two years. You look disheveled and hung over. And I read about it in Mom's diary."

His mouth drops open again. "She wrote that?"

"Yes."

He shakes his head. "Well, your mom was... she dramatized everything just like you do. Yes, I sometimes drink too much, but I'm not... an alcoholic."

"Then why have you hidden it from me all these years? Why do you hide your bottles in the dirty clothes?"

"I... didn't want you thinking you should drink!" His tone is defensive. He's angry.

But I don't care. This has to be said.

"People drink, Dad. Only people with problems hide it from others."

"That's simply not true! I said I'll cut back and I will." He gets out of his car and shuts the car door a little harder than needed.

I sit there for several seconds, hugging myself, wondering if telling him was wrong. Will he start drinking more now that it's out of the closet?

Damn! Shit! Damn!

Right then my phone dings with a text.

It's from Kelsey. Her message is short and to the point. *What the fuck? Are you okay?*

Closing my eyes, I lean back on the headrest. Less than two hours ago, witnessing Abby's crossing I felt powerful, capable, ready to take on whatever problem life and even death threw at me. Now I'm back to feeling as if I'm faking it.

• • •

"I would go with the beige sweater," Kelsey says.

I'm standing in the middle of my room, holding out two different tops.

She came over this morning to help me pick out my outfit for my date with Jacob tonight. She came over yesterday to get the story about the accident and me almost becoming a serial rapist's next victim. Which meant I had to lie to her too.

Added to all that, Dad's client, the convict, showed up while I was white-lying it to my best friend and pretty much securing my place in hell. I never looked at the spirit directly, but he never looked away from me. He knows... somehow, he knows I can see him. Sooner or later, I'm going to have to confront him.

But later is just fine with me. First let me get over nearly being raped and murdered.

Kelsey stands up from my bed and holds the sweater up to me. "You look... kind of angelic, kind of otherworldly. Spooky sexy. Something about how your hair color matches it."

I make a face at her. "Spooky sexy?"

She laughs.

"And I'm not angelic," I insist. With as many lies as I've told lately, I'm for certain hell-bound.

"Hey, the pizza's here," Dad calls up from the bottom of the stairs. He's been kind of distant and yet… clingy.

He's been extra quiet, but has hugged me more yesterday and today than he's hugged me in two years. I can't even say I'm mad at him, I'm more just worried sick. So far, he hasn't drunk in front of me, and the one time I tried to bring the subject up again, he shut it down. Fast.

"We'll be right down," I say.

I toss the sweater on my desk. When I do, my drawing pad falls open on the floor. Kelsey stares down at the picture I drew. Hayden's image stares back.

"Wow. You said you liked art, but I didn't know you rocked at it. That's fantastic." She picks the pad up. Her brows pinch together and her baffled gaze shifts to me.

"Why would you draw you a picture of Carter?"

I stare at her. "What? Who?" I suddenly remember who Carter is. He's Jacob's friend. "That's not him. It's… just some guy I dreamed up."

She shakes her head. "Then you dreamed up Carter, because… that's him."

My chest swells with the realization of what this might mean. "No." I sit down at my desk, my hands are shaking, but I have to know. I look over my shoulder at Kelsey. "What's his full name?"

"It's Carter…? Wait. Carter is his last name. People just called him by his last name."

"What's his first name?" I almost sound impatient. I am impatient. Because if Hayden is really Carter then… he's not dead. And *bam*, I remember how different he was from the other ghosts. I remember that I've been pushing him to cross over when what he needs to do is fight. Fight for his life.

"I don't remember his name," Kelsey says. "I think it starts with an H."

Hayden. Chills race down my back. Tears fill my eyes. It's Hayden. I know it's Hayden. But why did he lie about his last name? I look back at Kelsey. "What happened to Carter?"

"A car accident," she answers.

At least he didn't lie about that.

Oh, shit! It suddenly makes sense. He didn't attach himself to me through Dad, but through Jacob. I remember first sensing him the night I walked home from Kelsey's after putting the letter in her mailbox. I realize this is also the reason he kept telling me that Jacob was a good guy.

I Google Hayden Carter and when his picture appears on the screen, I gasp.

"No," I say out loud.

"No, what?" Kelsey asks.

I had forgotten she was there. I blink away my tears.

"Nothing." I exit the screen. Take one deep breath and swallow a lump of panic. "I bet I saw his picture somewhere and just drew it." I stand up, but I have to grab the back of the chair because my knees are jelly.

"Yeah," she says, but she's staring at me all weird like.

And I know she knows I'm lying. She's going to figure out just how big of a freak I am. But at this moment, right now, I don't even care. What I care about is Hayden. What I care about is figuring out what I'm going to do.

I have to go to him. Tell him not to cross over. Tell him to try to live. Once again, I've screwed up this whole ghost stuff. But I have to fix this. I have to.

I suddenly realize I'm just standing there, existing in my head, while Kelsey is watching me.

"You're freaking me out again," she says.

"Yeah," I say and suddenly I'm angry, not at her but at Hayden for lying to me. I take a deep breath and meet her gaze. "I'm a freak. I admit it. I'm sorry. I can't change it." I feel the tears rolling down my eyes.

"Hey," she says and hugs me. "It's okay. I still like you even if you are a freak."

"Thanks." I pull back and swipe my tears off my cheeks. But deep down I know it's not okay. And it won't be until I talk to Hayden. I can't have his death on my hands. I can't be the reason he gives up and dies. I'm supposed to help the dead, not encourage the living to die.

"Pizza's getting cold," Dad calls out again.

I run my fingers through my hair and give myself a mental kick in the ass. I have to keep my shit together in front of Kelsey and Dad. And Jacob. Because tonight, I have a date with him.

Sometimes my life is a mixed bag of good, bad, and ugly. Sometimes I've never felt more alive. Sometimes I feel as if I have one foot in the grave.

Thank you for joining me on this new journey with
The Mortician's Daughter *series.*

I hope you'll leave a review for One Foot in the Grave
online and also sign up for my newsletter at
www.cchunterbooks.com,
so you can stay tuned for more books in this series!

Keep reading for a sneak peek at my next release,
This Heart of Mine,
coming in hardcover from Wednesday Books
on February 27th, 2018,
and available now for preorder!

FROM THE

NEW YORK TIMES BESTSELLING AUTHOR

c.c. hunter

this

of

mine

a novel

c.c. hunter

NEW YORK TIMES BESTSELLING AUTHOR

AVAILABLE
IN HARDCOVER 2/27/18

WEDNESDAY

BOOKS

PROLOGUE

May 13th

"It's over, Eric. Accept it. Let it go, would you?" The words echo from a cell phone into the dark night.

Eric Kenner sits at the patio table in his backyard, listening over and over again to Cassie's voicemail. Listening to the pool's pump vibrate. Listening to the pain vibrate in his chest.

"I can't let it go." Pain tumbles out of him. It is so damn wrong. He can't accept it.

Glancing back, he sees the light in his mom's bedroom go off. It's barely eight. She probably took another Xanax. His mom can't accept things either.

Why did life have to be so damn hard? Was he cursed?

He hits replay on his phone. Hoping to hear a crack in Cassie's voice, something that tells him she doesn't mean it. There's no crack in her voice, just the one in his heart.

He bolts up, sending the patio chair crashing into the

concrete. Snatching the piece of furniture, he hurls it into the pool. The chair floats on top of the water. While he feels as if he's sinking, drowning.

He swings around and shoots inside. Moving through the kitchen, then the living room, he stops in front of the forgotten space that was his father's study.

His dad would have known what to do.

Eric walks in. The door clicking shut shatters the silence. The room smells dusty, musty, like old books. The streetlight from the front yard spills silver light through the window. The beige walls look aged. The space feels lonely and abandoned.

The huge clock on the wall no longer moves. In here, time has stopped—just like his dad's life.

Eric's gaze lands on the flag, the one the military handed him at his father's funeral. The thing sits on the worn leather sofa, still folded, as if waiting for someone to put it away.

They called his dad a hero—as if remembering him that way would make his death easier. It hasn't.

It would have been his dad's last mission. The day he left, he'd doled out promises—camping trips, redoing the engine of the old Mustang in the garage. Promises that died with him.

Moving behind the mahogany desk, Eric drops into his dad's chair. It creaks as if complaining he isn't the man his dad was. Leaning forward, Eric opens the top drawer.

Swallowing a lump that feels like a piece of his broken heart, his eyes zoom in on one item. He reaches in and pulls it out. It's heavy and cold against his palm.

He stares at the gun. Maybe he does know how to fix this.

If he can find the courage.

1

One month earlier
April 13th

"You lucky bitch!" I drop back down on my pink bed-spread, phone to ear, knowing Brandy is dancing on cloud nine and I'm dancing with her. I glance at the door to make sure Mom isn't hovering and about to freak over my language. Again.

She isn't there.

Lately, I can't seem to control what comes out of my mouth. Mom blames it on too much daytime who's-the-baby-daddy television. She could be right. But hey, a girl's gotta have some fun.

"Where's he taking you?" I ask.

"Pablo's Pizza." Brandy's tone lost the oh-God shriek quality. "Why... why don't you come with us?"

"On your date? Are you freaking nuts?"

"You go to the doctor's office, you could—"

"No. That's *hell* no!" I even hate going to the doctor's office. If people stare long enough they see the tube. But this isn't even about me. "I'd die before I get between you—"

"Don't say that!" Brandy's emotional reprimand rings too loud. Too painful.

"It's just a figure of speech," I say, but in so many ways it's not. I'm dying. I've accepted that. The people in my life haven't. So, for them, I pretend. Or try to.

"But if you—"

"Stop. I'm not going."

There's a gulp of silence. That's when I realize my "lucky bitch" comment brought on the pity invite. Brandy's worried I'm jealous. And okay, maybe I am, a little. But my grandmother used to say it was okay to see someone in a beautiful red dress and think, I want a dress like hers. But it wasn't okay to think, I want a dress like hers and I want her to have a wart on her nose.

I don't wish Brandy warts. She's had the hots for Brian for years. She deserves Brian.

Do I deserve something besides the lousy card fate dealt to me? Hell yeah. But what am I going to do? Cry? I tried that. I've moved on.

Now I've got my bucket list. And my books.

The books are part of my bucket list. I want to read a hundred. At least a hundred. I started counting after I got out of the hospital the first time I survived an infection from my artificial heart. I'm at book twenty-eight now. I won't mention how many of them were romance novels.

"Leah," Brandy starts in again.

The chime of the doorbell has me glancing at the pink clock on my bedside table.

It's study time. Algebra. I hate it. But I kind of like hating it. Because I hated it before I got sick. Hating the same things as before makes me feel more like the old me.

"Gotta go. Ms. Strong is here." I bounce my heels on the bed. The beaks on my Donald Duck slippers bob up and down. Lately, I've been into cartoon-character slippers. They make my feet look happy. Mom's bought me three pairs: Mickey, Donald, and Dumbo.

"But—" Brandy tries again.

"No. But you're gonna tell me everything. All the sexy details. How good he kisses. How good he smells. How many times you catch him staring at your boobs."

Yep, I'm jealous all right. But I'm not a heartless bitch. Well, maybe I am. Heartless, really *heart*less, but not so much a bitch. I carry an artificial heart around in a back-pack. It's keeping me alive.

"I always tell you everything," Brandy says.

No, but you used to. I stare up at my whirling polka-dot ceiling fan. Even Brandy's walking on eggshells, scared she'll say something to remind me that I got a raw deal, something that will make me feel sorry for myself. I'm done doing that. But I hate hearing that crunch as people tiptoe around the truth.

"Leah." Mom calls me.

"Gotta go." I hang up, grab my heart, and get ready to face algebra.

I really hate it, but it's number one on my bucket list—my last hurrah. Well, not algebra, but graduating high school. And I don't want a diploma handed to me. I want to earn it.

I spot Mom standing in the entrance of the dining

room turned study. She's rubbing her palms over her hips. A nervous habit, though I have no idea what's got her jittery now. I survived the last infection and the one before that. She hears my footsteps, looks at me. Her brow puckers—another sign of serious mama fret.

I stop. Why's she so nervous? "What?"

"Ms. Strong couldn't make it." She rushes off faster than her hurried words.

I hear someone shuffling in the dining room. I'm leery. Hesitant. I move in. My Donald Duck slippers skid to a quick stop when I see the dark-haired boy at the table.

"Shit." I suck my lips into my mouth in hopes I didn't say it loud enough for him to hear.

He grins. He heard me. That smile is as good as the ones I read about in romance novels. Smiles described as crooked, mind-stopping, or coming with a melt-me-now quality. I swear my artificial heart skips two beats.

He's one of the Kenner twins, either Eric or Matt, the two hottest boys in school. I used to be able to tell them apart, but now I'm not sure of anything. If I combed my hair today. If I brushed my teeth. If I have on a bra?

I close my mouth, run my tongue over my fuzzy-feeling teeth, trying to quietly suck them clean.

Glancing down, away from his eyes, I rock back and forth on my heels, my Donald Ducks' bills rocking with me. Should I run back to my room? But how pathetic will I look then? And if I do, he'll leave. Lifting my gaze, I realize I'm not sure I want him to go. I kinda like looking at him.

"Hey," he says.

"Hey," I mimic and realize I'm hiding the backpack behind my leg. I give my bright red tank top a tug down to cover the tube that extends from the backpack and pokes into me under my left ribcage. A hole that kinda looks like a second belly button. Yup, I'm hiding the very thing that's keeping me alive.

"Ms. Strong couldn't make it," he says as if reading my mood and realizing he needs to justify his being here. "She asked me to sub."

"For how many extra credit points?" I wait for him to tell me he did it just out of kindness. And, if true, it would mean he did it out of pity. I'm not sure I'd enjoy looking at him anymore. I'd rather be someone's means to a better grade. Brandy told me that everyone in school knows about my dead heart.

"Fifteen. I got lazy and didn't turn in some homework. You'll pump me up to a B."

"You should have held out for twenty."

He smiles again. "I don't think it was negotiable."

Moving in, I try to guess which twin he is. I try to figure out how to ask, but everything I think of sounds lame. *Let him be Matt.*

I had a thing for Matt since seventh grade. It might have been wishful thinking, but in tenth grade I thought he liked me too. Not that it ever went anywhere. He was football, I was book club. He was popular, I was... not. Then I started dating Trent. A guy in book club. A guy I let off the hook as soon as I found out my heart was dying.

"Your books?" he asks.

I don't understand the question, until I see he's pointing to my backpack.

Crap! I freak a little. I have several pat answers in my head that I came up with when Mom, afraid I was turning into an agoraphobe, insisted I get out of the house. But I can't remember them. The silence reeks of awkwardness.

So I go with the truth. "No. It's my… heart."

"Shit." He spills my favorite word.

I laugh.

His eyes meet mine and he smiles again. Yup, it's kinda crooked. My mind's not working. And I'm melting.

"Oh, you're joking," he says. "Right?"

I nod yes then shake my head no as if I don't know the answer.

His smile fades like a light on a dimmer switch. "Seriously?"

"Seriously." I move to the desk in the corner. One-handed, I pull my math book from a drawer and drop down in the chair across from him. My heart lands in the chair beside me, so he can't see my tube.

When I glance up, he's doing exactly what I expect. Looking at the books so he doesn't have to look at me. People have a hard time facing me, facing my death, maybe even facing their own mortality. I understand, but it still bothers me.

He turns a page. The silence is so loud, I can almost hear the page float down to find its place. "Ms. Strong said we should start on chapter six."

"Yeah." Disappointed, I flip my book open and consider letting him off the hook, telling him I've got this, assuring him I won't mention it to Ms. Strong. But I look up, and I'm suddenly feeling selfish.

Hey, he's getting extra credit.

He glances up, and before I can look away, our eyes meet and lock. And hold. Longer than they should, because it feels... too. Too much. Too intimate. As if we've passed some invisible barrier. Like when a stranger stands too close to you in line.

We both look away.

He smacks the book closed. He flinches.

"What happened?" He whispers the question. His tone sad, sweet, and somehow still sexy.

I admire that he asked. Most people don't.

"A virus. It killed my heart." I hate the haunted look I see in his eyes. The sexiness vanishes. "It's highly contagious."

The oh-poor-you look on his face flips right to fear. Joking with him feels right.

I lose it. A laugh bubbles out of me and I feel instantly lighter.

"Real funny." He chuckles.

A crazy thought hits, one that says there's something almost... rusty about his laugh. And bam, I remember. I feel like the heartless bitch I swear I'm not for forgetting.

Not quite a year ago, his dad, a soldier, was killed. I'd been in the hospital, right after my condition had been diagnosed. His dad had been on the news, where they showed the pictures of soldiers and asked for a moment of silence.

I feel my smile slip from my eyes, my lips, and fall completely off my face. I know the look he sees in my eyes is probably the same pity-filled expression I saw in his seconds ago.

"I'm sorry," I say. "About your dad. I just remembered."

Ah, hell. Now I made his smile fall off his face. I should've kept my mouth shut.

"Yeah." He looks back at the book. "It sucks."

"Sort of like this." I motion to my backpack.

He glances again at the chair holding my heart. "Was it really a virus?"

"Yeah. The virus caused Myocarditis."

His gaze sticks to my backpack. "How does it work?"

It's a question no one has ever asked. "Just like a heart. It's a pump. Sends my blood through my veins and throughout my body." I summarize the surgery to connect the pump that's in my backpack and the batteries I have to carry.

He makes a face, even rubs his chest as if feeling empathetic pain. "So you have a tube going inside you?"

I touch my shirt, right under my left rib, where the tube goes in. "Gross, huh?"

"Yeah, but it's keeping you alive, so… not really."

I agree. The hesitant footsteps easing down the hall pulls my gaze from his.

Mom stops at the door. "Do you guys need something to drink or eat?"

She's rubbing her palms on her jeans again. Her pinched maternal concern locks on me. She's worried I'm mad about his being here. It's odd that I'm not.

The only person from my old life I've allowed to be close to "Dying Leah" is Brandy. And the only reason I allowed it was because she wouldn't go away. Both Mom and Dad have been pushing me to get out some. Socialize. There was even mention of my going back to school. I nixed that idea really fast. I want to graduate, but facing my peers while carrying my heart… Unh, uhh. Not doing it.

I have good reasons too. In seventh grade, Shelly Black

had leukemia. She came to school bald, wearing a scarf. Everyone tried not to show her how difficult it was to see her that way. She wasn't even my close friend. But my heart hurt for her. I'd rather be alone than put people through that. Then I look at the dark-haired hottie sitting across from me and wonder if that's what he feels now.

Then again, he chose to come here. He's asking me questions and seems interested in my answers. And it feels good talking to him. Like I'm a normal high school kid talking to a friend. An extremely hot friend.

I'm still not going back to school, but why not take advantage of this?

"I have sodas and chips." Mom's voice drags me back to reality.

I wait for him to answer. He declines with a thank-you.

Mom leaves, and we dive into algebra. We spend the next twenty minutes reading examples; then I do problems for him to check and see if I understand. It's not really awkward, but it's tougher than it is with Ms. Strong. I can't concentrate on math, because I'm concentrating on him. About which twin he is. Matt? Eric? Eric? Matt?

I recheck my answers before I push him the notebook. While he's reviewing my problems, I'm studying him. The shape of his lips. The cut of his jaw. The slight five o'clock shadow that tells me he's shaving.

I rub my index fingers against my thumbs and peer up at him through my lashes.

"You got it." Pride sounds in his voice. His smile reflects the same emotion. He pushes the notebook back. "You want to do some more?"

I want to say no, but I'm afraid he'll leave. And I'm feeling greedier than ever. I want my forty-five minutes. "Sure."

Then without thinking, I blurt out, "Instead, can I just ask you something?"

We stare across at each other again. "If I can ask you something," he counters.

"Okay." I rub the soles of my slippers on the wood floor under the table. "Me first." How to ask it? "I... I used to be able to tell you and your brother apart. But now..."

He grins, but almost looks disappointed. "Now you can't? You don't know who I am?"

"Guilty." Frowning, I flatten my palms, now slick from nerves, on the table. "So which one are you?"

He shoulders back in the chair. His posture's crooked. One shoulder is higher than the other. Didn't Matt used to sit like that? "How did you tell us apart before?"

"You mean physically or your personality?" Now I'm thinking I should have kept my mouth shut.

"Both." Anticipation brightens his eyes.

It's as if my answer matters. As if I need to be careful what I say.

"Uh, Eric wore his hair a little longer. Matt's hair was a little curlier." Unable to stop myself, I look at his hair, remembering sitting behind Matt in English, studying how it would curl up, and wondering if it was as soft as it looked. A lot of girls, bolder than I, would play with his curls. I always wished I had the guts to do it. But I was gutless. The bravest thing I ever did in school was start a book club.

My gaze shifts away from his hair. "And one of you is a little broader in the shoulders."

"Which one?" He sits straighter, his chest lifts, his shoulders stretch out.

I'm scared to answer, but that would be awkward.

"Eric?" I try to read his expression, but he seems to purposely keep it blank. "Not that both of you aren't... buff," I say for a lack of another word and feel myself blushing, because buff sounds... sexy or something.

He grins. "And?"

"Personality wise, Matt's quieter, more of a thinker. Eric's more outspoken."

He picks up his pencil and rolls it between his two palms leaving me to think he's rolling my answers around in his head.

The pencil slows down. I swear my heart speeds up like my old one would have.

"So which one am I? Buff and outspoken or thin and quiet."

"I didn't say thin or quiet. I said less buff and quieter." The desire to say I preferred Matt over Eric tap dances on my tongue, but if he's Eric?

He laughs and that sound is like magic, less rusty, more melting.

I'm sure he's Matt. Eric didn't have the same effect on me. Maybe I imagined it, but I could swear that Matt actually... noticed me. I don't think I hit Eric's radar. He had too many cheerleaders falling all over him. Not that Matt didn't have the girls flashing him smiles and playing with his curls. He just didn't seem like it went to his head as much. Sometimes, it even looked like it embarrassed him.

My backpack beeps, shattering that comfortable silence that we'd finally found. The dreaded chirp lets me know that I have less than thirty minutes of battery life left. Panic flashes in Matt's eyes. Or is he Eric?

"It's normal," I say, but because of that noise, of that damn tube, of my own dead heart, I feel anything but normal.

"So is this like forever?" he asks.

I shake my head. "No, it's supposed to be until I get a transplant."

"Supposed to be?" His gaze sweeps over me.

I look toward the hall to make sure Mom isn't around. So far, the truth has worked with him, and I decide not to waver from my approach. "I have a kind of rare blood type. AB. The odds aren't great."

"AB?" His brow wrinkles. "It's not that rare. I have it. If it was a kidney, I'd give you one."

I laugh, but this one's forced. I hate thinking about a transplant. Not just because I don't think it'll happen, but because someone having to die to give me life is all kinds of wrong. And that's what my parents and even Brandy are doing. Sitting around hoping someone will die.

That's even worse than wishing warts on someone.

"But…" The pause seems to mean something. "You… you just stay on this until a heart's available."

Okay. The truth didn't work. "Yeah," I say what he wants to hear. What everyone wants to hear. Never mind I've had two infections due to the artificial heart and each one nearly killed me. Never mind that no one has lived more than four years with an artificial heart. Never mind that hundreds of AB-blood-type people are waiting for a new heart, a new life, a miracle.

He frowns. "The way you say it sounds as if you don't believe..."

I need to work on that. "I'm sure it'll happen," I lie, and then suddenly I don't want to. I don't have to. Not with him. I sit up taller. "Look, it takes a lot more energy to hope than to accept. I'd rather spend my energy enjoying what I've got now."

"That really sucks." His frown deepens.

"Yeah, it does. But I'm okay with it." And for the most part, I really am. At first I kept telling myself that I had to hope, that a heart would come. But the more I read about statistics, the more I came to realize that the odds of getting a heart were slim to none. And rather than fooling myself or sitting around being miserable, I decided to make the most of the time I have left. Hence the bucket list. And I'm happier now. Really.

He looks up at the clock. "I guess I should be going."

I want to tell him he doesn't have to rush off. How sad is it that this is the most fun and the most alive I've felt all year?

He stands up. I do the same, then slip on the backpack, always hiding the tube.

He moves down the hall. I follow. I'm staring at his hair, the way it flips up. Again hoping he's Matt. I'm so into his hair, I don't notice him swing around.

We run smack-dab into each other.

"Shit." He grabs me by my shoulders and pulls me against him. "Are you okay?"

His hands are on my upper arms. My breasts are against his chest.

Then bam! I feel something I haven't felt in a long

time. Excitement. My very own I'm-a-girl-and-you're-a-boy excitement. Not the borrowed thrill I get from reading romances.

I can smell him. Like men's soap, or deodorant; a little spicy, a lot masculine. The desire to lean in and bury my nose in his shoulder is so strong I have to fist my hands.

"I'm fine," I say. *Don't pull away. Don't pull away. Please don't pull away.*

He doesn't pull away. He gazes down at me. This close I can see he has gold and green flecks in his brown eyes. A voice inside of me says I should step back, but you couldn't pay me to move. I'm dying. Is it wrong of me to want this?

"I... I forgot my books." The words fall from his lips in an uncertain tone. The pads of his thumbs rub the insides of my arm. Just the tiniest, softest friction that feels so damn good.

I run my tongue over my bottom lip. "Oh, I... I thought you were going to kiss me." I hear my own words and wonder where I got the balls to say that.

His eyes widen. Not in an oh-crap way, but in a surprised kind of way. "Do you want me to kiss you?"

I grin. "If you're Matt, I've wanted you to kiss me since seventh grade."

His gaze slides lower to my mouth and lingers. "Is your heart strong enough?"

I burst out laughing. "Are you that good of a kisser?"

"Maybe." A smile crinkles the corners of his eyes. He leans down. His lips are against mine, soft and sweet. I slip into sensory overload. I lean in and open my mouth and ease my tongue between his lips. Yeah, it's bold, but it's not like I'll live long enough to regret it.

His tongue brushes against mine. One hand moves to my waist, the other slides back behind my neck. He gently angles my face to deepen the kiss. I feel it, every contact that is his skin against mine. I feel awesome. So freaking alive.

I get even ballsier and reach up and run my fingers through his hair. It's even softer than I thought it'd be.

When he pulls back, we're breathing hard, and we stare at each other. The dazed look in his eyes tells me that this wasn't a pity kiss. We start inching closer. His lips are almost on mine again when the sound of the front door opening shatters the moment.

We jerk apart and walk back down the hall to the dining room. He picks up his books.

My dad calls out to my mom.

I ignore it.

All of my attention is on the guy standing in front of me, his lips still wet from our kiss. I grab a pen off the table, scribble my number on a notebook paper, rip it out, and hand it to him.

"If you ever want to talk. About everything that sucks," I add. Then I worry that sounded stupid.

He takes the paper. Our fingers meet and I feel that magic spark and I don't care if it sounded stupid. I vow not to regret this. If he calls. If he doesn't. This was too good to ever regret.

We stare at each other again. I want to kiss him again so badly, I'm shaking. The sound of my parents talking in the kitchen echoes and invades this magical moment. I wish we were somewhere different. I wish... I wish... But before I stumble down that dangerous path of wishing for the impossible, I push it away.

He starts down the hall and I follow him to the door. He reaches for the knob then turns. We don't say anything, but we exchange smiles. In his eyes, I see a whisper of embarrassment, a touch of uncertainty, and a hint of something raw. I hope desire. He glances over my shoulder, as if making sure we're alone, then brushes a finger over my lips. Soft. Slow. Sensual.

I tell myself to memorize how it feels. This is the good stuff.

He turns and leaves, way before I'm ready for him to go.

I bolt to the side window, not too close in case he looks back, but close enough so I can watch him walking down my sidewalk. I watch him get in his car. I watch him drive off. I watch his car disappear down the road.

I lick my lips, still tasting his kiss. If I died right now, I'd go happy.

Mom and Dad's footsteps echo behind me. They say something, but I ignore them. I'm in that moment, reliving it. How his kiss felt. How his kiss tasted. How his hair felt. How sweet life is. It doesn't even matter that I'm dying.

I move in and press my forehead to the glass. It's cool, the April weather still holds a hint of chill in the air. Then I frown when I realize he never told me if he was Eric or Matt. I remember what I said about wanting Matt to kiss me since seventh grade. If he hadn't been Matt, he'd have told me, right?

My heart says it was Matt, but my heart isn't real. Can I believe it? Damn, I don't know who I kissed.

"Leah?"

I turn. Dad and Mom are staring at me, all happy like.

"That seemed to go well." Mom offers up a real smile. The kind that wrinkles the sides of her nose. It hits me then that I can't remember the last time her nose wrinkled like that. I put that on my bucket list. Give mom more nose wrinkles.

They look at me all goofy like. Part of me wonders if Mom saw us kissing. I don't care. If it makes her happy, I'd kiss him again. It wouldn't be a hardship.

"Yeah. It went well." Moving in, I hug her, then dad. It becomes one of those group hugs. I hear my mom's breath shake, but it's not the bad kind of shake.

"I love you both." Emotion laces my words. Happy emotion. Then I break free and me and my Donald Ducks bounce back to my bedroom to plug in my heart.

While it's not supposed to work like that, I'm sure that kiss ate up a lot of battery life.

Once I plug in, I pick up the phone to call Brandy to tell her my boy news. Then I stop. Knowing Brandy, she'd feel obligated to find out whom I'd kissed, and even try to push him to come back. Maybe I'll just keep this to myself. My secret. The one I'll take with me to the grave.

2

The pizza's cold, the consistency of cardboard. For a moment, Matt Kenner thinks he's cut into the box, but he eats it anyway. It fills the hole in his stomach, but not his heart. He wants to call Leah. Wants to see her again. Wants to kiss her again.

Wants to freaking pound his fist into the kitchen table. Death had already robbed him of his dad.

The thump of a car door shutting has Matt sitting straighter. The swish and thud of the front door opening and closing adds to the late-night murmurs of the house. His brother's footsteps clip across the wood floors as he no doubt follows the one light on in the kitchen.

Matt looks over. Eric stands in the doorway. Eric, the buffer, more outspoken twin.

Matt's mind rolls that around for a second. It bumps into his ego. But Leah had wanted to kiss him—not Eric. Most girls Matt dated came to him by the way of Eric. When they couldn't catch the eye of the more popular twin, they set their sights on him. He never blamed his brother, but who wanted to be someone's second choice?

"Hey." Eric's keys hit the table. He sees the pizza, goes to the kitchen candy drawer and pulls out a handful of M&Ms, then drops into a chair. Snatching a piece of pizza, he takes a bite, then drops three M&Ms into his mouth. He swears chocolate and pizza were meant to be eaten together.

Right then, stale beer and another unpleasant smell mingle with the cold-pizza aroma. If his mom were up, and aware, she'd give Eric hell for drinking and driving. She isn't up. Isn't aware.

She'd been like this ever since their dad died. Going to sleep by eight after crashing from Xanax, only to get up the next morning and load up all over again.

"Should you be driving?" Matt fills in for his mom.

"I had two beers." Eric's disapproving expression is one more reserved for a parent than a brother, but the look doesn't hang on. His brother has done his share of filling in when it came to Matt too.

Eric rears his chair back on two legs. "I thought you were going with Ted to stay at his dad's lake house."

"I changed my mind."

"Why?"

Matt's only answer is a shoulder shrug. After he'd left Leah's, he'd just wanted to feed his stomach and be alone.

"Were you talking to someone?" Eric eyes the phone in Matt's hand.

"No. Just thinking." Matt sits his phone down on top of Leah's number.

His brother, pizza balanced on his fingertips in front

of his face, studies Matt as if picking up on his mood. "About what?"

"Leah McKenzie." No real reason not to tell Eric.

"Who?" Eric shoves the pizza into his mouth, tosses in three candies, chews, then swallows. "Wait, isn't she that girl who's sick? The pretty one, dark hair and light blue eyes, but too shy."

Matt swipes his phone, pretends to read it, but his mind's on Leah. *Oh, I... thought you were going to kiss me.* She isn't shy anymore.

"You had a thing for her. Wasn't she the one you were trying to get the nerve to ask out but she started dating someone else?"

Matt feels Eric staring. "Yeah."

His brother takes another bite. Matt's ego feels dinged again. The day he'd been about to ask Leah out, he saw her in the school hall, standing shoulder to shoulder with Trent Becker. Matt had lost his chance. Which was the real reason he'd jumped at the opportunity to go to her house today. Yeah, he needed the extra credit, but he'd already resigned himself to getting a C.

"Why are you thinking about her?" Eric lowers the front chair legs, gets up, and pulls a soda from the fridge. "You want one?" he mumbles around a mouthful of pizza.

"Yeah." Matt takes the can, puts it on the table, palms it, and feels the cold burn on the inside of his hands. "I went to see her today."

"Why?" Eric pops the top on the soda, downs the fizzy noise, and drops back in the chair.

"Ms. Strong tutors her and couldn't make it today. She offered me extra credit to do it."

Eric's brow wrinkles. "Is she like dying sick, or just sick-sick?"

Leah appears in his mind, soft, smiling, and for some reason happy. "She doesn't look sick, but... she's got an artificial heart."

"Really? Like connected to a machine?"

"It's small, like a backpack. But..."

"But what?"

Matt spills, hoping it will lighten the weight in his chest. "She doesn't think she's gonna make it." Which is why he can't get how she could be happy.

"Damn." Empathy laces Eric's voice. He sips his soda and studies Matt over the rim as if he knows there's more to the story.

"I kissed her," Matt confesses. Keeping something from Eric is impossible. Identical twins know each other's secrets. That weird twin-connection thing. Mom used to tell the story of how Eric, only three, had broken his arm playing at a friend's house and Matt had come to her crying that his arm hurt before she'd even been notified. Matt couldn't remember it, so he wasn't a 100 percent certain it was true.

"Why?" Eric nearly chokes on the soda.

"She wanted me to. I wanted to."

Eric sets the can on the table with a half-full clunk. "No. You can't do this. Don't go there."

Matt stares at his unopened can. He wants to pick the damn thing up and throw it. "It's just—"

"No!" His brother's sharp tone brings Matt's gaze up. "Look at us. We haven't... We haven't gotten over losing dad. Mom can't handle another loss. You can't handle another loss. We gotta heal, damn it. No more death around here."

Matt stops short of taking his anger out on Eric. Hadn't he just said the exact thing to himself? Wasn't that why he hadn't already called Leah? "I know."

"Seriously," Eric says. "We can't take on more grief."

"I said I know!" Matt closes his eyes, then opens them, wishing he didn't see Leah's smile, didn't see her dreamy expression after he'd kissed her. Silence fills the yellow kitchen. The color reminds him of Leah's Donald Duck house shoes.

Eric finishes off the slice of pizza and then licks his fingers. Matt feels the slice he'd eaten, a lump in his stomach. The silence stretches out for too many long seconds.

"Where've you been?" Matt asks, before the silence gives away just how hard this is for him.

"Nowhere, really."

The vague nonanswer smells like a lie. Matt raises an eyebrow.

Eric shrugs.

Just like that, Matt knows where Eric's been. "You're seeing Cassie again?"

"Get out of my head." His brother drops the chair down on four legs with a clunk.

"Like you don't stay in mine!" Matt picked up his soda then slams it down. "What did you just tell me? That we need to heal. Cassie isn't what I call healing."

His brother squeezes his can. The crunch of aluminum sounds tense. "First, this thing with Cassie isn't what you think. Second, getting involved with someone who's dying isn't in the same category as Cassie."

Dying. Matt flinches. "Maybe not, and nothing against Cassie, but she dumped you twice, and you went into a funk both times."

"I told you, I'm not dating Cassie. It's not like that."

"Then what's it like?" Matt hears his mom's tone in his voice.

"She's dealing with something." Eric exhales as if he's been carrying around old air, or old pain. Matt feels it too.

"What kind of something?"

"Will you stop it!" Eric belts out then closes his eyes in regret. "She won't tell me. She won't tell anyone." His jaw clenches. "Everyone's saying she's been acting weird, so I talked to her, and something's definitely going on."

"Can't she turn to one of her friends for help?"

Eric's posture hardens. "I'm not going back to Cassie."

Yeah, you are. Matt can see it, even if Eric can't.

The *whoosh* of a toilet flushing from his mom's bathroom brings their eyes up and the tension takes an emotional U-turn. Not that it lessens, it just changes lanes.

Matt hates this lane.

His dad's death still hurts, but the way they're losing their mom is almost as bad. Instead of moving past the hole in her heart that their dad's death had brought on, she's curled up inside it. Lives and breathes the grief.

Matt exhales. "Did you call Aunt Karen?"

"Yeah." Eric shakes his head. "She going to call but she can't come down. She's working some big case." He pauses. "She came down twice last month. We can't expect her to do more."

Matt stares at his hands cupping the cold soda. "Then we have to do more."

Eric nods.

"Maybe we could get Mom out of the house tomorrow," Matt says. "Go see a movie and eat dinner out. I'll see if I can get her to go jogging with me. She used to all the time."

Eric runs a hand down his face. "We could take her to the plant store. She used to love working in the yard."

"Yeah." Matt closes the pizza box. "You want another piece?"

"Nah. I'm out of M&Ms. Besides, I went by Desai Diner and ate the food of the gods."

"That's what I smell." Matt's brother's love for anything curry, and chocolate and pizza, are probably the only two differences in their tastes. Well, that and girls.

Standing, Matt sticks the leftover pizza back in the fridge, then snags his soda and phone. His gaze falls to the scrap of paper with Leah's number that he'd hidden under his cell. He picks it up, wads it up, feeling the same crumbled sensation in his chest, and tosses it in the garbage.

Eric is right. When one person in this family hurts, they all hurt. He can't do that to them.

3

May 15th

Matt wakes up gasping for air. He blinks, trying to make out the images flashing in his head—images of running in the woods. Of fear. From what, he doesn't know. *Just a dream.*

Swiping a hand over his eyes, he sits up. Sharp stabbing pains explode in his head. He pushes his palm over his temple. Agony pulses in his head with each irate thump of his heart.

Though he's not certain why he's angry. He goes to get up, feels dizzy. Feels himself falling. But he's not falling. He still grabs for the dresser.

When able to walk, he heads to the bathroom in search of some painkillers. Swallowing two bitter pills without water, he stares at himself in the mirror. For one second he swears he sees Eric standing behind him; then he's gone.

Confused, he splashes cold water on his face. The pain fades but leaves a numb sensation.

He heads back to his room, stopping when he notices Eric's bedroom door is open. His brother sleeps with it shut. Matt peers in the room. The bed's unmade, empty. The clock on the bedside table flashes the time. Three a.m.

He walks to the kitchen thinking his brother is probably eating a bowl of cereal. The kitchen's as empty as the bed. The ice maker spews out a few chunks of ice. The heater hums warmth through the house, but Matt feels cold.

Frowning, he goes to peer out the living room window. His brother's car is here. Where the hell is he at three in the morning?

Damn him, he knows better than to stay out past midnight. Sure, Mom's no longer enforcing curfews, but they'd agreed to stick by the rules.

He shoots back to his room to call his brother. Eric's probably hanging with Cassie again. The 'not going back with her' promise hadn't lasted two weeks. This last month he's spent more time with Cassie than at home. And Matt sees the effect it's having on his brother. That girl isn't good for Eric.

He snatches up his phone already practicing the hell he'll give his brother, but then he notices he has a new text. From Eric.

When did that come in? Two fifty-three. Right before Matt woke up.

He reads the text. *I need…* Nothing more. Almost as if Eric had been interrupted and accidentally hit *Send*.

What did Eric need?

Matt hits the call button. One ring. Two. Three. It goes to voicemail.

Hey, leave a message.

"Shit!" Matt mutters. At the beep he says, "Where are you, Eric? Call me. Now."

Right then he feels his brother behind him. Relief washes over him.

"Why are you late?" He swings around. Eric's not here.

Not here.

Not. Here.

The pain in Matt's temple starts throbbing again. His stomach churns. He recalls the nightmare of running in the woods and, just like that, he knows. It hadn't been him in the dream. Eric.

Chills crawl up Matt's spine, his neck, all the way up his head. He can't breathe. His brother's in trouble. He knows it like his lungs know how to take air. Like his eyes know how to blink. Like his heart knows how to beat.

His grip on his phone tightens, and he considers dialing 911. But to say what? *My brother's not home?* Eric's only three hours late.

How can Matt explain this feeling? This emptiness, the not-here feeling that is spreading through him like a virus. His stomach lurches. He rushes to the bathroom, barely making it to the toilet before he pukes. The retching sound echoes in the dark house.

He wipes his mouth with the back of his hand. Tears fill his eyes. No!

How can he explain to the police the god-awful feeling that's telling him Eric isn't just missing? He's gone.

"Are you okay?"

Matt keeps his head over the toilet but glances at his mom. Perched at the door, she's wearing the sweats she wore yesterday. Her blond hair is a mess—she's a mess. "Are you sick, hon?"

He tries to find his voice, but can't. His throat isn't working. Not for talking. He pukes again.

Hands on his knees, his heart thumping in his head, he sees her move to the cabinet. She pulls out a washcloth, runs water over it, then steps closer.

She brushes the cold wet cloth over his forehead, then lovingly swipes his wet bangs from his brow. Her green eyes meet his. For the first time in forever, he sees a hint of his old mom. And yet he knows he'll be losing her again.

"What's wrong, Matt?"

"I'm sorry," Dr. Bernard says. To her credit she looks sincerely remorseful.

Thirty-six hours. That's how long it had been since Matt woke up knowing. That's how long it took for the doctors to tell Matt and his mom what he already knew.

"All of the tests confirmed my fears. There's no brain activity."

His brother's dead. Brain death they called it.

He and his mom had called the police. They didn't seem to take it seriously. That changed at six this morning. The cops showed up on their doorstep with news that Eric had been found at a roadside park. A gunshot to the head. They life-flighted him to a hospital in Houston, where the best doctors work. But not even the best could save him. He was gone.

The police had found the gun next to his body. The Glock had belonged to their father. Gunpowder residue had been found on Eric's right hand. One of the cops used the words "possible attempted suicide."

Now they'd change it to "suicide."

Matt couldn't wrap his brain around that. He didn't have the stamina to fight it yet. Fighting didn't come nearly as naturally to him as to Eric. But as soon as he could breathe right, he planned on correcting the police.

Yeah, Eric got into funks, and he'd been acting off with the whole Cassie problem, but to kill himself? Not Eric.

His brother fought and won at everything. School, girls, sports. He didn't know how to say quit, much less do it. Eric never gave up.

More important, he'd never leave Matt and his mom like this. He knew what it would do to them.

His mom lets out a soulful groan that sounds like a wounded animal. Aunt Karen wraps her arm around his mom. Matt had called his aunt first thing and told her they were going to need her. He didn't need her, but he needed someone to take care of his mom, because he couldn't. He couldn't console himself, how the hell was he going to console her?

Breathing hurt. Blinking hurt. Being alive hurt.

The doctor leaves. His mom and aunt stand in the middle of the room holding on to each other. There's still three cops hanging around. He wishes they'd go find out what happened instead of just standing here, watching their pain as if they feed on it.

Mom makes sad noises, and his aunt says, "I know. I know. I know."

All that Matt knows is his brother is dead. Gone. He drops into the chair, drops his elbows on his knees, and tries to get his lungs to accept air.

He stays like that. Eyes closed. Trying to shut everything out, but he can't. He hears his mom crying, he hears his aunt soothing, he hears his heart breaking. And in the distance he can almost hear the beeping of the machine that forces air into Eric's lungs.

Matt breathes in.

Matt breathes out.

With the rhythm of the machine.

That's all he can do. Breathe. And that doesn't feel normal.

He closes his eyes and almost goes to sleep for the first time since it happened. Waking him up are voices. He looks up. There's a lady in a suit telling his mom something. He doesn't want to listen, but his mom cries harder. What could they say now that would hurt more than what's already been said?

His aunt's gaze beckons him to come over. Her green eyes, eyes that look just like his mom's, have more soul, more life. She hadn't lost her husband and her son.

He stands and goes to stand by his mother.

"No," his mom says. "No."

"What?" he says.

The woman focuses on him. "I'm with the transplant center. I know this is very difficult, and your loss is so great, but you have a chance to save…"

"Yes," he says before the woman finishes.

In the back of his mind, he thinks of Leah and others who would get a second chance at life. But his heart hurts too much to think about her; he just knows that this is what Eric wanted.

"But I can't live with the thought of them taking…"

"Stop it, Mom!" Matt says. "Eric wanted this. You can't deny him that."

"I will not let them do this," his mom snaps.

He tries to find patience. Digs deep, but he doesn't find much. He curls his hands up. "Eric and I registered when we signed up for our licenses. He told me he wanted to do this. I'm not going to let you stop it."

"He never told me."

He might have if you'd ever come out of your bedroom. Thank God he finds the thread of strength not to say what he feels. Deep down he knows this isn't his mom's fault. It's not Eric's fault either.

"Well, he told me. It's on his license." He looks at the woman and sees she has Eric's license on her clipboard. He takes the board from her hand and shows it to his mom. Then he looks back at the woman. "Yes. The answer's yes."

The woman looks at my mom. Tears run down her cheeks. She nods, turns around, and buries herself in her sister's arms and sobs.

I'm reading a romance novel. The first kiss is about to happen. The phone rings. It's not him, I tell myself.

It rings again. I frown, now completely pulled out of the story. Not so much from the ring, but from hope that won't die. It's been a month.

It's not even my phone. He wouldn't call my home number.

317

Then I start ticking off every reason he would. He lost my cell number. He wanted to make sure that it was okay with my parents if he called me. Yup, sadly even after all this time, every time a phone rings, I hold my breath and wait for my mother to call my name and tell me it's for me. I allow myself to wish for something that I shouldn't.

"Leah!" My mom's voice rings all the way down the hall to my room. I suck in a quick breath, slap my romance novel closed, and look up as mom stops in my door. Mom with a phone in her hand. Mom with a strange look on her face. Hope flutters in my stomach like a butterfly beating its wings for the first time.

"Is it for me?"

She nods.

I smile. I stand up. That smile curls up inside my chest. I hold my hand out for the phone. I'm trembling inside. I try to think of what to say. I don't want to sound too eager, but...

Mom doesn't move. "Give it to me."

She blinks. "We... You. There's a heart available." Her voice sounds like she's inhaled helium.

It's not Matt, or Eric. It's... I digest what she said. Then it's like time stops. The air from my pink polka-dot ceiling fan whispers across my bare skin, and I feel the tiny hairs on my arms stand up. "You sure?" I shake my head, certain she's mistaken.

She nods. "Yes."

"Shit," I say, and hear it like it's too loud. My knees start to give, and I lock them. My plans hadn't included... living. It's not that it's an unwelcome change; it's just a huge change. One that includes… getting my chest cracked back open.

I drop back onto the mattress. The memory foam sucks me down. I'm stunned. I'm numb. Oh, shit! I'm scared.

My hands shake.

Mom smiles and cries at the same time. "Come on." She rubs her hands down the side of her pants. Up. Down. Up. Down.

I'm getting dizzy watching them, but I can't look away. I can't…

"We have to go. They want you there in an hour and a half. I'm calling your dad. Grab your bag from the closet. You're getting a heart, baby! You're getting a heart."

Standing, I feel numb and yet top heavy, as if I have too much emotion in my chest. I grab my extra battery that's charged and ready to go. I stick it in my backpack. I slip my shoes on. They feel too tight. Like they belong to someone else.

In less than five minutes we are out of the house. Dad works close to Houston. He's meeting us there. Mom keeps talking. I stop listening. I stare out the side window and watch the world pass by. Cars. Trees. Houses. People.

I wish I'd have remembered to bring a book. Something to help me forget this fear.

"It's gonna be fine," Mama says when we're a mile from the hospital, and I'm almost certain she's said it around a hundred times by now.

I want to believe her. I really try. I try not to remember the statistics of how many don't make it through the surgery. I try not to think about the person who just died. The person whose heart is going to be put into my chest.

I wonder how old they are? I wonder if someone is crying for them. Then my vision blurs and I realize I'm crying. Crying for them. Crying because I'm scared. Crying because if something goes wrong, I'll die. Today. I could die. Today.

I'm not ready. Maybe I've been fooling myself about accepting it. Or maybe it's just because I haven't completed my bucket list. I haven't graduated yet. I haven't read a hundred books. Haven't figured out if it was Matt or Eric who I kissed.

I haven't lived enough.

Matt stands in the hall, leaning against the wall. He ignores the nurses, doctors, the hospital sounds, and the smells. His mom and his aunt have gone into the room to say goodbye. They come out, looking older than when they went in. He tells them to go on back to the hotel. He wants to say goodbye alone. His mom argues. Then her sad eyes meet his, and she relents.

They start out, but his aunt swings around and hugs him. "You sure you're okay?"

There is nothing okay about this. But he forces the lie out. "Yeah."

He watches them walk down the long hall, getting smaller and smaller. Only when they turn does he walk into his brother's room. His lungs feel like they have liquid in them. He sits in a chair next to his brother's bed. He can't look at him.

The machine beeps, beeps, beeps and makes swishing sounds. Finally, he forces himself to watch his brother's chest go up and down. "Hey," he says. Not that he believes his brother is there. Or maybe he does.

He looks at his brother's face, almost completely bandaged. "A lot of damage," they'd said earlier.

Closing his eyes, Matt sits there, his heart beats with the machine. Thu... thump. Thu... thump. He closes his eyes. After a minute, or maybe ten, he opens them.

He looks again at his brother. It's him, but it isn't. His personality, his essence is gone.

Seeing the clock on the wall, he realizes his time is up.

"What happened, Eric?" The damn knot crawls up higher in Matt's throat. Tears fill his eyes. He touches his brother's hand. Matt's breath catches when it feels cold.

He glances back to make sure no one is standing outside the door. Then he stands up and moves closer to his brother's side. "You know, you told me when dad died that we just had to live for him. Well, now I've got to live for the both of you. That's hard to do."

Matt runs a hand over his face. His chest feels so tight he's sure it's gonna break. "I don't know how to be me without you."

His voice shakes. "I'm gonna try. I'll do right by mom." He pauses. "But I'm pissed at her right now. If she hadn't... I know you didn't do this. I won't stop trying to find out who did. I promise you. Now go hang out with dad. Tell him I love him."

He hears a slight shuffle and looks back. A nurse is in the doorway. Her eyes are wet. She walks up to him as if to hug him, but he holds out his hand.

He hurries out of the ICU and finds an empty family room. Dropping into a chair, he wipes the tears from his cheeks and tries to piece together what's left of his broken soul.

He leans back in the chair, closes his eyes, and attempts to smooth the emotional wrinkles from his head. Staring at the blackness of his eyelids, he lets his thoughts float away, feeling so damn tired. Maybe if he could sleep a few minutes…

Maybe.

He lets his shoulders relax. He's almost asleep when he sees it and feels it again. Sees Eric running through the trees. Fear swells in his chest, his brother's fear. He senses someone is giving chase. He can almost hear the thud of footsteps following. Who? Who would want to hurt Eric?

Matt shoots up from the chair. Runs a hand over his face. He feels Eric. Feels him here. "You trying to tell me something?" He waits for an answer and then… worries he's losing it.

Unsure what he believes, he heads to his car. The heat claws at his skin. The air feels thick. Sweat runs down his brow. He sticks his hands in his jeans and thinks about Eric's cold hand.

He stops walking, realizing he doesn't even know where he is. He looks around. His car isn't where he thought it was. He stands there, fisting his hands in his pockets. Then he remembers parking in front of the emergency room. He starts that way, through a maze of cars, hurrying to get out of the smothering air.

He rounds the corner of another building. Nearby voices float above the sound of traffic. Something familiar about the voices causes him to look up. He sees the dark-haired girl with a backpack about two rows over. Leah and her parents. His knees almost buckle.

His gaze stays on her, on the way she walks, a little slow, her shoulders slumped over as if she's carrying too much. And not all of it physical weight, but emotional.

Air, with the weight of cement, catches between his Adam's apple and tonsils. They're walking into the hospital.

Just like that he knows. Leah McKenzie is getting Eric's heart.

Eric wanted this. Matt wanted this. Yet an emotion he can't quite name pushes its way into his already crowded and clutching chest. Leah gets to live. Eric gets to die. That feels so unfair.

He waits for the three of them to get inside before he dares to take a step. Then he bolts to his car.

Climbing behind the wheel, he fists his hands onto the steering wheel, as if by hanging on to it, he's hanging on to his sanity. Five. Ten minutes later, he's still there.

Still hanging on.

He's not in a hurry to leave. Instead, he sits there trying to fit everything he feels in a nice, neat little package.

It won't fit.

It's not nice. It's not neat.

Even his father's death didn't hurt this bad.

ABOUT THE AUTHOR

C. C. Hunter is the *New York Times* bestselling author of over thirty-five books, including her wildly popular Shadow Falls and Shadow Falls: After Dark series. In addition to winning numerous awards and rave reviews for her novels, C.C. is also a photojournalist, motivational speaker, and writing coach.

In February 2018, Wednesday Books will publish C.C.'s contemporary young adult and hardcover debut, *This Heart of Mine*. C.C. currently resides in Texas with her husband, junkyard dog, Lady, and whatever wild creatures meander out from the woods surrounding her home. To find out more, visit www.cchunterbooks.com.

A BRAND NEW SERIES

FROM THE
NEW YORK TIMES BESTSELLING AUTHOR
OF SHADOW FALLS

THE MORTICIAN'S DAUGHTER

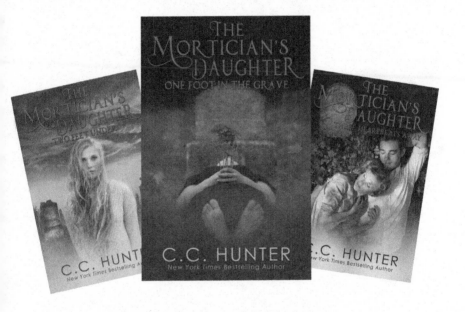

READ THE FIRST BOOK

ONE FOOT IN THE GRAVE
AVAILABLE OCTOBER 31st, 2017

CPSIA information can be obtained
at www.ICGtesting.com
Printed in the USA
BVOW03s1352241017
498515BV00001B/27/P